Power Wealth & Courage

EMPIRE OF THE LEGACIES ACADEMY
BOOK ONE

WRITTEN BY AWARD-WINNING AUTHOR

SUSAN HODDY

***Power Wealth & Courage*—Empire of the Legacies Academy**

First edition published in Australia in 2025

Text copyright © Susan Hoddy 2025

ISBN
978-0-9756369-3-0

Front cover image and book cover design created by Ammonia Book Covers
Editing by Debbie Phillips and Deb Klanfar from DP Plus
Formatting by Debbie Phillips from DP Plus
Printed by Ingram Spark, in Dandenong South, Victoria, Australia 3175

Susan's website https://www.susanhoddy.com

A catalogue record for this book is available from the National Library of Australia https://www.nla.gov.au

This book is dedicated to my wonderful Mum, who has always been there for me, and has supported my writing career. I hope we get the chance to meet again one day.
Love you always, Mum.

CHARACTERS IN THE STORYLINE

Hawk Ironclaw (Griffin)

Sully Valerith (half Griffin, half Lepidoptera Vampire, Fae)

Garrick Ironclaw (Stormclaw Aerie, Griffins' leader)

Elara Ironclaw (Griffin)

Rhydian Ironclaw (Griffin)

Drakon Ironclaw (Griffin)

Zephyrion Ironclaw (Griffin)

Rimmer Ironclaw (Griffin)

Eryndor Ironclaw (half Griffin, half Warlock)

Cryotusk (Artic Whale from Canadian waters)

The Griffin Soldiers: Draven, Kael

The Lepidoptera Vampires: Princess Violette, William, Grayson, Michael, Brock, Renee, Danielle, Stephen, Sharina, Shepherd, Christian, Kelan, Samantha, Samuel, Kiplin.

Tassone Boardman (Debauched Vampire)

Albinus Giordano (Human)

Elsie Brookton (Griffin)

Adrian Lachance (Warlock)

PLACES IN THE STORYLINE

Bagnolet, France
Olden Fjord, Norway
Stryn, Norway
Loen, Norway
Glittertind, Norway
Storvik, Norway
Norwegian Sea
Marigot Bay, Saint Lucia
Hollyburn Ridge, Canada

PROLOGUE

Hawk awakened with a jolt, his wings twitching instinctively as something cold and smooth coiled tightly around his body. The first sensation he felt was a suffocating pressure on his chest, and then a horrifying realization hit—the lower half of his torso was inside the gaping jaws of a massive python.

Its scales glistened in the dim light, a mosaic of black and green that shimmered as the muscles in its throat constricted, drawing Hawk further in. The snake's unblinking, lidless eyes reflected nothing but hunger, as its jaws clamped tight around its prey.

Hawk's heart pounded in his chest as he felt his hindquarters slip further into the python's maw, the rows of its backward-curving teeth preventing any easy escape. With his front claws still free, Hawk scraped them against the sheets, tearing through them as panic surged through him. His beak parted in a silent scream, his throat taut with effort, but no sound came—only raw agony carved into his face. His wings thrashed against the bed as he fought for breath, each movement desperate and wild. The pressure was unbearable, as his lion-like front legs kicked futilely.

What the fuck! This can't be happening ... a Griffin like me ... trapped by a python? NO! thought Hawk, trying to come to terms with what was going on.

With sheer willpower, Hawk forced himself to think past the panic. *Stay calm. Focus!*

The sharp talons, on his still-free front legs, were his best weapon. The snake's thick body had wrapped around him, muscles like iron bands, squeezing tighter with every second, but Hawk knew that he still had a chance, as it hadn't swallowed him fully yet.

With a snarl, he dug his talons into the python's head, aiming for its sensitive eyes. He felt a slight give, and the python recoiled, loosening its hold just a fraction. That was all Hawk needed. He tore at the serpent's face, the flesh parting under his sharp claws, blood spraying onto the bed. The snake hissed, a sound like air escaping a balloon, and its jaws slackened for a moment.

Hawk seized the opportunity, his powerful wings straining as he pushed himself backward, ripping free from the python's grip. Agonizing pain ripped through him as his flesh shredded against the serpent's fangs, and he slid from its mouth with a sickening, wet noise. Once free, his lion's paws found purchase on the floor, and he pounced with all the force he could muster, slamming his beak into the snake's skull with a sickening crunch.

The python's body coiled and thrashed beneath Hawk in a death throe, its last breath rattling through its twisted form, until the beast lay still; its lifeless body draped across Hawk's once-pristine bed. Blood pooled around Hawk, warm and sticky.

Panting heavily, Hawk stood victorious over the dead python, his feathers ruffled and soaked in sweat and blood. His sharp, bourbon-coloured eyes narrowed, as adrenaline and rage still pulsed through his veins.

"No one devours a Griffin," he spat, wiping the blood from his beak with the back of his paw.

Then, everything *stopped*.

In what seemed like slow motion, the python's body dissolved into mist, and the oppressive weight that had been around his chest, had vanished, and the blood on his claws faded as though it had never been there.

Hawk blinked, his heart still racing, and suddenly found himself back in human form, staring up at the familiar wooden beams of his bedroom ceiling. The soft embrace of his nest-like bed grounded him, and the torn sheets and blood had vanished, without a trace.

What the fuck ... I must have been dreaming, thought Hawk. His sweat-soaked body sat upright, and he raked a hand through his golden-blonde, shoulder-length hair. *What does this dream mean? And why am I dreaming of a primal, ancient predator?*

With a sharp breath, Hawk shoved the covers aside, and his feet hit the floor harder than he intended. The coolness of the room did nothing to soothe the gnawing unease tightening around his chest. Barely thinking, Hawk pushed himself up and moved toward the window, each step unsteady, as though the dream still had its hold on him.

When he reached the glass, he pressed both hands against it, as if seeking answers from the outside world. The pale light of dawn crept over the horizon, but it offered no peace, no clarity—only questions. Why was he dreaming of a python? And what did it mean?

CHAPTER ONE

"Come!" commanded Garrick Ironclaw, leader of the Stormclaw Aerie Griffins, hearing a knock at the door.

Hawk opened the large wooden door and walked toward Garrick, who was sitting behind his office desk. "Father ..." Hawk bowed his head slightly, then stood to attention.

"Yes?" prompted Garrick. He didn't look up from the paperwork he was reading.

"You asked to see me, Father."

"Right!" Garrick's, brown eyes scrutinized his son's demeanor. "We will wait for your mother. She needs to be included in this conversation, too."

"Yes, Sir," Hawk said, as he continued to stand to attention. He swallowed hard and wondered why he had been summoned to his father's office.

Garrick pushed his chair back and walked over to the expansive window situated behind him, which offered a captivating view of the Olden Fjord in Norway. With his gaze fixed on the majestic landscape, he stood with his back turned to Hawk, surveying his domain. When he heard footsteps on the marble floor, he turned and watched his wife, Elara, stride into the room.

"Let's get this over with, shall we," stated Elara, bluntly. With her silver locks bound loosely behind her, she gracefully approached her husband, taking her place by his side.

Hawk looked from his mother to his father, rolled his eyes and sighed. *Drama, drama.*

"Do you know why you are here, my son?" asked Elara Ironclaw.

"No … what is this about?" asked Hawk.

"We have made a decision." Elara's jade-green eyes looked from Hawk to Garrick, and back again, "You are next in line to our throne, but considering what has occurred here in the last few months, we do not think you are ready, or worthy yet, to take on any responsibilities of our kingdom."

Hawk sighed deeply and shook his head. "But, I …"

Garrick nostrils flared as he placed his right hand in the air, and his face assumed a resolute expression. "Just … listen … boy!"

Hawk's brow furrowed, and his nostrils also flared, but he waited for his mother to continue.

"The destruction you have recently caused, Hawk, is not beyond repair, but has placed a huge burden on us, and we wonder … well, if you are, or should be, the one to take over our kingdom; when we are gone, that is," Elara said, matter-of-factly.

"What! … May I speak?" charged Hawk as he looked from Elara to Garrick.

"Go ahead," said Elara, authoritatively.

"In my defense, what has occurred here lately is not entirely my fault," said Hawk. He looked from his mother to his father.

"That is where you are wrong, Hawk," interrupted Garrick. "Your selfish behavior and your arrogant ways nearly got us all killed. If your younger brother, Rhydian, hadn't stepped in, goodness knows what would have happened."

"For the sake of our entire kingdom, we cannot allow this attitude of yours to continue, Hawk," Elara stated firmly. "Your most recent reckless behavior; testing your abilities, it nearly destroyed the whole marketplace with a single swoop of your wings."

"But I have changed …" pleaded Hawk.

Elara interrupted his speech, "There are no buts here. We have given you enough time to change, and what have you shown us? Nothing!"

"Please … I can do this. Give me one more chance," begged Hawk.

"No! We have made our decision." She looked into his wounded eyes. "Instead of removing you from the ascension, we are going to send you away to an academy in France, where you will learn how to harness your powers, so that one day you will become a wise and responsible leader, one who can protect and serve our people, and who can work alongside others to achieve common goals."

Hawk sighed heavily. As his shoulders slumped forward, his eyes averted to the ground, and his chin rested on his chest.

"Please …" begged Hawk. He looked up at his mother and father with pleading eyes. "I can do better. Give me a chance to make this right."

"You leave in the morning," said Garrick, matter-of-factly.

"Yes, Sir," said Hawk. His dejected eyes filled with tears.

"Leave us, NOW!" bellowed Garrick. He waved Hawk away with his right hand.

Hawk nodded once, turned and walked toward the doorway. He knew that he could do better; but how could he show his parents this, when they were sending him away?

* * *

"Have you spoken with the academy about Hawk's attendance, and what is expected?" Elara asked Garrick, as she watched Hawk close the door.

"Yes. Violette is fully aware of what has transpired here, and she is mindful of what we expect from the academy," stated Garrick, looking at Elara.

"I hope Hawk can learn a thing or two there, and does us proud. I am still worried, though, whether we are doing the right thing, by sending him away," said Elara, her brow furrowed.

"One can only hope," Garrick replied sarcastically. "One can only hope."

CHAPTER TWO

Under the full moon's ethereal glow, the Seine River's silver waters shimmered like liquid stardust. Moonlight filtered through drifting clouds tinged with golden hues, casting a spellbinding reflection across the river's surface. Beyond the riverbanks, distant gray mountains loomed majestically, as Hawk Ironclaw, who was wading through the water, caught sight of the faint glimmers of light that illuminated his path forward.

"Thank you, Cryotusk. I would have been lost without your directions, and I have enjoyed our time together," Hawk said. "But I should be fine from here."

"Anytime! Well … I had better be heading back home to Canada," Cryotusk said. He indicated to the pendant that Hawk was wearing, a silver triquetra pentagram, that incorporated the sun, moon and a star, which was resting on his bare chest. "May it grant you good luck, strength and safe travels, Hawk."

"Thank you." Hawk nodded once to the arctic sea creature, and swam towards the shoreline.

It had taken Cryotusk and Hawk four days to fly and swim from Norway to Bagnolet, and Hawk was looking forward to eating something a bit more nourishing than raw fish. He also intended to enjoy a well-earned rest.

* * *

Samuel watched the tall, broad-shouldered male, walk naked out of the water, and stride toward him. "Hawk … welcome!" Samuel held his hand out for Hawk to shake.

"Yes! And you are?" asked Hawk, choosing to ignore Samuel's friendly gesture. He shook the water from shoulder length hair, as he came closer to the six-foot-tall, broad-shouldered Vampire.

"Samuel Gramaze. I have been instructed by the Head Chancellor to bring you back to the academy."

"Right! Are they for me?" Hawk asked, indicating to the towel and clothes Samuel was holding.

"Yes," Samuel said, handing them over. "Your bags turned up yesterday from Norway, and I have put them in your room at the academy."

"Great!" Hawk said. He wiped the water from his body and shrugged on the clothes.

"Follow me," Samuel said. He turned toward the lights in the distance. "Are you hungry from your long journey?"

"A little bit. Do your servants know what my dietary requirements are?"

"Servants! We don't have servants at the academy."

Humph, who does this joker think he is? Royalty? thought Samuel, not knowing he was speaking to the prince of Norway, and the son of two powerful Griffins.

"You will need to let the kitchen staff know your food requirements," stated Samuel.

"Right!" Hawk rolled his eyes, and took a deep breath in, then out, as he strode through the sand barefoot, with the towel slung over his shoulder.

I wonder if they have ambrosia here? thought Hawk.

* * *

Samuel stopped at the edge of the tall eastern hemlock and sycamore trees that bordered the property in front of them, and waited for Hawk to join him. "We will have to wait here for a few seconds until the wards around the academy are taken down."

"What are you talking about?" Hawk asked, as he walked past Samuel toward the invisible wall, without a care.

"Wait!" Samuel commanded. His deep blue eyes opened wide, and he quickly grabbed the back of Hawk's T-shirt, pulling him to a halt. "Do you have a death wish, man? Didn't you hear what I said?"

Hawk shrugged Samuel's hand away. "Yes, I heard you." Hawk glared at Samuel with contempt.

"Watch!" Samuel bent down and picked up a small stone from the ground and threw it toward the trees.

Hawk took a sharp breath in and his eyes widened as he witnessed lightning strike the stone. With a cracking sound, it disintegrated as it hit an invisible wall. Turning to Samuel, he said, "Fuck … thank you. I am in your debt."

Samuel sighed deeply and ran his fingers through his dark brown hair.

Violette … I have Hawk with me. Please take down the wards, mind-thought Samuel to the powerful Lepidoptera Vampire princess, who was next in line to the throne at the Gramaze coven.

Within seconds, Violette appeared at the edge of the trees, seemingly out of nowhere. The young, dark-haired female, who was dressed in black leather battle gear, extended her hands, commanding the ward to open a door-sized hole, only big enough to allow them to walk through.

"Who is that?" Hawk asked, watching her every move.

"You'll find out soon enough. Follow me," Samuel replied. He walked toward the invisible wall opening.

Hawk didn't argue, instead he did as he was instructed and followed Samuel.

* * *

Once they were through the ward, Violette turned to the new inductee, and said, "Welcome, Hawk. My name is Violette Castell. I'm Head Chancellor here at the Legacies

Academy." She held her hand out for him to shake. Ever since Violette opened the academy, twenty years prior, she'd made it a point to personally greet each new student—young adults, who were legacies of supernatural beings from around the world, attending the academy for the first time.

Hawk shook her hand firmly, and looked past her, to where three others stood in the shadows. "Thank you."

"You will do well to listen more closely from now on," Violette said, authoritatively. "You are free to go anywhere that students are permitted on campus, but you are never to leave this estate without my permission. No supernatural being or human can pass through the invisible wards we have around the academy. So don't even try. AM I MAKING MYSELF CLEAR?"

"Yes Ma'am ... crystal clear," Hawk said, his lips twisting. *Who in the fuck does this bitch think she is talking to? Doesn't she know that I come from a royal Griffin lineage?*

Violette's Lepidoptera Vampire abilities allowed her to hear his thoughts, but she chose to ignore them.

"Right. Now that is sorted, let's get you settled into your room," Violette said. She commanded the wards to close behind them. "Come this way."

As they walked, Violette started her usual orientation talk, covering the 'four Cs' at the Legacies Academy, and how important they are to all students.

"Our philosophy is governed by four Cs. The first C is 'classification', categorizing something or someone into a certain group or system based on certain characteristics. Next is 'compliance', ensuring that you adhere to all national, and international regulatory frameworks and policies. Then, there is 'connection', the sense of closeness and belonging a person can experience when having supportive relationships with those around them. And, finally, 'culture', all the ways of life, including arts, beliefs and institutions of a population that are passed down from generation to generation."

Hawk nodded once in her direction, but he had stopped listening somewhere around the second C.

* * *

With the spring night's breeze gently blowing, Hawk walked along-side Samuel on the tree-lined, gently sloped cream pathway, their footsteps echoing. Ahead of them was an enchanting French Gothic Revival-style building. "Is that the academy or the dorms I see in front of us?"

"Neither," Samuel replied, as he looked up at the rough-hewn stone buildings illuminated by floodlights.

Hawk raked a hand through his hair and rolled his eyes in disbelief at how he was being received, especially as he was a Griffin, with powerful parents. He was used to servants bowing at his feet and people treating him with respect, not being treated like a nobody.

What were my mother and father thinking sending me here? wondered Hawk.

"I think you may already know the answer to that question, Hawk," said Violette, firmly.

Humph! thought Hawk. His eyes narrowed in defiance, signaling his protest, when he realized that she had eavesdropped on his thoughts.

CHAPTER THREE

Hawk watched the wooden door to his room close, and listened to the footsteps of the Head Chancellor and her entourage eventually quieten on the tiles in the dorm's hallway. *Thank God they have gone!* Plonking himself down on the queen-size bed provided, which had not been made up yet, but had a sheet, duvet and pillows stacked neatly near the headboard, his shoulders rounded and he sighed heavily.

The first chance I get, I am out of here. This place is a joke, thought Hawk, feeling frustrated at the lack of control he had at the moment, over his own life or future.

As he looked across the room, he spotted an unmade second queen size bed, with charcoal-colored bedding, which had a black bedside table next to it, and a digital clock on top. *What the ... looks like I have a roommate.* Hawk sighed and rolled his eyes, at the annoyance of having to share a room with someone else. He was then drawn to a magnificent picture hanging on the wall beside the bed. Standing, he headed over to get a better look.

Hawk frowned as he looked closer at the picture. The image captured a luxurious two-story mansion mid-explosion, with debris scattering across an ice-covered lake, reaching the surrounding snow-laden trees. Captivated by the sight of this picture, his eyes darted to the right-hand corner of the frame, where a name was engraved. *Photographer: Kiplin Cooper.*

"Hmm ... Impressive, Kiplin Cooper. I wonder where this photo was taken?"

As he scanned the room further, Hawk noticed his suitcases next to a dark-colored tallboy, which was situated near the opening of the room's wardrobe. *I will deal with them later.* He then spotted an expensive digital camera sitting on top of the tallboy. Hawk walked over and picked it up to look it over. "Nikon … hmm; someone's got good taste." Given that photography was one of Hawk's passions, which his father would no longer let him pursue, he was captivated by the feel of the camera and imagined its capabilities.

Brought back to reality when he heard voices coming from outside the bedroom window, Hawk replaced the camera on the tallboy and walked over to the open window. Peering out, he realized that it was only a couple of other Supes, who were playing around with their magic and laughing.

"Keep it down, will ya!" yelled Hawk, from the open window.

The three male Supes looked up at Hawk, nodded in his direction, chuckled, then quietly walked away.

Idiots! … I wonder if I can get a decent flat white in this shit hole. Or even some food. I am starting to get a bit hungry. He headed towards the door. *Maybe I can take a better look around whilst I'm at it.*

* * *

"I hear you're getting a new roommate," Samuel said to Kiplin, as he aimed, and lobbed the basketball toward the hoop.

"Yeah, and apparently he is arriving at the academy tonight," Kiplin said, as he caught the rebound off the backboard. "The Head Chancellor told me he's from Norway." Bouncing the ball with one hand, he then tossed it toward the hoop and watched it glide through.

Samuel caught the ball as it fell through the hoop's net and threw it toward Kiplin. "Lucky shot."

"Humph, not from where this Lepidoptera is standing," Kiplin said, smirking, as he held his hands out to catch the ball from Samuel.

"Must be my turn," Sully said, stepping in front of Kiplin, at Vampire speed, grabbing the basketball before Kiplin could catch it. "Snooze you lose." She ran up to the hoop and threw the ball with ease into the net.

Samuel snickered as he watched his adopted sister take the shot.

"Hey … no fair," Kiplin complained, his hands resting on his hips.

"So … what else do we know about this new roommate of yours?" Elsie queried, joining them on the court. Elsie gracefully folded her Griffin wings against her back, retracting them as she descended onto the solid concrete ground. Like a magical illusion, the wings seamlessly disappeared, blending into her back as if they were never there.

"Not much, besides the fact that his luggage turned up yesterday. A bit strange that his stuff turned up before him," Kiplin said, watching Elsie resume her human form. "What have you been up to tonight, Elsie?"

"I was guarding Head Chancellor Violette," Elsie replied, retracting her eagle-like claws.

"She was working with me. I had to greet the new guy down by the river," Samuel said, remembering the egotism of the newbie, Hawk.

"Down by the river?" Kiplin queried.

"Yeah, apparently he flew and swam all the way from Norway to Bagnolet," Samuel said.

"What? No way!" scoffed Sully, skeptical that anyone, even a Supe, could fly and swim that far.

"I'm telling you, he did. I saw him walk out of the water." Samuel placed his hands on his hips.

"I'd like to meet someone who can fly and swim that far," Sully said, in admiration. *I wonder what supernatural creature he is?*

"Looks like you'll get your chance; here he comes now," Samuel said, spotting Hawk walking toward them.

Elsie, Kiplin and Sully turned to watch the tall, muscular, male walk toward them.

Cute! thought Sully, as she watched him swagger over.

Samuel's Lepidoptera ability to hear Sully's inner musings, about what she thought of another boy, brought a sense of amusement to his lips, and he couldn't help but grin.

* * *

Well, Father, you wanted me to mingle with like-minded supernatural creatures. Here goes. Hawk's curiosity piqued as he came to stand in front of the four of them, on the tree-lined, concrete basketball court, situated at the rear of the academy.

"Hawk … this is Elsie, Kiplin and Sully," Samuel said, gesturing to each of them in turn.

Kiplin offered his hand. "Good to meet you, roomie."

"Ah … good to meet you, too," Hawk responded, shaking Kiplin's hand, realizing he was the photographer of that awesome picture. Leaning in, he extended his hand to Elsie and Sully. "Nice to meet you both."

"You too. How's the unpacking going?" Sully asked, admiring his bourbon-colored eyes.

"I haven't started. Thought I'd have a look around the grounds first," Hawk said, looking into her jade-green eyes.

"I'm surprised that the Head Chancellor didn't offer to have someone show you around," Elsie said.

"Ah, that's because I told her I didn't need anyone's help, and that I wasn't staying long anyway," Hawk replied, crossing his arms over his chest.

Kiplin's brow furrowed as he questioned, "What makes you think that you won't be staying long?"

"I told my father that I wouldn't be here long. Not that he agreed. He seems to think that I need some worldly mingling with other Supers, and to learn some life lessons. Or something like that. Humph …" Hawk rolled his eyes. "So … what do you all do for fun around here?"

"Fun? You've misunderstood the purpose of this place," stated Samuel, his tone tinged with a hint of surprise. "We're all here for one reason, and that is to learn and train in combat, and to hone our abilities, so that we can eventually control our powers and go out on missions," Samuel explained. Hawk's unfamiliarity with the academy surprised Samuel, especially given the widely recognized motivations that led most other supernatural creatures to enroll there.

"Humph … right!" Hawk raised his eyebrows. "I certainly won't be needing any combat training. Where I come from, we're taught that from an early age." He looked at each of their faces to see their reaction. "Well, I'll leave you to it. Just thought I'd come over and see what the go is here." Without another word, Hawk strode off toward the trees that surrounded the property.

"Who does that guy think he is?" Sully asked quietly. She tried to use her Lepidoptera ability to read Hawk's thoughts, as she watched him walk away.

"I know … conceited much? You should have heard him down at the river tonight. I think he must come from some sort of privileged life," Samuel said. He shook his head.

"Don't judge him yet, guys," Kiplin said, raking a hand through this blond hair, and hoping that this would be the last roommate that he would have to get to know and share with.

Could you read his thoughts, Samuel? questioned Sully to her brother, as she pushed her deep red hair behind her ears.

No. He must be blocking us, thought Samuel.

Hmm … I wonder what his story is? thought Sully.

* * *

Hawk's stomach growled in acknowledgement of the delicious aromas that wafted through the academy dining room, as he retrieved a cold bottle of water out of the fridge and placed it on his tray. Near the center of the well-lit area, long counters displayed an assortment of delicious and healthy options in bains-marie. Hawk selected a large white bone china plate from the bottom shelf, and surveyed the assortment of labeled trays to see what delectable options were available for his meal.

There is enough food here for a king, thought Hawk.

After he scooped a few of the healthier options onto his plate, he moved along to select a knife and fork, and looked around at the spacious area designed to accommodate the numerous students at the academy. The room was set with small square white tables, each having four chairs. Hawk noticed that it seemed quiet, with no one in sight, and half of the dining room was in complete darkness, as he placed his tray full of food on a table and seated himself. As he shoveled food into his mouth, and looked around at the empty room, Hawk thought, *I know it's late, but where is everyone?* Shrugging his shoulders, he then noticed Sully walking into the dining room.

Sully waved to Hawk, smiled, and continued on toward the coffee machine.

"Would you like a coffee, Hawk?" Sully called out, as she stood in front of the machine.

"Sure. Thanks! White, with two sugars. And can you make it strong," Hawk replied.

"Okay!" Sully said, as she positioned two large cups under the machine.

* * *

Sully placed the hot cup of coffee on the table in front of Hawk. "Here you go."

"Thanks," said Hawk. He pushed his empty food tray over to one side and picked up the cup of coffee.

"My brother, Samuel, tells me that you're from Norway. Which part? Sully asked, sitting across from Hawk at the table.

"Olden Fjord," replied Hawk, his Norwegian accent apparent.

"Ah, right. It must have taken you a while to fly and swim from there to Bagnolet?" asked Sully, placing her cup of coffee on the table.

"Yeah, about four days," Hawk replied.

"Wow … I can't even imagine flying or swimming for that number of days. Why didn't you take a jet here instead?"

"Honestly, I don't know where my father's head was at, when he suggested that I fly and swim to Bagnolet. I would have preferred to use a jet, but he insisted that I should spend some time exploring the skies and ocean." Hawk shook his head and sighed.

"Parents can be a bit of pain in the ass sometimes, I know," said Sully, remembering all the times her adopted father, William, wouldn't let her do certain things. "Did you fly and swim here with family or someone else?"

"I flew some of the way by myself, and then I swam with an arctic whale the rest of the way. Cryotusk, he is one of my kingdom's allies, and knows the oceans well. He is from Canada," said Hawk.

"Oh, right! How was the food, compared to your home?" asked Sully. She indicated to the empty tray.

"It was good, actually. Especially the ambrosia. One of my favorites," said Hawk. He leaned back in his chair and took a sip of his coffee. "Mmm, just what I needed."

"Oh, that's good," said Sully, as she studied his facial features. "So … I believe you are sharing with Kiplin."

"Yeah, I think so. Hey … is it always this quiet at night in the dining room?" said Hawk.

"Yes, it's always quiet this time of night. They mainly leave the area lit up and food out for the older Supes who are coming in late from assignments. Tomorrow at breakfast, you will see what it's really like here. Busy as hell. The academy has over a hundred young Supes at the moment," said Sully.

"Right! That makes sense," said Hawk.

"Have you got your training time table yet?"

"I think it might be in the welcome package that the Head Chancellor gave me. But I don't think I'm going to need it. I'm going to give my father a ring soon, and explain that I don't want to stay here. I am sure he will tell me to come back home," said Hawk.

"That's a shame. I was looking forward to getting to know you better. I'm sure if you give it a chance here, you'll soon realize that it's not half bad," said Sully, remembering her first few days at the academy, and how she didn't feel like she fit in, even though she had lived with the Gramaze coven Lepidopteras for the previous five years.

"Maybe," said Hawk. He pushed his chair back and picked up his tray. "What do I do with these?" He indicated to his dirty plate, cutlery and tray.

Sully pointed to an empty rack over next to the bains-marie. "On the rack over there. The kitchen staff collect them and wash them."

Hawk looked in the direction she was pointing. "Oh, right. Thanks!"

"I'm going to head back to my dorm room now. See you possibly tomorrow sometime," said Sully, standing.

"Probably not."

"Sleep on it, before you ring you family. You may find in the morning that you're feeling better about being here," Sully suggested.

"Doubt it," stated Hawk, in a monotone voice. His negative expression showed, as he crossed his arms over his chest.

"Your choice," Sully shrugged. She smiled, and walked away from him, toward the dorm rooms.

Stubborn male!

CHAPTER FOUR

Kiplin woke the next morning to the sound of a door closing, and an empty room. Sitting up, he looked over at Hawk's rumpled bed, and the suitcases that were still situated near the tallboy dresser.

I wonder where Hawk is off to this morning. Kiplin raked a hand through his hair and sighed. *I might have a shower, and then chase up my roomie.*

* * *

Kiplin found an anxious Hawk, holding a tray of food, looking around the noisy dining room for somewhere to sit. With over a hundred supernatural creatures in the dining room, it was impossible to find a seat where he could be by himself.

"Looking for a quiet pew, man?" asked Kiplin, who was now standing behind Hawk with his own breakfast tray in hand. "Good luck with that!" Kiplin was able to read Hawk's mind with his Lepidoptera abilities.

"Yeah … I think I might go sit outside," said Hawk.

"Mind if I join you?" asked Kiplin.

"Humph … that's up to you," said Hawk, walking away. He rolled his eyes and sighed hard.

Someone got up on the wrong side of the bed today, thought Kiplin, as he followed Hawk outside.

"So … how are you settling in, man?" asked Kiplin, as he sat across from Hawk at a wooden table in the courtyard.

Hawk didn't answer. He didn't look up either, just kept shoveling food into his mouth.

"How are you settling in, man?" asked Kiplin, again.

"I heard you the first time," grunted Hawk. He continued to eat his breakfast.

"Well …?" Kiplin prompted.

Hawk didn't answer.

What is this dude's problem? thought Kiplin.

As Kiplin delved into Hawk's open thoughts, Hawk's desire for solitude became apparent, and Kiplin came to the realization that his queries would remain unanswered. Standing, he collected his tray of food and silently retreated from the table.

Talk about fucking rude, thought Kiplin.

Everything alright? Samuel reached out to Kiplin. He had heard his friend's thoughts from across the court-yard.

Yeah, all good, man. He'll come around when he's ready.

But as soon as Kiplin thought it, he heard an argument erupt behind him, accompanied by the sound of shattering furniture. Turning around, he witnessed Hawk being aggressively attacked by three other supernaturals in the court-yard. Abandoning his tray, Kiplin rushed to Hawk's aid, knowing well from past training sessions that these were no ordinary Warlocks, but formidable wielders of magic.

"Get the fuck off him!" yelled Kiplin, using his Lepidoptera strength to forcefully yank two of the Warlocks away from Hawk.

"What do you care, Lepidoptera?" asked the first Warlock, with a furrowed brow, steadying himself.

"Mind your own business," said the second Warlock, dusting himself off.

"This is my business, dickhead," Kiplin replied, pulling the third Warlock off Hawk.

Kiplin held out his hand, and helped Hawk up off the pavement.

"Thanks," said Hawk, standing. He clenched his fists beside his body.

"Don't thank me yet," stated Kiplin. He was well aware that these three troublemaking Warlocks, recent additions to the academy, were far from trustworthy.

"You three!" shouted Chancellor Michael, the academy's combat trainer, from across the courtyard. "You will report to the Head Chancellor's office, now." His intense Lepidoptera Vampire blue eyes watched the three Warlocks' reaction, as he came to stand before them.

"But …" said one of them.

"There will be no *buts* here. Report to the Head Chancellor, NOW!" He pointed toward the office and watched the three frustrated Warlocks, walk away. "Kiplin, Hawk, I want an explanation."

Kiplin gulped hard and nodded yes.

Hawk sullenly waited to see what was going to happen.

"I would like an explanation, Hawk," Michael repeated. His nostrils flared, as he looked around at the wooden table and seats that were destroyed.

"I don't have to explain to you," stated Hawk, his brow furrowed, his arrogance showing. "You're not my father."

"You will explain, or you are gone," replied Michael, in a heated voice.

"Fine with me," said Hawk, matter-of-factly. He turned and walked off towards his dorm room.

With Vampire speed, Michael grabbed hold of Hawk's shirt and pulled him back toward him. "Where do you think you're going? I haven't finished with you yet." He shoved Hawk down on the wooden seat near them.

"Listen … I didn't start the fight with the Warlocks. I was eating my breakfast when they attacked me," said Hawk, looking up at Michael. "Anyway, what does it matter. I am fucking out of here." He got to his feet.

"He's telling the truth, Chancellor," said Kiplin, as he wondered what punishment would be handed out for fighting.

They are telling you the truth, Michael. I saw what happened, and this was not Hawk's fault, mind-thought

Samuel, from across the court yard. He had been watching the whole situation unfold in front of him, along with others.

"Right," said Michael, his brow furrowed, as he looked from Hawk to Kiplin. "You will report to the training and combat room. NOW, HAWK!"

"For fuck's sake … I didn't even do anything, and now I have to train? What sort of academy are you running here?" demanded Hawk, his fists clenched beside him.

"You will do as you are told, legacy," said Michael, sternly. "Kiplin, show Hawk where the training and combat room is."

Hawk's nostrils flared, and he clenched his jaw. *Why has my father sent me to an academy that is run by imbeciles?*

"Yes, Sir," said Kiplin. He knew better than to argue with one of the many powerful Gramaze coven Lepidopteras. "It's this way, Hawk. Let's go." He pointed toward the academy.

"Well … what are you waiting for; get going. NOW!" stated Michael, listening to Hawk's thoughts about leaving.

Michael watched Kiplin and Hawk, walk toward the right-hand side of the academy.

Samuel … organize for this mess to be cleaned up, thought Michael, as he looked across the court-yard at the broken furniture.

Yes, Michael, Samuel responded.

Breathing a heavy sigh, Michael visualized and remembered the details of Hawk's file sitting back on his desk. *I'm glad I read this boy's file before he entered the academy. If today is anything to go by, we certainly have a lot to teach him.*

CHAPTER FIVE

"You are one formidable warrior, Chancellor," stated Hawk, who had been surprised by the high level of combat training he had received. Despite the sweat glistening on his forehead and the visible signs of fatigue in his upper body resulting from the intense one-on-one combat training he had undergone with Michael, Hawk remained enthusiastic and determined to continue his training.

Michael nodded once. "That will be all for this morning, Hawk. But I want to see you here again this evening. I think I can teach you how to hone those skills of yours better. In the meantime, keep out of trouble."

"Humph … It seems to follow me, I know," said Hawk, smirking.

Kiplin, it will be your job today to keep an eye on Hawk, mind-thought Michael.

Yes, Sir, mind-thought Kiplin, who had been standing on the sidelines watching them train. He knew better than to argue with the third-in-command for the Gramaze family Vampire coven.

"Showers are this way, Hawk," said Kiplin, indicating to the doorway to the left of the room.

"Ah, right. Thanks," said Hawk.

* * *

"Are you ready to go?" asked Kiplin, standing near the dirty towel basket in the shower room.

"Yeah," said Hawk, throwing his towel in the basket. "Just need to get my dirty clothes, then I'm good to go."

"Good. Lunch will be ready in the dining room by the time we get there. You hungry?" asked Kiplin.

"Yeah. Hey … watch where you're going," said Hawk, to the Warlock who had shoulder bumped him as he walked past.

"You fucking watch where you're going, asshole," replied the bare-chested Warlock, who had a towel wrapped around his bottom half.

"Asshole … humph … what is your problem, you mother-fucker?" asked Hawk. He recognized the Warlock from earlier that morning as one of the individuals who had attacked him.

"You are!" The Warlock assumed a stance, ready to fight.

"Just ignore him, Hawk. He's not worth your effort," said Kiplin, now standing in front of Hawk.

Fuck off, Warlock, otherwise I will report you to the Head Chancellor, mind-thought Kiplin. His eyes bored into the Warlock's, locking onto them with unwavering intensity.

Realizing Hawk had a Lepidoptera Vampire as reinforcement, the Warlock recoiled his stance.

"Humph … yeah, you're right, he is not worth it. Let's blow this joint," said Hawk, picking up his dirty clothes, shoulder bumping the Warlock as he walked out of the shower room.

"What was that dude's problem?" asked Kiplin.

"Fucked if I know. As I said to Chancellor Michael earlier, trouble seems to follow me," replied Hawk, as he walked up the steps.

* * *

"You guys up for a few hoops later?" asked Sully, as she passed Kiplin and Hawk walking out of the training room.

Looks like Hawk has changed his mind about leaving, thought Sully to herself.

Hawk breathed in her cinnamon scent, and eyed her slender body up and down.

"Maybe," said Hawk. He wasn't one for joining in, at this stage.

"Sounds like a plan," said Kiplin.

"Great! Catch up with you later," said Sully, continuing on into the training room.

Hawk watched Sully's long, deep red hair sway down her petite, muscular body as she walked away.

"Like what you see?" asked Kiplin, smirking. He had watched the way Hawk was looking back over his shoulder at Sully, as they walked toward the dining room.

"Humph …" Hawk raised his eyebrows, and smirked.

* * *

"So … what is next on your time-table?" asked Kiplin, as he sat next to Hawk at a dining room table.

"It looks like I have a class called *Supes*," replied Hawk, looking at his piece of paper. "Are you taking that class?"

"Ah, right. Yeah, that is a class everyone here takes," said Kiplin, picking up his bacon-and-egg sandwich. "It's a walk in the park. You only have to sit and listen; that's all."

"Hmm … not one of my strong suits," stated Hawk, as he picked up his bottle of water and unscrewed the lid.

"You guys got Supes next?" asked Elsie, sitting at the table across from Hawk and Kiplin, with her lunch tray.

They both nodded yes as they ate their lunch.

"Yeah, me too. I think it's about Warlocks today," said Elsie, pushing her shoulder-length, brown hair behind her ears.

"Should be interesting," said Hawk, remembering the run in he'd had with the three Warlocks earlier that morning, and one of them again in the shower room. Strategically, Hawk was hoping that this class could give him the upper hand he needed to deal with the Warlocks.

"Where's Sully?" asked Elsie, picking up her fork.

"Last time we saw her, she was going into the training room," said Kiplin.

"Here she comes now," said Hawk, watching Sully's every move.

"Hi, guys," said Sully, looking around the dining room, as she sat at the table next to Elsie.

"Have you got Supes this afternoon?" asked Elsie.

"Yep. But I'm not sure how long I will be able to sit still in there. It's a bit of a snore, you know," said Sully, leaning into Elsie.

Elsie snickered and said, "Today is all about Warlocks, so it should be a bit more interesting than usual."

"Maybe," said Sully. Her eyes sparkling as she glanced across the table at Hawk, smiled and nodded once.

"Well, I'm out of here," said Hawk, pushing his chair back and standing. He picked up his tray and walked toward the bin.

Sully and Elsie's brows furrowed.

"What is his problem?" asked Elsie quietly, leaning into Sully.

Sully shrugged, not knowing why Hawk had left so quickly.

"Wait!" said Kiplin, quickly pushing his chair backwards. Leaving his tray, he followed Hawk from the dining room and into the hallway. "What's the rush?" Kiplin grabbed hold of Hawk's arm.

Turning around, Hawk asked, "What is that woman's problem?"

"Who are you talking about?" asked Kiplin, his brow creased.

"Sully, you idiot," replied Hawk, wrenching his arm from Kiplin's grip. "She keeps giving me a flirty look."

"I hadn't noticed."

"And what's with that scent of hers?" asked Hawk. "She smells like cinnamon."

"Again, I haven't noticed. Maybe it's a new perfume."

Maybe it's just me that can smell it, thought Hawk.

"I think so," said Kiplin, who knew the real reason why.

"What …?" Hawk's brow furrowed. "Did you hear what I thought?" *Fuck, I forgot to block him reading me.*

"Yeah. I thought you knew. All Lepidoptera Vampires can hear your thoughts, that's unless you block them out. Oh, except for the older Lepidopteras. They can usually read you, even if you do block them," said Kiplin.

"Hmm … that's something I will have to remember," stated Hawk, who had been relaxed until now, and forgotten to block anyone from reading his thoughts today. *Fuck, this is not what I expected today. I will have to be more vigilant.*

"You will figure it out eventually," said Kiplin, not wanting to let on who at the academy would be able to read Hawk.

"Man, that's annoying," said Hawk, walking away. Looking over his shoulder at Kiplin, his brow furrowed, shaking his head. "Keep out of my thoughts," he yelled.

Kiplin watched Hawk quickly stride away, and rolled his eyes. *He sure has a lot to learn.*

CHAPTER SIX

"Glad you could join us, Hawk," said Michael, when he noticed Hawk standing on the sidelines in the training room. "Ready to get your ass kicked?"

"Humph ..." sneered Hawk, taking his shirt off and discarding it on the floor. "Bring it on."

Michael smirked. "That will be all for the moment, Sully. You can watch how it's done."

"Yes, Sir," replied Sully, who had been training with Michael. Wiping the sweat from her brow, she stood on the sidelines with the other Supes to watch.

Nice pecs, Hawk. I'd love to rub my hands over them. Woo wee, sizzle ... get a hold of yourself, girl, thought Sully, who gulped hard, and imaginary slapped herself.

Michael gestured with one hand to invite Hawk to join him on the floor. "Here, boy ... catch." Michael threw a black-and-gold sheathed sword in the air toward Hawk.

Hawk caught the sword in his right hand and inspected the hand-crafted medieval weapon Michael had selected for training. A Dirilis Ertugrul. "I see you know your swords, Chancellor." Taking the sheath off, he quickly discarded it on the floor and stood in a ready position.

Michael, who was bare chested, wearing only tattered denim jeans, selected a fourteenth-century hand-crafted Longsword from the wall behind him, turned and asked, "Are you ready?"

Hawk nodded once and smirked.

Michael held his sword firmly in front of him. "En garde!" Keeping his sword in motion, and continually changing his guard and stance, he thrust his sword toward Hawk's body.

Hawk countered by raising his sword high and striking horizontally. His blow offset Michael's, and the tip of his sword swished past Michael face, missing him by inches.

"Not bad … for a beginner," scoffed Michael, his sword raised in front of him.

"I am no beginner. We train at an early age where I come from," stated Hawk, his brow furrowed. He lunged forward to strike at Michael's upper body.

Michael countered Hawk's blow. With swords crossed in front of them, and their faces close to each other for what seemed like seconds, Michael smirked and pushed Hawk to the floor with ease.

With his nostrils flared, Hawk quickly got to his feet, and with an almighty scream, he lunged at Michael again.

This time, Michael stepped out of the way of his sharp blade, and let Hawk pass him by. "You will have to do better than that, boy."

Turning, Hawk steadied himself and brought his sword up to meet his lips. Clearing his mind, he called upon his Norwegian blood-lines, which gave him strength and clarity. Lunging forward once again, he tried to thrust the Dirilis Ertugrul into Michael's chest. This time he missed Michael by inches.

But before Hawk could steady himself, he was knocked to the ground by Michael. As Hawk lay on the ground, with his face planted into the concrete floor, Michael pressed his sword firmly to the back of Hawk's neck.

"Do it!" Hawk jeered, loudly. "Come on, I dare you."

Michael took his sword away from Hawk's neck, and Hawk rolled onto his back. "Get up." Michael held his hand out to Hawk.

"I don't need your help," said Hawk, as he quickly got to his feet. The clenched knuckles of his left hand were white as he steadied himself, and his sword in his right hand. Without a word, his left fist connected with

Michael's jaw, knocking him off his feet. Hawk, then placed the tip of his sword firmly to Michael's neck, just piercing the skin.

Quicker than the eye could see, Michael released himself from Hawk's sword tip, and now had him restrained, with his hands behind his back, both their swords discarded on the floor.

By this time all the other Supes in the room, who had previously been training, had stopped to watch the combat between Michael and Hawk. Each was cheering on their favorite.

"You will do well to remember who is friend or foe here," Michael whispered into Hawk's ear.

Hawk tried to wriggle free. "You are not my friend."

Michael released Hawk and pushed him forward. Picking up his own sword off the concrete floor, he said authoritatively, "Get your sword."

Hawk collected his sword from the ground, and with a surge of adrenaline, he swiftly executed a powerful swipe of his blade, aiming it directly at Michael's head.

Michael countered by striking Hawk's blade. Watching the fire in Hawk's eyes ignite each time he tried to attack, Michael blocked his every move.

The training session stretched into an hour, with neither Michael nor Hawk letting their guard down again. With sweat beading on their upper lips and brow, and a glistening sheen on their muscular upper bodies, neither were prepared to give in to the other.

"Very good, Hawk. But you will never be able to beat me, boy. You need to stop thinking before you strike, because I can see every move you're about to make, before you make it," said Michael, taking the final blow, knocking Hawk's sword out of his hand in a downward motion.

Hawk knew exactly what Michael meant.

Bloody Lepidoptera! Should have guessed, thought Hawk, his brow furrowed.

Michael raised his eyebrows and sneered. "Yes, that is correct, and I am honored to be one."

Hawk rolled his eyes. *I can't seem to get away from these eavesdroppers.*

"I think that will be all for tonight, Hawk. You can go and have a shower now," said Michael. He stepped back and placed his sword on the wall behind him.

"Fine by me," grunted Hawk, leaving his sword and its sheath on the ground, collecting his shirt.

Sully frowned as she watched a defiant Hawk show his arrogance to Michael, and wondered why Hawk hated eavesdroppers, especially as he didn't block anyone from his thoughts, whilst he was training.

The room full of Supes parted, as Hawk stormed through them, and strode angrily into the shower room.

CHAPTER SEVEN

Hawk sat on a slatted wooden bench near the river and watched the moon's reflection on the water. He was overcome with a desire to be home in Olden Fjord, with his own kind. He missed the respect from others, and the familiarity of his kingdom and the freedom to fly and swim. A river cruise boat made its way past him, lights blazing, and for one minute he wished that he was on it.

So peaceful ... thought Hawk.

Without a word spoken, Sully placed her hand on Hawk's shoulder. She had been listening to his thoughts as she approached him.

Hawk jumped, turning quickly to stand at attention, with his fists raised. When he saw it was Sully, he took a deep breath in, then out, rolled his eyes and lowered his fists. "What do you want?"

"Well, hello to you, too," said Sully, her hands on her hips.

"Look ... I just want to be left alone. Okay?" stated Hawk, sitting back on the wooden bench.

"You have come to the wrong place for that," said Sully, as she sat on the bench next to him. "Peaceful, isn't it?"

"What?"

"The river."

Hawk didn't say anything for a few seconds, instead stared out across the water.

"I miss the ocean," said Hawk, turning to Sully. "I love the feeling it gives me when I'm swimming. My wings, they feel rejuvenated, cleansed."

"Yeah, me too," said Sully, nodding. "Ever since they put the wards up, I haven't been able to go for a deep swim."

Hawk frowned. "You like to swim in the ocean?"

"Sure. I find it exhilarating. Must be the Griffin in me," said Sully, turning to Hawk.

She's a Griffin. Hawk's frown turned into a grin. "Where are you from?"

"France, stupid. Where else would I be from?" asked Sully.

"When you said you have Griffin in you, I surmised you must be from my home country, Norway," said Hawk.

"Ah, right! My Father was born in Norway and he was a Griffin. But my home country is France, because this is where I was born," replied Sully.

"That explains it. So … why did they put the wards up, anyway?" asked Hawk.

"From what I hear, there was an attack on the academy one night, about a month ago. Since then, the wards have been up for our protection."

"What … what sort of attack … what happened?"

"I don't know much about it. But I think Samuel knows. His father is head of the Lepidopteras, here in Bagnolet."

"Right!"

"So … it looks like you have changed your mind about staying," stated Sully.

"I didn't have much of a choice. My father said no to me returning home," said Hawk. He rolled his eyes and sighed heavily.

"Well, I'm glad you're staying."

"Thanks!" said Hawk.

"You did really well in training today."

"You think?"

"Yeah, but be careful, though. Chancellor Michael is not someone to mess with. He is third-in-command of the Gramaze Lepidopteras, you know," stated Sully.

"Noted," said Hawk, nodding. He knew the Gramaze family history all too well.

"Are you up for a few hoops tonight?" asked Sully.

"Nah, I might give it a miss," replied Hawk, as he turned back to the river.

"Are you sure?"

"Yeah. I'm not in the mood for that tonight." Turning to Sully, he softened his tone and asked, "So … how long have you been at the academy?"

"Nearly a year."

Hawk's brow furrowed. "Really … why so long?"

Sully rolled her eyes and stepped down off the wooden bench. *Bloody nosey parker.* "Well, I will see you in the morning. I need to catch up on my sleep."

"You didn't answer my question," stated Hawk, standing.

"Maybe another day," said Sully. She walked toward the academy.

"Wait … I will walk with you," said Hawk, following her. "What's the big secret."

With her Lepidoptera Vampire speed, and faster than his eyes could follow, Sully ran toward her dorm room. "No secret," she called out.

Even though Sully felt some sort of connection to Hawk, through their Griffin cultural heritage, she wasn't about to tell him much about herself, until she got to know him a bit better. She had learned at an early age to always keep people at a distance, that was until she got to know them better.

"What the fuck … where's she gone?" said Hawk, looking around the grounds. "Women." He shook his head.

"You know she is a Lepidoptera, right?" asked Kiplin, who had appeared behind Hawk, from what seemed like nowhere.

Hawk jumped. "Man … that's not cool. You fucking scared the shit out of me."

"Sorry, but I've been trying to track you down," said Kiplin.

"And … now you have found me."

"The Head Chancellor wants to see you," said Kiplin, grabbing hold of Hawk's arm.

Hawk looked down at Kiplin's hold on his arm and shrugged him away.

"What in the hell does she want, now?" asked Hawk. He rolled his eyes and sighed. "I really don't want to hear any more BS about the four Cs of this academy, or what she expects from me."

"I don't know. I've only been asked to bring you to her. Don't kill the messenger, man."

Hawk sighed. "Right!"

"Follow me," said Kiplin. He walked toward the middle of the academy, where all the chancellors were housed.

Hmm … it's interesting that Sully is a Griffin and a Lepidoptera! thought Hawk, walking beside Kiplin.

* * *

"Come!" said Violette, upon hearing the knock at her office door.

Kiplin opened the door and gestured for Hawk to go in. "Catch up with you later."

As Hawk walked through the doorway and into the Head Chancellor's large office, he was immediately surprised to see how it held an embodiment of both darkness and sophistication, with a distinct aura of mystery that filled the air. The ancient oak furniture exuded an old-world charm, with ornate wooden desks and chairs that bore the signs of time. Arrayed along the walls were towering shelves, holding a treasure trove of what looked like ancient volumes of arcane knowledge and dusty grimoires.

"Ah, Hawk. Follow me," said Violette, authoritatively. She walked toward the doorway. "You are required too, Kiplin."

Kiplin nodded once. "Yes, Ma'am."

Without another word spoken, they followed Violette down a long, dark corridor, and then down some concrete stairs, which led them to a narrow, brick-lined, low-lit passageway, that seemed to go on forever. Arriving at a thick metal door, which could only be opened by the strength of a Lepidoptera Vampire, Violette turned to Kiplin and Hawk, and said, "This door leads into the Gramaze mansion, which is next door to the academy." She opened the door and led them to an operations room, where several Vampires were waiting. Hawk recognized Michael, but not the others.

"Hawk ... this is our coven's leader, William Gramaze," said Violette, gesturing to the brown-haired, seven-foot-tall Lepidoptera Vampire standing before them, dressed in leather attire that portrayed a blended elegance, power, and an unmistakable air of danger, embodying a formidable figure.

Hawk nodded once to William.

"Kiplin, I believe you have already met our leader," said Violette.

"Yes, I have, Head Chancellor," said Kiplin, turning from Violette to William. He stood tall and nodded once to William. "Good evening."

"Take a seat, Kiplin and Hawk," said William, his demeanor intense and focused.

"I prefer to stand. What is this about?" asked Hawk, eager to get this over with.

Hmm ... just like your father; straight to the point, thought William.

Kiplin stood silent beside Hawk.

"Brock, bring it up on the screen," instructed William, turning to the explosive's expert and IT specialist for the Gramaze Lepidoptera Vampire coven.

Brock pressed the enter button on his keyboard, replaying the CCTV recording.

The bewildered look on Hawk's face morphed to shock as he watched his home-land under siege. "This can't be happening," said Hawk, raking a hand through his hair, watching the screen even more closely.

"I am afraid that is not the worst of it. Elara Ironclaw has been taken," said William, turning to Hawk.

"What … how?" asked Hawk, his nostrils flaring. "Whoever has my mother will pay if she is hurt in any way. What do you know so far?"

"We know that Garrick Ironclaw has been wounded. Actually, he was the one to alert us that he needed our help," said William.

"Fuck … who would dare do this?" queried Hawk, his brow furrowed as he shook his head in disbelief that this could even happen to his powerful Griffin parents.

"That's what we are going to find out. I have known your parents for hundreds of years, and in all that time, I can't say that I have ever seen a situation like this, where they couldn't take care of themselves, and their land."

"I can't say that I have either," said Hawk.

"I have summoned a Warlock to create a portal for my family and me to go to Norway to help find your mother, and also to help bring the country back into some sort of order. I will require your assistance with the lay of the land. Are you with us?" said William, radiating authority and strength.

"I am ready, Sir, and … I thank you for your support. But I do need to retrieve my weapons from the academy," said Hawk. He turned and walked toward the glass sliding doors of the operations room.

"We already have your weapons bag here, Hawk." William turned to Michael. "Michael, show Hawk and Kiplin where our combat room is, so they can get changed into suitable battle gear, and Hawk can retrieve his weapons."

"Yes, Sire. Follow me, Hawk and Kiplin," said Michael. He walked toward the glass sliding doors.

"Yes, Sire. Follow me, Hawk and Kiplin," said Michael. He walked toward the glass sliding doors.

CHAPTER EIGHT

Warlock Adrian Lachance, who was Violette's adoptive father and had been a good friend of William Gramaze for numerous years, gestured with his hands, and uttered the command that brought the shimmering blue-green portal to a close behind them. "What now, William?"

"We wait here for Garrick Ironclaw to contact us," said William, noticing Hawk clutching his head. He knew the feeling of dizziness all too well from previous portal travels.

Michael, help Hawk with that, will you, mind-thought William.

Yes, Sire, replied Michael. He watched Hawk sit on the edge of a large spherical granite boulder near the shoreline and vomit.

Looking out and into the distance, William watched an eruption of fire just off Olden Fjord, with bright orange flames, and smoke rising into the air. An intense crackling and popping sound filled the air, as sparks soared into the sky, disappearing into the vastness above, leaving a heavy scent of burning wood.

Grayson, Samantha, Christian, Danielle ... form a protective border around us, mind-thought William to his Lepidoptera coven. He knew they were vulnerable out in the open, near the ocean.

Brock, Stephen, Sharina ... get the weapons ready. Sully, Samuel, Elsie, Kiplin ... you will stay with me, mind-thought William to the youngest legacies of the academy, and his coven.

Everybody quickly did as they were instructed by the powerful three-thousand-year-old Lepidoptera Vampire leader, and waited for further orders.

* * *

William watched as the foaming waves receded from the shoreline, their rhythmic retreat leaving dark, glistening stones in their wake. The crunch of footsteps on the beach's pebbles broke the stillness behind him. Turning sharply, he spotted two figures emerging from the shadowed depths of Olden Fjord. Bare-chested and powerfully built, the men's human forms glimmered in the pale moonlight, rivulets of water cascading down their skin. Yet, what drew William's attention most were the massive wings unfurled from their shoulders—dark as midnight, their feathers tipped with silvery light, glistening like shards of starlight.

With a practiced motion, William retrieved his sword from the sheath strapped across his back, the blade catching the moon's glow. His coven followed suit, their movements sharp and disciplined as they drew their weapons in unison. "State your business!" William demanded, his voice steady and commanding, radiating an aura of unquestionable authority.

The two strangers halted at the water's edge, their wings stretching slightly before stilling. Denim jeans clung to their long legs, the shredded hems brushing against the wet stones. Then, a faint glow began to emanate from their backs, casting ethereal reflections across the rocky shore. Each took a deep breath, and with a roll of their powerful shoulders, their wings quivered and began to retract. The feathers seemed to dissolve into a silken shimmer of light, melting seamlessly into their skin. As the glow faded, only faint scars in the shape of wing joints remained—a subtle but unmistakable mark of their Griffin heritage.

"William?" asked the first one. His brown eyes widened with a mix of surprise and relief, when he noticed the large group of well-built Lepidoptera Vampires waiting behind William, their weapons drawn.

"Yes!" replied William, abruptly. He held his sword in place.

"I am Draven." He placed a hand over his chest. "And this is Kael." He gestured to the tall, black-haired male standing beside him. His tone grew firm as he added, "We are soldiers of Garrick Ironclaw. You'll need to come with us."

William sheathed his sword and walked toward them, with Sully, Samuel, Kiplin and Elsie behind him.

When William reached the two soldiers, Draven held his hand out to clasp forearms with William. "Thank you for coming. We will need all the help we can get."

"Anytime! I believe Elara Ironclaw is missing," said William, grasping Draven's forearm.

"Yes. We have only now discovered where she is being held," said Draven. "Where is Hawk?"

"Here!" called Hawk, as he approached them. "Where are my mother and father, Draven?"

Draven lowered his eyes and bowed his head slightly to the Griffin prince. "Your father told us to bring you back home."

Hawk grasped Draven's arm firmly. "I'm not going back home. We will be searching for Elara Ironclaw. Are we clear?"

"Yes, Hawk," said Draven, bowing his head once. "Your mother is being held on a yacht about twelve miles out to sea." Draven indicated to the dark inky ocean.

"We believe, from our sources, that she is alive. But we don't know for how much longer," said Kael.

"Has father sent anyone for her?" asked Hawk. He looked from Draven to Kael.

"We don't know," said Kael, his brown eyes looking from Hawk to Draven for support. "We were told to come and collect you and take you back home. That is all."

"As I said, I won't be returning home until we find my mother. You know how important she is to our kind, and to me," expressed Hawk, heatedly.

Draven and Kael both nodded in agreement.

"Well, what are you waiting for … go and organize some of our soldiers to help you with this," ordered Hawk, shooing them both away.

Draven and Kael looked at each other and gulped. They both knew that if they didn't do what was expected of them by the prince, the son of their leader, then they would be brutally punished by him.

"Hawk, I think you are forgetting one important detail," said William, placing his hand on Hawk's shoulder.

"And that would be?" asked Hawk, shrugging away William's hand, his arrogance showing.

"We need a boat to be able to rescue your mother. We are strong, but none of my family can swim that far out, except for Sully," said William.

Hawk looked from William to Sully. "You will come with me, Sully."

"She won't be going anywhere with you, Hawk. I am the one in charge of this mission, and I will be giving the instructions, not you. ARE WE CLEAR?" William's broad shoulders towered over Hawk as he stood directly in front of him.

Hawk's nostrils flared, and his hands fisted, not showing any sign of intimidation as he looked up at William.

Fucking Lepidoptera. You are not my superior. I should put you down, thought Hawk.

"Humph … go for it, boy," said William. His scowling blue eyes turned ebony red, and they bore into Hawk's skull to create pain and discomfort. One of William's many Lepidoptera Vampire abilities to control the situation at hand.

Hawk clutched his head as the excruciating pain William inflicted on him became more intense by the second.

Realizing what was about to happen, Draven and Kael quickly stood in between William and Hawk.

"I don't think that this is going to help the situation, Sir," stated Draven.

"You will do well to listen to your people, Hawk," stated William. His ebony red eyes returned to blue.

Sully and Samuel looked at each other in disbelief and shook their heads.

What is that dude's problem? thought Sully to Samuel.

Whether it's out of sheer ignorance or naivety, he seems oblivious to who he is dealing with. Attempting to intimidate and threaten our father will yield no positive outcome for him. Hawk should consider himself fortunate that our father's allegiance to his parents and their kingdom outweighs any desire to impart a valuable lesson upon him, thought Samuel to Sully.

Agreed! thought Sully.

"Kael, can you find us a small boat?" instructed William.

"Yes, William. I will be back in a few minutes," said Kael. He ran toward the shoreline. Kael knew better than to argue with the powerful three-thousand-year-old Vampire, whose reputation was well known, and who had come to help them.

"Humph." Hawk strode off toward the inky black ocean.

"I'm sorry, William, for the treatment you have received here tonight from Hawk. Even though he is next in line to the throne, he is still a boy and inexperienced with his actions and the consequences," said Draven, with a look of concern creasing his forehead.

"Hmm … he sure needs a lesson or two. But I am certain, amongst other things, that is why his mother and father sent Hawk to the academy," said William, with his hands on his hips.

"Correct!" said Draven, remembering the trouble Hawk had caused and the lack of commitment to their culture that Hawk had shown in previous years. "But more importantly, we are hoping to get Elara Ironclaw back, and to also bring our kingdom back under control."

"I agree." With his Lepidoptera night vision, William watched Hawk, who was now in the water, summon some sea creature friends, and then Kael turn up in a metal dinghy.

Draven heard the sound of the outboard motor on the dinghy and turned to see what was happening behind him. "Looks like we are ready to go," said Draven to William.

"Yes, I can see that," stated William.

"Adrian, Christian, Danielle, Elsie and Kiplin, I need you to hold this position," William commanded, his voice firm and authoritative. "Guard the beach diligently until we return. Stay vigilant and be prepared for any unexpected developments."

Addressing the rest of the group, he continued, "The rest of you, follow me." With determined strides, William made his way to the water's edge, the others falling into step behind him, eager to heed his command and face whatever lay ahead.

As each supernatural creature stepped into the dinghy, William's authoritative voice resonated with clear instructions, ensuring they understood their mission and what was expected of them once they boarded the vessel.

"We will embark on this mission together. May our abilities combine and our determination prevail," said William, casting a glance at each member of the team, radiating confidence and conviction.

They all cheered loudly and fist pumped the air.

CHAPTER NINE

"Stop here, and cut the engine, Kael," Draven commanded, his voice steady and low, as the semi-lit vessel came into view in the deep waters of the Norwegian Sea.

Kael obeyed Draven's instructions, cutting the engine and bringing the boat to a halt. The dinghy continued to rock and sway, caught in the relentless rhythm of the choppy seas.

Draven surveyed the scene, absorbing every detail. The tension in the air was palpable as his focus shifted to the vessel ahead, where Elara Ironclaw was being held against her will. "Prepare yourselves for what lies ahead, everyone. We must free Elara, and restore the balance that has been disrupted," said Draven, his voice a quiet, yet resolute whisper.

His words resonated with everyone, their faces reflecting unwavering determination. As they readied themselves, Draven's eyes scanned the semi-lit vessel, mapping out their approach and formulating a plan.

"Let's go," said Draven, as he jumped into the water.

The icy ocean water churned as the Griffins and Lepidoptera Vampires jumped in, without hesitation, from the dinghy into the water.

William surfaced first, scanning the vessel ahead. The others emerged beside him, their movements smooth and controlled. "Stay together, everyone," stated William to everyone.

The darkness of the night embraced the Griffins and Lepidopteras, yet their determination burned brightly, guiding their every move. In the depths of Norwegian Sea, where the power of nature converged, they ventured forth, ready to confront the forces that had imprisoned Elara, and restore the harmony of Olden Fjord, Norway.

* * *

They climbed aboard silently, using a steel ladder that dangled into the water from the stern of the sleek white superyacht.

Hawk was first on board, creeping up on a muscular guard, and placing him in a headlock, to render him unconscious. He then gestured for Draven and Kael to follow him down the left-hand side of the yacht.

William used his Lepidoptera Vampire mind-talk abilities, to instruct his family to spread out and find Elara, all while keeping a watchful eye on their collective progress.

As each of them searched throughout the vessel's four decks and rooms, they came across a few more security guards and easily overpowered them.

Humans! thought Grayson, William's second-in-command, his brow furrowed. He had been expecting other supernatural creatures, and a lot more resistance than they were encountering.

This seems a little bit too easy, Lepidopteras. Stay focused and be prepared for anything. Keep your wits about you, thought William to his family, cautioning them as they all reached the top deck.

The air crackled with apprehension as William's words echoed in his coven member's mind. Each of them bound by their extraordinary Lepidoptera lineage and unwavering loyalty, they understood the gravity of the situation. The seemingly smooth progress raised concerns, and their instincts told them to remain vigilant. They affirmed their understanding with a resolute thought, reinforcing their determination to face whatever challenges awaited them. They harnessed their collective strength, drawing upon their unique individual abilities to be ready for any sudden turn of events.

* * *

"She's not here, anywhere. What the fuck is going on?" asked Hawk in a low voice, standing next to William. But as he said this, there was an explosion at the back end of the yacht. Steadying himself, Hawk turned toward a white light at the front of the yacht, and watched as his unconscious mother was carried toward a shimmering portal, by a man whom he had not seen or heard from for hundreds of years: his adopted older brother, Eryndor.

Hawk's voice pierced the air, desperately echoing, "Eryndor, STOP!" His every stride carried a sense of urgency as he sprinted toward them, driven by a steadfast determination to intervene.

But Eryndor didn't acknowledge Hawk. Instead, the Harbinger of Shadows crossed the threshold, and an enigmatic force enveloped him, shrouding him from sight. Abruptly, the portal sealed shut, severing any connection to them.

The sudden closure left Hawk standing on the edge of the deck, disbelief etching deep lines on his face. Raking a hand through his hair, he sighed. "Fuck!" *What does he want Mother for?*

"That's a good question," said William, placing a hand on Hawk's shoulder. "More importantly … we need to move. This vessel is going down."

Let's go, Lepidopteras, thought William to his coven.

William's coven moved as one, plunging into the abyssal depths, as the super-yacht started to break in half.

"Shit … Draven, Kael, we need to get the hell out of here!" Hawk's voice thundered with urgency, his words echoing through the air. The realization of the yacht's teetering balance sent shockwaves of fear and adrenaline coursing through his veins, propelling him into immediate action, diving into the frothy waters below.

Draven and Kael, attuned to the gravity of the situation, wasted no time in responding. Their shared instincts kicked in, urging them to flee from the impending disaster that lurked before them.

With their Griffin wings extended, they propelled themselves into the murky depths. The explosive force behind them tore through the air, finally shattering the yacht into two separate halves. Flames engulfed the broken vessel, casting an eerie glow that danced upon the waves before it succumbed.

Amidst the chaos, a sense of camaraderie cemented their resolve. Hawk, Draven, and Kael shared an unspoken bond, a deep trust in one another that further fueled their determination.

Everyone found themselves surrounded by an eerie stillness, the echo of the explosion reverberating in their ears. In the watery silence, they embraced the weight of their narrow escape, understanding that their lives had been spared by a mere fraction of time and circumstance.

"Shit, that was close," said Hawk, as he bobbed up and down in the water. "Thank you for the heads-up, William."

"You are welcome. Who was that malevolent harbinger that had your mother?" said William, treading water.

"My older brother … his name is Eryndor. I have not seen him for years. I didn't even know he was still alive, until now. Apparently, Mother and Father banished him from our kingdom hundreds of years ago, for atrocities he committed against our kind."

"What do you think he wants with Elara?" asked William.

"I'm not sure," said Hawk, shaking his head. "She must have something he wants."

"What makes you say that, Hawk?" asked Grayson, as he trod water next to William.

"From what I know, and according to our ancient folklore, Eryndor is the Harbinger of Shadows—a powerful and foreboding figure who doesn't just dwell in darkness, but commands and shapes it to his will. When my parents banished him, he vowed to return and conquer the earth, claiming everything and everyone on it," Hawk said, looking from Grayson to William.

"He sounds like a creature who doesn't deserve to be on this earth. But more to the point, what does he want from your mother?" queried Grayson.

Hawk casually shrugged his shoulders.

Maybe the Twin Icefire Blades, thought Hawk.

He scratched the back of his head feeling perplexed, accompanied by a sense of unease in his gut. Eryndor's abduction of his mother had caught him off guard, leaving him deep in thought, as he scrambled to find a plausible explanation.

"Who, or should I say what, are the Twin Icefire Blades?" asked William.

Ah, fuck ... I forgot about blocking. Now they have heard my thoughts. Hawk's brow furrowed.

"You Vampires really need to learn some boundaries, you know," said Hawk, shaking his head.

"I need an answer, boy," demanded William, firmly.

Hawk rolled his eyes. "They are ..." He took a deep breath to steady his thoughts. "It's not something I am meant to discuss, unless ..."

"Unless, what?" asked William, his tone abrupt. William punched his fist on top of the water and splashed it in Hawk's face.

"Unless our family is threatened." He wiped the water from his face and sighed deeply. "The Twin Icefire Blades are called *Eisvarda* and *Blaznira*. They are two of the most sacred and powerful possessions of the Norwegian people, created by the Smith Elders," said Hawk, whose body had now turned into Griffin form.

"What does that have to do with your mother?" asked William, frowning.

"I could be wrong, but I think that now Eryndor has returned, he could be looking for more power. And the Twin Icefire Blades can give him exactly that. From what I have overheard and know from my ancestry, my mother knows where the Twin Icefire Blades are hidden and how to extract them. This is the only reason I can think of for Eryndor to take her. Maybe my father would know more," said Hawk.

"Right … that would make sense. Let's make our way to see your father, and then we can come up with a plan of attack," said William.

"Yes, Sir," Hawk replied solemnly, his voice laced with concern. "I can't help but worry about my mother's well-being as we embark on this search. Hopefully she will still be alive, by the time we find her." As he spoke, the vivid image of his mother's motionless form being carried through the portal by Eryndor filled his mind, intensifying his unease.

"We can't let fear cloud our focus," William said, his eyes narrowing. "We will find Elara, I promise. Eryndor may be a force to reckon with, but we're not without our own strength." He gestured to his Lepidoptera coven. "Your mother's a strong woman, and she's survived worse than this. We'll get her back; I have no doubt."

"I want to believe that, William," Hawk said, his voice low but resolute. "If it's up to me, Eryndor won't get away with this."

William held Hawk's gaze, his expression firm and unwavering. "He won't," he said with quiet conviction. "But we need to move quickly and strike with purpose. Whatever he throws at us, we'll be ready."

Hawk's jaw tightened and the weight of his determination was clear in his stance. "Then let's make sure we're ready. My mother's life is on the line."

Griffins, Lepidopteras ... let's get back to the dinghy, and we will head to shore, mind-thought William.

Without hesitation, the group moved as one, swimming through the water with silent precision, as they swam back to the waiting dinghy.

Hawk reached it first, gripping the edge and hauling himself aboard before extending a hand to William. One by one, the others climbed in, their movements swift and practiced.

As soon as they were settled, Draven took up the anchor, and his sharp gaze flicked toward the distant shoreline. "No sign of pursuit," he murmured.

Kael nodded, his body still dripping as he settled into place. "Then let's move before it changes."

William cast one last glance at the looming vessel, before it finally went under. *Time to go.*

With that, the dinghy cut through the water, slipping toward the shadowed coast.

CHAPTER TEN

"My Lord," the soldier spoke with reverence, his voice filled with loyalty and respect. With a deep bow, he acknowledged his leader, who stood at the top of the elegant gray marble stairs.

The Griffin leader's gaze was fixed upon the captivating view of Olden Fjord, stretching out into the distance. "Yes!"

"William Gramaze is here to speak with you. He has Hawk with him, too."

"Show them in," said Garrick. The powerful Griffin turned toward the grand chamber, a space rich with ancestral heritage, wisdom, and spirituality. As the guard opened the heavy wooden double doors, Garrick watched his visitors enter.

William and Hawk walked toward Garrick, who was now standing at the bottom of the stairs.

"Father ..." stated Hawk. He bowed his head and knelt before Garrick in respect.

Garrick placed his hand on Hawk's shoulder and said, "Rise."

With no words spoken, Hawk did as he was instructed and stood to attention.

"William ... it is good to see you, my friend. It has been a while," said Garrick, holding his hand out. "Thank you for coming so quickly."

"Only too happy to help out, my friend," replied William, shaking his hand. "It's good to see you have healed well."

"Thank you. Being a Griffin sure has its advantages," replied Garrick.

"Have you heard from Eryndor yet?" William had contacted Garrick on the way to discuss what had transpired on the yacht.

Garrick's nostrils flared at the mention of his adopted son's name. "No, not yet. I am wondering why he has caused all this havoc in my land, and has taken Elara. I mean, what good will she be to him?"

"I think I may be able to answer that," said Hawk eagerly, looking at his father.

"Hold your tongue, boy!" said Garrick, angrily.

Hawk bowed his head, lowered his eyes, and took a deep breath to try and calm himself, as his fists clenched beside him in annoyance. The constant disregard and infantilization from his father had worn him down. The weariness of not being heard, of being dismissed as a child, had taken its toll on him.

"The boy might be on to something, Garrick. Just hear him out," stated William.

Thank you, William, thought Hawk.

William nodded once towards Hawk.

"Well ..." said Garrick, as he looked to Hawk. "What crazy idea have you come up with, now?"

"Listen ... I want to find mother as much as you do, but ..." began Hawk, heatedly.

"You had better curb your tongue, boy. I won't tolerate insolence," interrupted Garrick. A blue electricity emanated from his body as he crossed his arms over his chest. He had not forgotten the disrespectful way Hawk had acted in the past, nor his arrogance.

Hawk took a deep breath and steadied himself. "Do you think mother may have been taken because she knows where the Twin Icefire Blades are?"

Garrick Ironclaw opened his mouth to say something and then closed it. Frowning, he raked a hand through his short graying blond hair. "Hmm ... you could be on to something there, Hawk. Actually, it would make sense. Eryndor would be needing more power to stay topside, and take over my kingdom. Fuck! I should have killed that little piece of shit when he caused so much trouble years ago, rather than complying with the council's decision to exile him." Garrick pictured the destruction wreaked on his kingdom, and the citizens who had been murdered at the hands of Eryndor, and shook his head.

"Do you know where these Twin Icefire Blades are, Garrick?" asked William.

"Absolutely! But it will take us days to get there. And in the meantime," Garrick raked a hand through his hair again and sighed heavily. "Once Eryndor has what he wants, he will kill Elara."

"I won't let that happen, my friend," said William.

"He will pay with his life, if he harms my mother," said Hawk. Anger ignited within him, evident in the tightening of his jaw, as he remembered Eryndor carrying his unconscious mother into the shimmering portal.

"We have a Warlock with us and he can create a portal to this place. My family are outside waiting for instructions. Let's go," said William. He started for the doorway.

"Excellent," said Garrick, following William. "Come Hawk, you may learn something."

Hawk rolled his eyes, but followed William and his father through the lavish mansion, and then outside to where the Gramaze coven and the kingdom's soldiers were waiting.

* * *

As Hawk stepped through the shimmering portal, he quickly surveyed the chaotic battle scene that was set out before him.

What the fuck?

Hawk realized that Eryndor had wasted no time in launching an ambush, catching everyone off guard as they set foot on the mountainous snow in Hollyburn Ridge.

The air crackled with the sound of clashing weapons and war cries, which filled Hawk with a mix of determination and concern for everyone.

With his heart racing, Hawk retrieved his sword from the gilded scabbard he was carrying on his back and ran toward the battle. The clash of steel echoed across the mountainside, as Hawk's skills as a warrior were put to the test. He parried blows, dodged incoming strikes, and sought openings to strike back.

As his senses heightened, he remained vigilant, scanning the battlefield for any sign of a potential advantage. However, his focus was abruptly interrupted by the sound of someone calling his name.

Hawk ... this way ... over here, thought William, noticing Hawk, as he wielded his own sword straight through one of Eryndor's soldiers.

Hawk shook his head, scowling as William's thoughts invaded his mind. He had always hated anyone prying into his head. *Get the fuck out of my head, Lepidoptera.*

Distracted by William's mind-chatter, Hawk watched a sword swoosh past his face at lightning speed, the deadly strike of the white-eyed creature just missing him by inches. Reacting swiftly, he instinctively took a step back, distancing himself from the immediate danger. The encounter had caught him off guard, but he refused to let fear consume him. As he attempted to retaliate, he was effortlessly thwarted as the creature skillfully disarmed him, sending his weapon clattering to the ground. Hawk's mind raced, as he searched for an alternative course of action.

"Get the fuck away from him," commanded William, as he plunged his sword through the creature's back, and watched his body fall to the ground.

Hawk looked from the creature lying on the ground to William and gulped. "Thank you."

"Stay with me, and we can fight these creatures together," said William, acknowledging the other creatures that Eryndor had summoned.

"Yes, Sir," said Hawk. His solemn gaze scanned the lifeless bodies strewn across the blood-stained snow. With a determined nod, he reached down to retrieve his sword, feeling its familiar weight in his grasp, and joined the Lepidoptera leader to fight the white, glazed-eyed creatures in front of them.

With every swing and strike, the clash of metal echoed across the desolate mountain. Their movements were choreographed in harmony, each anticipating the other's actions. Hawk's blade sliced through the air, cleaving through the eerie creatures with precision. William's swift strikes followed suit, his weapon leaving trails of crimson in its wake.

As their adversaries faltered, the creatures' numbers dwindled beneath the relentless onslaught, and the atmosphere shifted. Where Eryndor's creatures were once fearsome and dominant, a palpable change rippled through the battlefield. The Griffin's embodiments of ancient power, and the Gramaze Lepidoptera coven, guardians of all, felt a surge of renewed hope coursing through their celestial veins, as the mountain quietened.

"What are these creatures?" asked Hawk, as he watched the last one fall.

"They are human. But I think Eryndor has them under his control," answered Samuel, who had overheard the conversation, as he came to stand next to William, with Sully and Elsie. "Don't worry, they are no match for my family or yours."

"Human!" said Hawk. His brow furrowed. "That doesn't seem possible."

"Eryndor must be controlling them," said Garrick, as he came to stand next to Hawk, holding his bloodied sword.

"Eryndor must be holding Elara nearby, because he had this area well-guarded before we stepped through the portal," said William, looking around at the blood-stained snow, and the decapitated bodies lying everywhere.

Keep your wits about you, Lepidopteras, thought William to his coven. The weight of uncertainty loomed over him, and he understood the importance of being proactive rather than reactive.

Sire ... where to now? mind-thought Grayson to William.

Firstly, I want this mess cleaned up, before anyone else sees this. Quickly and quietly, people. Then, we can regroup and discuss our plan of attack. I want everyone on the same page. I am sure this fucker will have some more surprises in store for us, mind-thought William, to his Lepidoptera coven and Griffins. He watched as everyone swiftly swung into action, clearing away the lifeless bodies strewn across the ground and working to erase the crimson stains from the snow within minutes.

With William's and Garrick's forces combining to confront Eryndor, they all understood the importance of devising a cohesive strategy to effectively put an end to Eryndor's control. They recognized that defeating Eryndor would require a combination of careful planning, collaboration, and utilizing their unique strengths.

CHAPTER ELEVEN

"Eryndor ... show yourself." Garrick's voice carried a firmness that demanded Eryndor's attention. Standing resolute in front of a towering wall of ice, Garrick exuded an aura of authority and determination. Hawk stood steadfastly by his father's side, ready to support him at this crucial moment.

The freezing wind whipped past, and silence fell upon them, as they waited at the base of Hollyburn Mountain, with tall snow-covered pine trees all around them.

"Show yourself, fucker!" shouted Hawk. His deep voice echoed throughout the jagged peaks, reverberating into the silence.

The ground rumbled, and a sense of anticipation filled the air, as a large door made entirely of ice, its surface glistening with a faint blue hue, slowly slid open in front of them. This man-made subterranean tunnel, built and utilized by the Canadian Armed Forces, served as a storage facility for weaponry and numerous artifacts.

Hawk quickly glanced at his father, and then inside to what looked like a vast, dark opening through the mountain. There in front of them stood two glazed-eyed, solidly built soldiers, both dressed in Roman attire, dark brown leather battle gear with their fully automatic rifles drawn, pointing toward them.

"Drop your weapons," said one of the soldiers, as he waved the tip of the gun at them.

"Like fuck we will. Where is Eryndor?" demanded Garrick.

"Drop your weapons, or you die. Your choice," said the soldier.

Hawk's eyes widened in alarm as he caught sight of a crimson dot materializing on his father's forehead. A surge of fear coursed through him, and he swallowed hard, the lump in his throat almost choking him. *Sniper?*

Garrick's gaze darted toward Hawk's chest, where he noticed an identical red dot materializing. The realization struck him like a lightning bolt.

Shit, Eryndor must have deployed sniper soldiers, concealed nearby, thought Garrick.

With no other choice, Garrick and Hawk discarded their weapons onto the snow beside them.

"Get moving," said the other soldier, pointing his rifle at them, indicating they should walk inside the mountain, while the other soldier collected their weapons off the snow, and followed them inside.

Cautious, Garrick and Hawk walked inside to where a railcar was waiting for them. The two soldiers prodded them in the back with their riffles, herding them into the railcar. As it started to move along the track, Garrick and Hawk were held at gunpoint in their seats by their captors.

* * *

"Let's go everyone. We need to get inside," commanded William, as he and his family, and Garrick's soldiers, moved faster than the human eye could perceive, toward the large door of ice, which was slowly closing in front of them, slipping inside the granite rock lined, darkened tunnel.

Kael fumbled in the dark to activate his phone's torch. Once he had turned it on, the blackened tunnel lit up, and he watched some of the Gramaze Vampires, who had the power of night vision, walk toward a railcar, which was big enough to fit both groups.

"Brock, Stephen and Sharina, I want you to wait here and guard the entrance. Adrian, you will stay with them. When we are on our way back, I will give the go-ahead, and you will need to get the portal ready. The rest of you will come with me. Are we clear?" commanded William.

They all responded together, "Yes, Sire."

* * *

The railcar came to a stop on the tracks at the end of a dimly lit concrete-lined tunnel. Looking all around, William noticed another railcar, and a steel ladder, which went from the bottom of the tunnel to a ledge a few meters above them. Without a word, William signaled for everyone to either climb the ladder or jump up to the ledge.

With their weapons drawn and ready for anything, both groups noticed a distinct rotten egg smell in the air.

"Father … what is that smell?" Samuel asked William.

"Hydrogen sulfide," said William, looking all around. "See the yellow deposits on the granite rock face; well, they are sulfur crystals, that release sulfurous gases."

"Ah, right," said Samuel, fascinated by the information.

"Listen up, people. If you haven't already noticed, this is probably an active volcano. The sulfur smell is a good indication of a potential eruption. So, let's get on with what we came for, and get the fuck out of here quickly," commanded William.

"Sire … it looks like there is a door over here," said Grayson, walking over to a metal door, on his left. Noticing a green button on the wall, he pressed it, then watched the thick metal door slide upwards. To his surprise it opened into a long, dimly lit, lead-lined hallway, with polished concrete flooring.

William and the others hastily moved to join Grayson.

"Wait!" ordered William, pushing past everyone. He picked up a rock from the ground and threw it into the hallway.

Sparks flew at the rock, and to their surprise it disintegrated in front of everyone's eyes.

William took a deep breath inward. "Just as I thought—booby-trapped. Christian, bring over the decoder."

"Yes, Sire." Christian retrieved the decoder from his backpack. Opening a separate USB port panel, which had been hidden in the wall next to the green button, Christian hooked up the decoder to the electronic screen in front of him, and then waited for the decoder to discover the four-digit code it required.

William and Christian watched until the decoder eventually found the last digit. As it clicked into place the hallway lit up brightly. Picking another rock up from the ground, William once again threw it into the hallway; this time it didn't disintegrate, instead it landed on the concrete flooring.

"Let's go everyone, but keep your wits about you," said William. A steely determination flickered in his eyes, conveying his resolute focus and readiness for the task ahead. With a confident stride, he led the way into the hallway, his countenance radiating a blend of leadership, caution, and a hint of underlying concern.

Christian swiftly detached the decoder, ensuring its safety within his backpack. With a decisive motion, he pressed the button located on the opposite side of the hallway, commanding the metal door to seal shut behind them. Without hesitation, he joined the others, striding purposefully into the expanse of the elongated corridor.

* * *

"What the hell!" yelled Grayson, his voice filled with alarm and disbelief, as the ground beneath him suddenly began to tremble violently.

"We need to find Garrick, Hawk and Elara and get the fuck out of here," said William, knowing that there could be an eruption at any time.

"But what about the Icefire Blades and Eryndor, William?" asked Kael. A grave and somber expression clouded Kael's face as he imagined the potential devastation that Eryndor could unleash upon not just their homeland, but the entire world, should he acquire the Icefire Blades. The weight of the responsibility to prevent such catastrophic consequences was evident in his furrowed brow, and the determined set of his jaw.

"You know damn well what our mission has been, Kael. Don't fret about that," said William.

Kael's nostrils flared in frustration, and he nodded once to William. He had no choice other than to follow, and help with the planned mission, even if he didn't agree.

As they all got closer to the end of the hallway, Grayson lifted his hand in the air to signal for everyone to keep quiet. He could hear voices nearby. Peering through a small glass opening in a doorway, he spotted Elara, her arms stretched above her, her wrists shackled to forged chains that descended from a pulley in the ceiling, her body in a barrel of water, which was up to her waist. He then watched her body convulse as the person in front of her electrocuted her again and again, until her body became limp, and she was rendered unconscious.

Fucking bastard! mind-thought Grayson.

William didn't need to see what was happening on the other side of the doorway, as he read Grayson's mind and felt the pain.

Get in there, NOW! screamed William through mind-thought to Grayson.

Grayson broke through the door at Vampire speed and held the man responsible up in the air by his throat. "How dare you treat Elara with such disrespect."

Kael and Draven watched as the ghostly eyed man struggled to break himself free from Grayson's hold. Soon enough Grayson had snapped his neck and discarded his lifeless body to the corner of the room.

"Your Highness, are you okay?" asked William, who had ripped the forged chains off Elara, and laid her limp body gently on the ground.

But she didn't answer.

"Danielle … come, she needs to be healed," instructed William.

Danielle, an immortal healer of supernatural beings, knelt beside Elara and placed her gentle, Lepidoptera hands on Elara's chest. A soothing warmth flowed from her fingertips as she closed her eyes, channeling her innate healing energy. Her hands glowed softly, radiating a luminescent light, as streams of white healing energy cascaded over Elara's body, wrapping her in a cocoon of restoration. The air grew still, filled with a serene calm, as Danielle's connection to her gift deepened.

Slowly, Elara's eyes fluttered open, their depths now shimmering with renewed vitality. The heavy weight of her burdens seemed to momentarily fade, replaced by a quiet sense of relief. Her steady, rhythmic breaths reflected a restored life force, with the healing energy weaving through her being, and rekindling her strength.

As the white rays of healing energy flowed, Danielle knew that her efforts were not only restoring Elara's well-being but also reaffirming the sacred bond between humanity and the earth. In this moment of healing, Danielle and Elara shared a profound connection, bound together in their shared devotion to preserving the sanctity and harmony of the natural world.

Sully, Elsie and Kiplin, who had gathered by the side of the room, exchanged astonished glances, captivated by the extraordinary spectacle before them. As relatively inexperienced individuals in the realm of missions or their powers, they were amazed by the healing abilities demonstrated by the Lepidoptera Vampire, an unprecedented sight in their limited encounters so far.

"William …" Elara recognized his face, as she sat up sluggishly, and held her bloodied head. "Where am I?"

"You are in Canada, your Highness. Where are the Icefire Blades?" asked William, who was kneeling next to her.

"Don't worry, William; they are still in a safe place. Eryndor … where is he?" asked Elara, her brow furrowed.

"Let's get you out of here, Elara," said William, picking her up in his arms. "We can talk about Eryndor later."

"NO … we must kill that evil bastard. He will pay for what he has done," said Elara, struggling free of William's arms.

"Your Highness …," said William.

"Don't *Your Highness* me. Where is Garrick?"

"He has been taken by Eryndor's soldiers, along with Hawk," said William. He watched the reaction on her face.

"What! Hawk … how is that possible? We sent him to the academy in Bagnolet. What the hell is going on?" Elara's nostrils flared, as a purple electric lightning source shimmied across her body.

Elara listened as William explained in detail the events that had transpired since their arrival in Olden Fjord, as per Garrick's request.

Absorbing every word, Elara recognized the importance of the information and the significance of the mission they were on. Her eyes held a mix of wisdom and concern, understanding the gravity of the situation and the potential consequences that loomed.

As William described the current whereabouts of Garrick and Hawk, Elara's expression mirrored the emotions that surged within her—a blend of hope for their safety, and a determination to assist in any way possible.

CHAPTER TWELVE

"Where are they?" shouted Eryndor, as he slashed a braided leather bullwhip across Hawk's abdomen.

"Fuck!" Hawk's body convulsed in pain.

"He doesn't know anything," shouted Garrick, hearing his son's pain, and watching his abdomen bleed through his torn clothing.

"You had better tell me, Garrick, otherwise Hawk will die in vain," warned Eryndor. He whipped Hawk belligerently once more.

"Go to hell, you fucker," screamed Hawk. "I would rather die than have Father give you the location of the Twin Icefire Blades." He sobbed through the pain, and tried to break free from the mystically forged chains that held him and his father upright against the concrete-lined wall.

"Let him go and I will tell you," Garrick said, looking from Hawk to Eryndor.

"Do you think I am stupid? I know what you are up to, Garrick, or should I say, Father." Eryndor's gaunt face sneered. "Even Mother, your Elara, tried to give me a cock-and-bull story about the whereabouts of the blades. But I didn't believe her either." Eryndor turned the bull whip on Garrick, slashing him across the chest. "I will only release Hawk once I have the Twin Icefire Blades and not before." A smug look crossed his face. "But then again, maybe I won't." His sickening laugh echoed throughout the room.

"You will pay for what you have done, Eryndor," yelled Garrick, trying to break free of the chains. "I will make sure of this."

Eryndor snickered and said, "It will be you who pays, Garrick." He then slashed Garrick across his bloodied chest once more, and watched with delight the pain his father was enduring.

Without warning, the metal door to the room they were held in burst open and was torn off its hinges.

"Get the fuck away from them," commanded William to Eryndor. The seven-foot-tall Lepidoptera leader stood in the doorway with his family behind him, their swords drawn.

"Ah, the cavalry has arrived," said Eryndor, sarcastically. He swiftly waved his hand in front of him and created a portal to carry him to his next destination.

Fuck! thought William, his nostrils flared. He hurried toward the shimmering portal and tried to stop the Harbinger of Shadows. As he thrust his sword toward Eryndor, the portal closed, and his sword dropped to the ground. "Shit! That fucker is going to pay when I get my hands on him." He then rushed over to Garrick and Hawk and broke their bloodied bodies free from the chains that had held them captive.

Danielle! mind-thought William.

Danielle rushed over to Garrick and placed her healing hands over his bloodied chest, watching his wounds disappear.

"Don't worry about me, attend to the boy," said Garrick to Danielle, his voice hoarse as he looked over at an unconscious Hawk.

Sully's brow furrowed and tears formed in her eyes when she realized Hawk had been tortured. *Hawk ...!*

Elara knelt beside her son and wept. With her bottom lip quivering, she held his hand in hers, and cried, "Hawk!"

Danielle quickly moved over and knelt next to Hawk's seemingly lifeless body, and moved her hands slowly up and down his torso. When his bloodied wounds healed, but he didn't wake, Danielle closed her eyes and chanted, *Ong Ma Lee Bae Mae Hong*, an ancient healing ritual.

But Hawk still didn't wake.

Strands of Danielle's blonde hair began to rise, as if lifted by static electricity, as she continued to chant the spiritual healing ritual over and over. *"Ong Ma Lee Bae Mae Hong."*

"What are you doing, stupid woman. That is not working," screamed Elara, through her sobs. She pushed Danielle's healing hands away in frustration.

Danielle looked at Elara and shook her head.

"Elara … you will desist," shouted Garrick, as he rushed over to their son.

Elara bowed her head and lowered her eyes.

"Go ahead, Danielle," said Garrick, who had every faith in her ability to heal Hawk.

With a look of determination, Danielle nodded once and resumed the chant. *"Ong Ma Lee Bae Mae Hong."*

After a few more uneventful moments, Garrick said, "What is going on? Why isn't he waking?"

Danielle blocked his questions out of her mind and continued to chant.

"Answer me, woman!" cried Garrick.

Danielle opened her eyes and scowled at Garrick, as she kept her healing hands on Hawk.

"Just give her a few more minutes, Garrick," demanded William.

"What is all the fuss about?" asked Hawk, opening his eyes. He slowly sat up and looked around the room.

"Oh, thank the gods," said Elara, who was still holding Hawk's hand.

Hawk smiled at his mother. "Thank goodness, you're safe, Mother."

"And you, *sønnen min*. I am relieved that you are okay," said Elara. She looked over at Danielle, "Thank you."

Danielle smiled and nodded once at Elara.

"Where is Eryndor?" asked Hawk.

"The fucker escaped through a portal," said William, holding his hand out to assist Hawk to stand.

"Shit … did he get his hands on the Twin Icefire Blades?" asked Hawk, standing slowly, without taking William's hand.

"No," said Garrick, helping Elara up off the ground.

Hawk breathed a sigh of relief. "Thank the gods!"

"What now, Sire?" asked Grayson.

"Back to Garrick and Elara's homeland. But first, I wanted to ask Elara something. Why did Eryndor take you instead of Garrick?" asked William, as he looked from Elara to Garrick.

"Why do you ask?" enquired Elara.

William looked between them again.

"Well, you both knew the Icefire Blades were meant to be here, in Hollyburn Ridge. So again, I will ask, why did he just take you? queried William.

"I don't know. What are you suggesting, William?" said Elara, her nostrils flaring.

Garrick looked from William to Elara and asked, "What have you done?"

"Besides having the Icefire Blades moved from here a millennium ago? Nothing!" She looked at Garrick sheepishly.

"What?" grunted Garrick. For thousands of years, he had always believed that the Twin Icefire Blades were in Hollyburn Ridge.

"I don't believe you, Elara," said William, with his hand on his sheathed blade. He had read her mind, so he knew she was hiding the truth.

She took a deep breath in, then out. "Fylgja told Eryndor where the Icefire Blades are being held." Elara looked at Garrick with a furrowed brow.

"What, or should I say who, is Fylgja?" asked William.

"My spirit guide, who travels with me," replied Elara.

"What trickery is this?" queried William, his blue eyes scowling at Elara.

"What the fuck, Elara! How can that be?" said Garrick. He had known for many years about her spirit guide. But he didn't know that Fylgja could communicate with others. "How did this happen?"

"When I was being electrocuted, Fylgja could feel that I was dying. And to save herself and me, she made her presence known to Eryndor and that's when she told Eryndor where the Icefire Blades are. I'm sorry, Garrick," said Elara. She lowered her head in shame.

"For fuck's sake … is any of this true?" William asked Garrick. He raked a hand through his brown hair.

"I'm afraid so, my friend," said Garrick, turning to William. His lips pressed in a thin line and his jaw tightened. "Elara will have to deal with Fylgja later. In the meantime, we need to come up with a plan to stop Eryndor. I don't want to even contemplate what he will do if he finds the Twin Icefire Blades. We definitely won't be able to defeat him then."

"What … that doesn't make sense. If Eryndor already knew where the Twin Icefire Blades were, then why did he continue to torture us all for information," asked Hawk, as he looked from Garrick to Elara.

"Maybe he didn't trust what Fylgja had told him," Elara suggested.

"Yeah, or maybe the sick fucker enjoyed watching us squirm in agony," said Hawk. His nostrils flared and he shook his head.

"Let's get the fuck out of here. We can talk about this on the way to the portal, and decide how we are going to stop Eryndor, and hide the Twin Icefire Blades somewhere safe again," said William.

"Sounds like a plan, my friend," said Garrick. He walked toward the doorway with Elara and Hawk.

Brock, Stephen, Sharina; we are on our way back. We have Garrick, Hawk and Elara with us. Be ready to portal out of here, mind-thought William to his Lepidoptera coven.

They all acknowledged his order.

Adrian ... mind-thought William, walking toward the doorway.

Yes, William.

Get the portal ready for our return. I will give you the coordinates once we get there.

Yes, William, Adrian responded.

CHAPTER THIRTEEN

"My Lord will not be happy about that," said the soldier to the captain, as he watched the anchor being dropped from the bow of the vessel into the ocean off the North Sea.

"What won't I be happy about?" asked Eryndor. As he stepped forward, the shadows around him writhed and stretched unnaturally, as though alive, creeping toward the ship's captain and the soldier, like grasping hands.

"My Lord, I didn't see you there … umm … well … the captain, he was telling me that because the seas are rough out here today, that we will not be able to see anything by sonar," said the soldier. "And, in fact, he told me that … that we wouldn't be able to use the submersible until it cleared." The soldier gulped hard and lowered his eyes.

"I don't care for excuses, and I am not paying you, captain, to tell me that we can't see what's at the bottom of the seabed. I want the submersible lowered, NOW," said Eryndor, authoritatively. His spine-chilling eyes bored into the captain's skull.

"Yes, Sir. But …" The captain clutched at his head.

"Just do as I have instructed you, captain," demanded Eryndor, his voice cold and unyielding. A dark, writhing shape, like the silhouette of a skeletal figure, seemed to crawl beneath his skin, rippling across his torso before sinking back into the shadows within him.

The captain gulped hard and his eyes widened, then he nodded once. *I wish I had never taken on this damn job. No amount of money is worth me losing my life over. And my family ... what would they do without me? What was I thinking?*

"Well, what are you waiting for?" asked Eryndor, impatiently.

"Yes, Sir," said the captain. He walked over to the white-under-water submersible, which was on the deck, and lowered it slowly into the water with the ship's crane.

As the submersible bobbed up and down in the rough seas, Eryndor's soldier climbed aboard the vessel and opened the hatch for Eryndor to step in.

"Keep guard whilst I am under the ocean. I don't want any surprises when I come back up. Do you hear me?" said Eryndor to the soldier, as his body floated down inside the submersible.

"Yes, My Lord," replied the soldier. He watched the door close, and then he locked the outside handle of the submersible's hatch. Scrambling back up the ship's ladder to the deck, the soldier watched the submersible dive into the water and disappear from sight.

Fortunately, I possess the necessary skills to maneuver this submersible, otherwise, recovering the Twin Icefire Blades would have been impossible, thought Eryndor.

Eryndor couldn't help but contemplate the price he would make his parents pay for robbing him of his Griffin prowess to explore the depths of the ocean, when he was banished.

Even though he was the Harbinger of Shadows and had been banished from Norway by his adoptive parents years ago, Eryndor despised the limits on his Griffin abilities. He hoped acquiring the blades would provide him with the crucial enhancement necessary to gain additional abilities that could help him take over, not only the Norwegian kingdom, but also the world.

Eryndor turned the sonar on and steered the submersible deep into the waters off the North Sea.

* * *

"Where are we, Hawk?" asked Sully, her voice filled with curiosity, as she emerged through the portal beside him. Her gaze swept across the breathtaking scenery that unfolded before her.

"We are in Norway, my home. This place is called Olden Fjord. Beautiful, isn't it?" said Hawk, looking at Sully.

"So beautiful ... and peaceful," said Sully, stepping onto the green grass. "Did you spend much time here when you were growing up?" Sully breathed in the salty air, as she walked toward the crystal-blue ocean.

"No, not really. Father always had my brothers and I in combat training. And, with all that is going on, only now do I understand why most of our lives he has been hard on all of us," said Hawk, as he walked beside Sully.

Stopping at the shoreline, Sully hadn't even heard what Hawk had said about his training, as she looked out to sea in wonderment, yearning to be swimming in the deep ocean.

"Sully, Hawk, over this way," gestured Samuel, who was standing with William and Elsie, near the pine trees.

Hawk nodded to Samuel, grasped a dazed Sully's arm, and pulled her toward where everyone else was standing.

* * *

"Can you sense Eryndor's presence, Elara?" Garrick asked, his voice low.

Elara had always been able to feel her sons' presence on Griffin land or sea, even Eryndor's. But this ... this was different. As her gaze drifted toward the horizon, a shiver ran through her, a chill that seemed to seep into her very bones. She knew—Eryndor was nearby.

"He's out there," she murmured, her finger pointing to the depths of the ocean, where the waters seemed unnaturally still.

"Would you like me to go and search for this worthless piece of shit?" Hawk asked his father. He was ready to show his father that he was prepared for anything, even if it meant he was to die for his family and country.

Garrick's brow furrowed, as he searched Hawk's thoughts, and realized that he would put his life on the line for not only his family, but his country as well. Placing his hand on Hawk's shoulder he said, "Eryndor … he would kill you, my son."

"I am ready, father," Hawk declared, his demeanor resonating with soldier-like determination, as he locked eyes with Garrick.

"Yes, I can see that. But what you don't fully understand is that Eryndor will be more powerful than ever, once he has the Twin Icefire Blades. You won't stand a chance of defeating him by yourself. None of us will."

"How are we to stop him, then?" queried Hawk, frowning.

"William and I have discussed a plan of attack," said Garrick, looking from Hawk to William.

Hawk looked at William and nodded once in his direction.

You will come with me, Hawk. I will be happy to have you on my team, mind-thought William to Hawk.

Uh huh … please … I don't like the mind thing, Hawk mind-thought to William. Even as a child, he had hated anyone intruding on his thoughts, and now that he was older, it drove him crazy.

William smirked and nodded once to Hawk.

Get ready, Lepidopteras. We have one chance to get this right, mind-thought William, to his family, who had already been given their orders.

Garrick stepped away from Hawk and said, "Gather around everyone. I want to discuss our future."

CHAPTER FOURTEEN

The eager-to-please soldier unlatched the white hatch of the submersible, and Eryndor soared upward, his movements swift and formidable, before landing on the ship's deck. In his hands, wrapped in a swirling dark mist, he held a long, intricately carved wooden box. The shadows around him seemed almost alive, writhing as if to shield him from the clashing forces contained within.

"My Lord …" The soldier bowed his head and lowered his eyes.

"Tell the captain to take us back to the shore," said Eryndor, matter-of-factly.

"Yes, Sir," said the soldier. He hurried below deck to find the captain.

But Eryndor wasn't about to wait for the ship to arrive at the shore, neither did he want to share what he had found below the ocean's currents. Instead, he created a portal to carry the wooden box and himself to the shore.

* * *

Eryndor's senses, although already sharpened as he stepped through the shimmering portal, failed to warn him of the ambush. In an instant, his hands were wrenched apart, and glowing mystical chains bound him to the rugged mountainside of Olden. Elara's power pulsed through the bindings, unyielding and absolute. His gaze dropped to the carved wooden box, now lying in the sand before him, its presence taunting him. Snarling, he twisted and strained against the chains, shadows writhing around him as he fought to break free.

"Once I break free, you will pay with your life, Elara," grunted Eryndor.

"Eryndor, it is you who shall pay. Allowing you to live all those years ago was a grave error, and it is a mistake I refuse to repeat." He watched Elara clench her right hand into a ball and thrust a lightning bolt at his upper abdomen.

"Ah, fuck …" Eryndor's face contorted in pain. "Is that all you've got, bitch?" He strained against the chains, twisting and pulling with all his might, but each movement sent a jolt of searing energy into his wrists and ankles, the mystical bindings biting into his shadow-wreathed limbs with every futile attempt to break free.

Ignoring his comments, Elara said, "Grab the box, Hawk."

But before Hawk could even start to run toward the box to retrieve its contents, William Gramaze quickly stopped him in his tracks.

Wait!

Hawk did as William instructed, though he couldn't ignore the pull of the power radiating from the wooden box—unlike anything he had ever encountered before. His eyes remained fixed on the box as it slowly opened, revealing a brilliant light. A blade rose into the air, floating effortlessly.

Elara … Elara Ironclaw, come to me. We are one, called the *Eisvarda* blade.

Everyone on the beach heard the voice calling Elara.

"Elara, NO," shouted Garrick, as he watched a dazed look come over her face, and her long silver hair start to rise in the air. She no longer had control of her mind and was walking directly toward the blade. Without hesitation, Garrick rugby tackled Elara to the ground. As she tried to break free from his hold, he slapped her face.

"What the fuck, Garrick. Get off me," yelled Elara, as she came out of the trance-like state. She tossed him to the side and pushed herself to her feet.

Eryndor smirked as he watched on in amusement. *Power, I want some of that.* Wriggling, he eventually broke free from the chains on his ankles and then his wrists.

"Oh no, you don't," said William. Using his Vampire abilities, he held his hand out to stop Eryndor from moving, then drew his sword from its sheath and held it to Eryndor's throat.

"You are no match for me, Lepidoptera," said Eryndor, smirking. He used his powers to turn the sword on William. "Now who is in control, Vampire?"

"Get the fuck away from my father," cried Samuel, who used his own sword to cut off Eryndor's hand.

William jumped to his feet, collected his sword from the ground, and stood beside his son with his sword drawn.

"Fuck …" screamed Eryndor, clutching his left wrist. "You will pay with your life, boy." Quickly and without a word he created a portal.

Samuel ran toward the portal to try and stop Eryndor, but it closed all too soon in front of his eyes and Eryndor was gone. "Shit!"

"Are you both unharmed?" Garrick inquired, his voice laced with concern, as he positioned himself beside William and Samuel.

William looked from Samuel to Garrick and said, "Yes, we are fine."

"Let's get the hell out of here, and find this other blade before Eryndor does," stated Garrick. He watched Elara kneel beside the carved wooden box, with the first blade in it, close the lid and fasten the latch. Elara caressed the intricate wooden pattern on the lid with her fingertips and looked off into the distance.

Adrian, create the portal to transport us all to the next destination, mind-thought William.

Yes, my friend, replied Adrian.

* * *

"Where is the *Eisvarda* blade, Elara?" asked William, as he watched her step out of the portal, and onto the bridge.

"What … what are you talking about? It's here, in my hands," said a dazed Elara. Even though she had been the first one to step into the portal, carrying the wooden box, she was the last one to step out of the portal at the other end.

"What the fuck … it's not in your hands. Are you blind, woman?" asked William, his brow furrowed.

Elara looked down at her hands. Bewildered, she realized that the carved wooden box and its contents were missing. Panicked, she looked back at the shimmering portal and ran back toward it. But it closed as she neared it, as Garrick pulled her backward.

"What are you doing? That portal could have cut you in half," said Garrick, holding her arm.

Elara flinched away from Garrick. "The *Eisvarda* blade … it's inside the portal." She turned to Adrian. "Open the portal up, Adrian. I need to retrieve the sacred blade."

"Elara, are you alright?" asked a worried Garrick.

Elara frowned, closed her jade-green eyes, and rubbed her temples. "Of course I'm all right." Her memories of the portal transport then came flooding back. "Oh, shit … Eryndor has the first blade."

"What the hell … how did this happen?" asked Garrick, with his hands on his hips.

Elara gave a blow-by-blow explanation of the mind control Eryndor had exerted over her, and what happened when she entered the portal.

Adrian! mind-thought William. His nostrils flared as he listened to Elara recount her interaction with Eryndor, of how he had lain in wait, and was able to take the first blade from her during the portal transportation.

Adrian gulped hard. *Shit!*

Shit! Is that all you have to say? … I will deal with you later, mind-thought William.

"Now that Eryndor has the first blade, it is only a matter of time before he finds the second one," said Elara, realizing Eryndor had probably walked out of the portal ahead of them all, and was now searching for the second blade. "By the way, Eryndor has grown back his left hand. I don't know how; I just remember seeing it when he was inside the portal."

"How is that possible?" queried William, his brow furrowed.

"I don't know. What I do know is that the *Eisvarda* and *Blaznira* blades will be drawn to each other, now that they are in the same region. And I am sure Eryndor knows this from our cultural history," said Elara.

"Right, well it would seem that time is of the essence. Let's get moving," said William, hearing the roar of the nearby waterfall and looking at his surroundings. "Am I right in surmising we are at the Kleivafossen Waterfall?"

"Yes. The other blade is not too far from here," said Elara, pointing to the rock-face tunnels inside Kleivafossen Waterfall.

"You lead the way, and we will keep guard until the blades are recovered," said William.

Elara gave a single nod in acknowledgment before proceeding across the bridge, where rustic lanterns lined the path. Their warm, flickering glow cast a soft, dim light, gently illuminating her way across.

CHAPTER FIFTEEN

"Ah … finally, my beauty," Eryndor whispered, his voice tinged with anticipation, as he unlocked the intricately carved wooden box. With bated breath, he revealed the resplendent *Eisvarda* blade nestled within. A triumphant gleam danced in his eyes, as his fingertips traced the flawless craftsmanship of the weapon; its long, broad blade radiated a lustrous sheen from its darkened, polished-steel surface. The blade bore the weight of ancient symbols, etched into its very essence, signifying the awe-inspiring power it possessed. Securing the lid once more, he retrieved the other wooden box, which held the legendary *Blaznira* blade, from the ground in front of him. With a confident gesture, he extended his hand, invoking his arcane abilities to conjure a portal with a single gesture.

Eryndor …

A perplexed expression crossed Eryndor's face as he swiftly withdrew his hand and scanned his surroundings, searching for the source of the voice that had interrupted this moment. His heightened senses sharpened further, alert to any sign of presence. A surge of suspicion coursed through him as he gradually comprehended that no one was there to confront him.

"Reveal yourself!" he demanded, his grip on the two ornately carved boxes tightening as he held them protectively against his chest.

Eryndor …

"Show yourself," Eryndor demanded again, as his eyes darted all around the tunnel.

Suddenly, and without warning, Eryndor found himself violently thrust into the air, suspended above the ground by an unseen force. As his body hovered, a brilliant white light began to radiate from the previously sealed wooden boxes, which had opened upon hitting the ground.

Why have you interrupted our slumber?

As Eryndor's body hung in the air, suspended like a marionette puppet, he felt a strength like no other, which held him in place. He couldn't move his body or hands to escape. His eyes darted everywhere, as the voice spoke, once again.

Why have you woken us?

"To draw from your power," said Eryndor, now realizing he was hearing the voice of one of the blades.

Is that so? Then what can you offer us in return?

"A lifeline to both worlds, above and below," said Eryndor.

Your offer is minimal ... and we suspect you are offering something you can't give.

"Believe me, I can and will be able to offer you this, once I have your powers," promised Eryndor.

Prove it!

Eryndor's body was dropped to the ground, beside the two carved boxes. He quickly got to his feet and tried to summon a portal.

What the hell is going on? thought Eryndor, when the portal didn't appear.

Well ... we are waiting.

Eryndor knelt on the ground and looked upon the Twin Icefire Blades. "My powers ... they've been drained." As Eryndor's fingertips made contact with the blades, an electric energy surged forth from the ancient weapons, crackling and arcing with a life of its own. The sheer force flung Eryndor backward, his body colliding forcefully with the unforgiving wall of the tunnel.

"Ah, fuck," said Eryndor, his brow furrowed as he tried to stand.

Stunned and disoriented, Eryndor struggled to regain his footing, the echoes of the surge still reverberating within him. Despite the pain and momentary setback, a wicked smile twisted across his lips. The jolt he had experienced was but a taste of the raw power contained within those blades, a testament to their untamed might. With renewed determination, Eryndor rose from the tunnel floor, his eyes ablaze with a hunger for power. The path ahead may be treacherous, but he would embrace the challenges, wielding the blades as instruments of his malevolence.

Eryndor harbored a sinister ambition to rule Norway, with all its citizens under his dominion. In his twisted mind, the betrayal of losing his rightful place as heir to the throne only fueled his relentless pursuit of power. He would stop at nothing to see his dark aspirations realized, ready to manipulate, scheme, and overcome any obstacle in his way. Driven by a longing to reclaim what he thought was his and a thirst for domination, Eryndor pressed forward on his treacherous quest for both power and the crown.

You will pay for this trickery.

"I was not trying to deceive you. I need some of your powers so that I can portal us out of here," said Eryndor, with his hands on his hips.

You will need to earn it first, before we hand over to you any of our powers.

"What do you want me to do?" asked Eryndor.

Besides your word that this is not a trick, we require safe passage to a place of our choosing.

"I can promise that I will be able to provide a safe passage to anywhere, once I have some of your powers," said Eryndor, who was not usually a man of his word. He was, after all, a deceitful Harbinger of Shadows, whom you would never trust.

Then we have a deal.

"Why would you believe or trust anything this evil creature says? He can NEVER be trusted!" Elara interrupted, stepping out of the dark tunnel into the light, with Garrick by her side. They had been listening to the conversation between their adopted son and the two ancient blades, biding their time to see what would unfold.

Eryndor was thrust against the tunnel wall by the Twin Icefire Blades.

Ah, there you are, Elara. Come to us.

In a dazed state, Elara floated in an upright position above the ground and was pulled toward the opened carved boxes.

With his fists clenched, Garrick was held in a standing position by the blades, unable to move his limbs.

I see from your memories that you were the one to let Eryndor know each of our locations. Why would you do this?

"I am deeply sorry, *Blaznira* and *Eisvarda*. It was not my intention, at all, to let you fall into the hands of the Harbinger of Shadows," said Elara. She was pulled into a kneeling position next to the open carved boxes. "My spirit guide gave your locations to Eryndor. But … please … don't punish her. Fylgja still has much to learn."

Garrick tried to wriggle free from the powerful hold the blades had on him, but to no avail. "If you so much as touch my partner, I will …"

Hold your tongue, Garrick.

In an instant, and without warning, Garrick lips were sealed shut. A look of fury and frustration twisted his features as he vehemently shook his head, attempting to break free from the blades' grip on his speech. Yet, his efforts proved futile against the overwhelming power emanating from the ancient weapons.

Elara … we require safe passage to a place of our choosing. Can you assist us with this?

"Yes. And I promise your locations will never, ever, be revealed again," said Elara, looking at each of the blades.

"It doesn't matter where you hide them, I will eventually find them again," Eryndor smirked, as his body hung from the tunnel walls. *Their power will be mine!*

Enough ... be gone, roared the *Blaznira* blade, commandingly.

And with that said, Eryndor's body was thrust down into the sewers of hell by the Twin Icefire Blades.

"I will return," screamed Eryndor. His voice echoed throughout the tunnel.

"Now, let's find a secure location for both of you." Elara spoke with determination. "Where would you prefer to be placed?" she inquired.

CHAPTER SIXTEEN

With Eryndor banished to the depths of hell, and the Twin Icefire Blades securely concealed, the resilient citizens of Olden emerged from their places of refuge and began the arduous task of rebuilding their shattered community. Days had passed since havoc was wreaked by Eryndor, and now a sense of determination filled the air as the loyal citizens worked tirelessly to restore what had been lost. Through sweat and perseverance, the scars of destruction gradually gave way to signs of rejuvenation. The sound of hammers pounding, saws cutting, and voices uniting filled the once desolate streets. The community came together as one, rebuilding homes, mending infrastructure, and restoring the vibrant heart of their town.

Olden, Norway, once again stood as a testament to the unyielding spirit of its people. A community reborn from the ashes, unified by the shared experience of overcoming adversity, and ready to embrace a brighter future.

"I want to thank you and your family for everything you have done to help me and my people," said Garrick to William. He held his hand out to clasp forearms with William. "I don't think we could have defeated Eryndor without your support."

"You are welcome, my friends. Anytime!" William looked from Garrick to Elara. "I must admit I was a little bit surprised when I got the call from you, explaining you had been wounded and your country was under attack. I suppose being that you are a powerful Griffin warrior, I just … well, I would never have expected that you would have needed our help." William grasped Garrick's forearm, then held his hand out to Elara.

"Believe me, I was as surprised as you were. Fortunately, I heal quickly. We will be better prepared if anything like this were to happen again," expressed Garrick.

"Yes, and we would also like to thank you and your family for staying and helping rebuild our small villages," said Elara, taking William's hand.

"I am sure you would have done the same, if the situation provided itself, Elara. My family and I are only too happy to help," said William, shaking her hand.

"It's a pity you have to leave so soon. But I do understand you have a city of your own to protect, back in Bagnolet," said Garrick.

"Yes, and speaking of Bagnolet, will Hawk be returning with us, and training back at the academy?" queried William.

"Elara and I have spoken about this, and … even though Hawk seems to have grown a lot in the last month, we still think it would be beneficial for him to return with you," said Garrick. He sighed heavily.

William nodded and said, "He does seem to have a VERY big chip on his shoulder … is there any reason why?"

Elara looked at Garrick, raised her eyebrows and twitched her lips. "I will let you explain, Garrick."

"Right! Well, when Hawk was little, he was the perfect child, but in his early teens, he became such a handful. He wouldn't listen; he didn't want to take on our Norwegian culture, and he even tried running away and moving in with another family. Of course, that didn't work either, because even they couldn't put up with his arrogant ways," said Garrick, remembering how, out of all his children, with the exception of Eryndor, Hawk was the most difficult one to raise.

William snickered, and remembered just how problematic Sully had been, when her foster parents were killed, and he first took her in. "Well, that is most teenagers, until they learn some life lessons. Don't you think?"

"Yes, but with Hawk, his arrogant and over-confident, self-centered attitude has gotten him into all sorts of situations. An example of this was just before we sent him to Bagnolet; he nearly killed all the sea creatures in the Olden Fjord. Hawk's shortcomings in listening, processing information, and considering the broader implications of his actions demonstrate his unreadiness to ascend to the throne. To become a worthy king, he must overcome his arrogance, cultivate humility, and develop a deep sense of responsibility toward his kingdom and its inhabitants," said Garrick, his brow furrowed. "Only through growth and introspection can he mature into a leader capable of making informed, compassionate decisions that benefit his people and the world around him. We think time at the academy and being around other Supes may help him to grow and become someone our people can learn to trust. Especially as he is next in line to our throne."

"From what I have seen so far from Hawk, I do believe he has changed. But only time will tell. How does he feel about going back to the academy?" asked William.

"He is not thrilled about the idea," said Elara. She sighed heavily. "In fact, in the last couple of days, we haven't been able to get him to leave his room. And the only person he has let into his room has been your daughter, Sully."

"Yes, and I believe from speaking with my son, Samuel, that Sully has been spending a considerable amount of time with Hawk," said William, his nostrils flared.

"How do you feel about this, William?" asked Elara.

"I am not overly worried. Unfortunately for them, when we return to the academy, they will not be spending much time together at all."

"Right! Can I ask that you keep a close eye on Hawk, then?" asked Elara.

"You don't need to worry; he will be fine. Our instructors and Head Chancellor will not only be taking care of his training and learning, but also his egotistical ways. Hawk will be quite busy when he returns to the academy. Also, Kiplin, Hawk's roommate, has been at the academy for a while, and has been given strict instructions to look after him and help him settle in," said William.

"Thank you, my friend," said Garrick, placing his hand on William's right shoulder.

"You are welcome. Just one thing, though …" said William, looking from Garrick to Elara. "When it's time to leave for Bagnolet tonight, you can say your goodbyes, but I want you both to leave Hawk to me."

"What do you have planned?" questioned Elara.

"You will see soon enough," stated William, his expression a mixture of confidence, and a knowing smile.

* * *

Hawk found solace in the comfort of the cushioned window seat, and stretched his legs out before him. With a contemplative gaze, he peered out across the expanse of the Olden Fjord. The deep blue hues of the water and the untamed ruggedness of the shoreline beckoned to him, captivating his senses in an inexplicable way. Every fiber of his being felt the magnetic pull, as if the very essence of the place was summoning him to immerse himself in its beauty and mystery.

I sure will miss my hjem *and* familie.

Taking a bite of his apple, Hawk leaned back, his eyes fixed on the enchanting canvas of the sky. Shades of blue, pink and orange painted the heavens, as the sun descended behind the majestic mountains. The tranquil scene unfolded before him, a breathtaking display of nature's artistry. With each passing moment, the sky transformed, casting a warm glow that embraced the landscape and whispered of the impending twilight.

"Knock, knock," said Sully, opening Hawk's bedroom door. Her brow furrowed when she noticed him sitting alone, looking longingly out the window. She closed the door behind her, and headed over to him. "Are you okay?"

"Yeah, I'm fine."

"You don't look fine!" exclaimed Sully, sitting next to him on the window seat.

"It's … well … I will miss my home and this," said Hawk, pointing to the Olden Fjord waters.

"I don't blame you. It sure is beautiful." Sully looked out at the sunset that was painting the calm water's edge. "I love swimming in the ocean because it always makes me feel alive."

"Yeah, me too. So … what can I do for you?" asked Hawk, looking into her jade-green eyes.

"Umm … I have been asked to come and get you. Apparently, we are departing soon, and William would like to talk with you before we all leave," said Sully.

"Oh, right! What does he want to chat about?"

She shrugged her shoulders. "No idea!"

Hawk swung his legs over the side of the window seat and placed his feet on the ground. Standing, he walked over to his packed bags, which were on his bed.

Why won't father let me stay? I have proven myself over and over. What more does he need? thought Hawk.

Sully listened to Hawk's thoughts and walked toward him. Placing a hand on his right shoulder she said, "I am sure you will be able to return home soon enough. And in the meantime, well, you have a few good friends at the academy who will watch your back, and can be your wingman, or woman." She smirked, as Hawk turned around.

Hawk nodded and smiled. "Thanks, Sully. I sure do appreciate our friendship. And yes, you can be my wing-woman, anytime." He leaned in to give her a heartfelt hug.

Sully smiled and nestled into his muscular body. "I suppose we had better get going. William will be wondering where we are." She slowly pulled away from Hawk's embrace, picked up one of his bags, and headed toward the doorway.

"Okay," said Hawk, picking up the other bag.

* * *

"Ah, there you are, Hawk," said Garrick, who was standing with Elara and William, in the main hall. "Well, son, I am sure we will see you again soon. Do us proud at the academy." He extended his hand toward Hawk.

"Yes, Father," said Hawk, shaking Garrick's hand.

Elara leaned into Hawk for a hug. "Goodbye, my *sønn*. Look after yourself and, remember, you are attending the academy for a reason. And that is to better yourself! We look forward to your return."

"Yes, Mother," said Hawk, embracing her.

"Before we go, Hawk, I wanted to speak with you about something I think you may be interested in, back at the academy," said William.

"And that is?" Hawk asked in a matter-of-fact tone, clearly unaware of what William was about to propose.

"It's an important role at the academy," said William. He watched Hawk's demeanor change. "At this stage, it's more of an apprentice role, but it could turn into an instructor role; that's if you are up to the challenge."

"What would I need to do?" asked Hawk.

"We need someone to train the younger Supes in combat. Would you be interested in this role?" asked William.

"Sounds interesting! When would I start?" asked Hawk.

"It would be as soon as we arrive back at the academy."

"Right!" Hawk smiled. "So … you said that it would be an apprentice role, at first?"

"Yes. We can iron out all the details later. For now, I just wanted to see if you were interested."

"Yes, I'm definitely eager to take on this role you're offering, and I thank you for the opportunity, Sir. But …" he hesitated for a few seconds, "I am wondering why you would choose me for this role? I am sure there are others at the academy you could have chosen?" Hawk looked from William to Sully, smiled, and then back to William.

"Hmm …" William's brow furrowed as he thought about it for a few seconds. "I think you have something to offer that no others can at the academy, and not only that, I think that you have demonstrated in the last month that you are quite capable of becoming a formidable ally to our family. And that is something that I would like to pursue further."

"Oh, right!" Hawk responded, impressed that the leader of the France Lepidopteras even thought of him this way.

"As I said, Hawk, the role starts as soon as we get back to the academy. But for now, we need to get going."

"Ready whenever you are, Sir," said Hawk, eagerly. He looked from William to his parents and smiled.

Sully, who was standing next to Hawk, smiled and said, "Congrats."

"Thanks," said Hawk.

"Adrian … transport us back to Gramaze mansion," instructed William.

"Yes, William," said Adrian. He placed his hands out front and commanded a portal to open.

William watched the shimmering portal open, and then turned to Garrick and Elara and said, "Well, my friends … call me if you need us to come back. We are only too happy to help, anytime."

"Thank you, William," said Garrick.

"Yes, thank you, William. And thank you for offering Hawk a lifeline at the academy," said Elara. She leaned in to give William a hug.

"I will keep you updated on his progress," said William, as he pulled away from her embrace. "Sully, Hawk … our transport awaits." The seven-foot-tall Vampire walked toward the shimmering wall of the portal that glistened in front of them.

As they walked through, Adrian followed, and with a wave of his hand, commanded the portal to close.

"I hope he does us proud," said Garrick to Elara, as they watched the portal close.

CHAPTER SEVENTEEN

Five months had elapsed since their departure from Olden, Norway, and in that time, William's decision to invite Hawk to join the academy as an instructor had proven to be a resounding success. Hawk had seamlessly transitioned into his new role, exceeding William's expectations at every turn. His training expertise and natural aptitude for teaching made him an invaluable addition to the academy's faculty. The students flourished under his guidance, benefiting from his knowledge and the unique perspective he offered. Surprisingly, he demonstrated remarkable patience with his students—an ironic contrast to the impatience he had once shown his own teachers. It was a testament to how much he had grown, not just as a warrior, but as a leader.

"That will be all for today, everyone," said Hawk, standing tall, as he looked around the combat room at the young, inexperienced Supes. Hawk smirked, as he remembered his own first day in the combat room, training with Michael. "Return your equipment to the weapons room, and then you can head to the showers."

Without hesitation, they all did as he instructed.

"Well done, Hawk." Michael's voice resonated through the training room as he emerged from the shadows. For months, he had carefully watched Hawk's progress, guiding him through the arduous journey of mastering combat techniques and imparting his own wisdom to his eager pupils. Now, standing shoulder to shoulder with him, Michael couldn't help but express his pride. "You certainly have come a long way and surpassed all expectations."

"Thank you, Chancellor. I do enjoy the responsibility of training them and witnessing their progress," said Hawk. "And now I feel like I have a purpose in life."

"Yes, I can understand that. And I think that you definitely have changed, Hawk. I remember a young, arrogant boy who gave me grief and told me that he didn't want to be here, and now, well … you have certainly grown as a person, and should be proud of what you have achieved," said Michael.

"Thanks. I appreciate your generous words. I don't think my parents would agree with you, though," said Hawk. He sighed deeply, and watched some of the young Supes, walk into the shower room. *Especially after all the grief I caused them. What was I thinking?*

"Yeah, parents can be frustrating sometimes. I do remember what mine were like, that is before they were murdered by the Debauched Vampires. But I think I would rather put up with that, than not having them here at all," said Michael, picturing his parents' faces.

"Sorry for your loss, man. That must be hard!" said Hawk, his brow furrowing.

"Yeah, it was, and still is. I am just lucky that William took me in and turned me," said Michael, remembering that day.

"What … you mean you were human?" queried Hawk, who couldn't fathom why any human would want to become a Vampire. He knew from studying Vampire history and listening to others talk, that there were a lot of regulations and controls in place for the Lepidoptera Vampires.

"Yes, I was. But I don't regret being turned into a Lepidoptera Vampire. In fact, it was probably the best thing that could have happened to me," said Michael, proudly.

"I don't see how you could be happy about it. I mean, you have to drink blood, right?" said Hawk, his ignorance showing.

"It's not that bad!" said Michael, smirking.

"It is from where this Griffin is standing!" Hawk quivered all over. "What year were you turned?"

"In 1921. I was about twenty years old when this happened," said Michael, remembering the horrific accident and the life-threatening injuries he'd received from being pinned under a horse and carriage. Michael explained in more detail to Hawk, about what had happened that day, to not only himself, but also his parents, who were sucked dry by the Debauched Vampires.

"I can't even imagine what that must have been like. Are all Lepidopteras born this way; human I mean?"

"No. Some of us are the offspring of our Queen. So born a Lepidoptera … like my life partner," said Michael, picturing Violette, Head Chancellor at the academy and also next in line to take over as the Lepidopteras Queen.

"Queen … life partner?" Hawk frowned.

Michael explained to Hawk how a Lepidoptera finds his life partner, how they're attracted to each other's scent, and about the butterfly markings on the back of their necks that solidify their powers and attraction to one another.

"Humph … unbelievable. That certainly is different," said Hawk, raising his eyebrows and smirking.

Sully … her scent is like cinnamon.

"Cinnamon, hey?" teased Michael.

Hawk rolled his eyes. "Man, keep out of my thoughts. You know I hate it."

"You know she's William's daughter, don't you? I'd be careful, if I were you," said Michael.

"Dude, there is nothing going on between us. I don't even think of her that way, anyway."

Michael grinned. "Humph."

"What?"

"If you can smell her scent, Hawk, then I would say she's your life partner. Put it this way: I can't smell her scent when I am around her. Do you know if any other Supes can smell the cinnamon scent, like you do?"

"Come to think of it, no. Shit … what am I going to do? I never, ever, have thought of her that way. We're only good friends," said Hawk, remembering how Sully had been supportive, and had helped him settle into the academy over the past five months.

"You can fight it all you want, but the attraction you will eventually feel toward her will be what brings you two together. Believe me, I know from experience," said Michael, recalling when he first set eyes on Violette in the gardens at her foster parents' mansion, many years ago, and how her alluring frangipani scent, and their attraction for one another had started. "Speaking of Sully, here she comes. Good luck! I'll see you tomorrow." Michael smirked and quickly walked away to the weapons room.

Hawk rolled his eyes and tried to calm himself.

"How's it going, Hawk?" asked Sully, as she walked toward him from the stairs that led down into the training room.

"Yeah, good. And you?" Hawk felt his cheeks redden, as he breathed in her scent.

"Good. What are you up to tonight?"

"I was going to do some laps in the pool, and then I was thinking about watching a movie," said Hawk.

"Oh, right. Would you mind if I join you?"

"The more, the merrier. I could meet you down at the pool in say, twenty minutes, if that's okay," said Hawk, noting the clock on the wall behind Sully that said it was eleven-thirty. "I just need to catch up with Kiplin first."

"Okay. No probs … see you in a little while," said Sully.

"Sounds like a plan. Catch you soon."

She watched Hawk, walk toward the doorway of the combat room. *Cute ass!*

Why the hell did Michael tell me about the Lepidoptera connection thing? Shit, what am I going to do? I won't be able to get her out of my head now. Hmm, but it does explain a lot, thought Hawk, as he walked away from

Sully, toward his dorm room. He had spent a lot of time with Sully since their return from Norway and they had become close, but he had always thought of them as good friends, nothing else.

Luckily, over time, Hawk had become proficient at blocking anyone from listening to his thoughts, when he remembered. Otherwise, Sully would have heard his inner thoughts about their friendship, and the turmoil he felt about their connection.

* * *

Sully checked her mobile phone. *12.01am. I wonder where Hawk is*, thought Sully, as she waited for him near the long, olympic-sized pool. A few minutes later, she checked her phone again. *Hmm, no message from him.* With not a soul in sight, Sully decided to take a seat on one of the lounge chairs and check her social media while she waited for Hawk to arrive.

Sully ... help, said a faint voice.

Sully stood to attention quickly and wondered where the voice was coming from. Looking all around, she said, "Who's there?"

Help ...

"Show yourself," said Sully, standing with her feet apart, and her fists clenched by her side. She knew from previous experience that a cry for help didn't always mean someone was hurt or even needed her help.

Sully ...

She then recognized the faint voice. *Hawk ... where are you?*

"Behind you," said Hawk, as he staggered toward her.

Turning around, Sully watched Hawk limp slowly toward her. His face was dripping with blood. He had been beaten so badly that his bruised eyes were almost closed from the swelling.

"Hawk!" screamed Sully, as she ran toward him.

Hawk dropped to his knees in front of her.

Sully laid Hawk on the concrete, knelt beside him, and placed her hands over his face and body. Drawing upon her newly acquired Lepidoptera Vampire healing abilities, taught by Danielle, she chanted a ritual, and watched his face mend and the deep gashes on his upper torso vanish.

"How are you feeling?" asked Sully, her brow furrowed. She stroked the side of his face and looked into his bourbon-colored eyes.

Hawk sat up slowly. "Better. Thank you." He watched the concern on her face.

Sully leaned in to give Hawk a comforting hug.

"I'm all right. You don't need to worry," said Hawk, embracing her. Pulling away slowly, he looked into her jade-green eyes. "Truly, I'm fine."

Sully sat back on her heels and sighed. "Who did this to you? What happened?"

"I'm not sure," said Hawk, raking a hand through his golden-blond hair. "All I remember is I was sitting over there, waiting for you to come," he pointed to the wooden table and chairs near the pool. "And the next thing I knew, a dazzling blue, gem-like bird, you know like a Grandala, had landed on my arm. Then another one landed on my right shoulder. I sat there wondering why these beautiful birds had chosen me to land on, and why they were so far from their home country. I was mesmerized by them. But then I felt something attacking me from above. You know, like we learnt recently at the academy, when an Australian Magpie swoops you and its beak nips at your scalp."

Sully brow furrowed as she nodded in agreeance, not knowing what to say.

"As I tried to shoo the bird away from my head, I felt the other one on my shoulder strike my neck with its beak. It hurt like hell. But when I tried to stand up, my body felt like it had been drugged. I couldn't move properly, so I couldn't get away from them. The three of them kept attacking me. As I was about to pass out, I heard voices talking, which was a bit strange. I'm sure I heard one of them say that Eryndor would be pleased with their work. I don't know … this is all so strange, Sully."

"So … let me get this right," she took a deep breath. "You're saying that three birds that looked like Grandala attacked you, but they were really humans and could talk?"

"I think so. Oh, I don't know …" said Hawk, raking a hand through his hair again. "I know this sounds bizarre, but that's what I remember from the attack. The next thing I knew was when I woke up with all these injuries."

"Oh, I believe you, Hawk. I'm just puzzled about why Eryndor would send others to harm you. It doesn't add up," Sully remarked, placing a reassuring hand on Hawk's shoulder. "I think we should report this to the Head Chancellor, don't you?"

"NO … I would rather not," Hawk responded, his voice laced with concern.

"What? Why not?" asked Sully, frowning. She knew from previously living with the Gramaze Lepidoptera coven that when something like this had happened, it should be reported.

Hawk sighed. "Listen, I'm finally settling in here and, well … I don't want to be sent home, or kept in some safe place, while they figure this out. Please, Sully …"

Sully sighed heavily and thought about it for a few seconds. "We really should report this, Hawk. Whoever did this to you is obviously living here at the academy, and I'm worried they could really hurt you, or worse still, kill you. And I'm afraid that they could harm others, too."

Please don't report this, thought Hawk.

Sully listened to his plea and watched the wave of sadness on Hawk's face.

"If I don't report this, can you guarantee me that you will be a bit more aware of what is going on around you. I don't want anything happening to you, Hawk. You mean a lot to me, you know."

"I mean a lot to you?" He gulped hard. "Well, then, I will do as madam is asking." He bowed his head to her and flashed a smug grin.

Sully slapped his arm. "Smart-ass!" Standing, she held out her hand. "Come on, let's get you back to your room."

Hawk took her hand and stood up slowly. Cringing from the pain as he stood next to Sully, he said, "Fuck!"

"Lean on me. I can continue to heal you as we walk to your room." Sully leaned into Hawk's side and placed one arm around his back, and the other hand on his abdomen.

"Thank you," said Hawk, as he placed his arm around her shoulder for support.

They navigated the dimly lit corridors of the academy, concealed within the shadows, ensuring that Hawk's injuries remained hidden from prying eyes.

* * *

"Dude, what happened to you?" Kiplin exclaimed, springing off his bed as Hawk stumbled into the room, his clothes covered in blood. Sully was right behind him, her face etched with concern. Kiplin hurried toward them, his worry mounting with each step.

"He was attacked," said Sully, lowering Hawk to the edge of his bed.

"Ah, shit," said Hawk, as he lay on his bed.

Sully placed her hands over his body once more, to finish healing his deep wounds.

"Who did this?" Kiplin demanded; his eyes fixed on the bright light emanating from Sully's hovering hands as it flowed into Hawk's battered body.

"Believe it or not, three grandala birds," said Sully.

"Really?" Kiplin questioned, frowning as he wondered how Grandala birds could have even entered the academy grounds, especially with wards placed around them.

"Yes, really," said Sully, as she watched the pain on Hawk's face dissipate. "How's the pain?"

"Yeah, better," said Hawk. He sat up slowly and pushed himself back against the headboard.

"Kiplin, can you get a wet cloth so I can wipe this blood from Hawk's head?"

"No problem," Kiplin replied. He raced into the bathroom and was back within seconds with a washcloth and some first-aid supplies. "Here you go."

"Thanks, Kiplin," said Sully, taking the white cloth and pouring some antiseptic on it.

"I don't understand, how did three birds do all this damage?" asked Kiplin, as he watched Sully clean the blood from Hawk's head and face.

Hawk relayed the attack to Kiplin in detail.

"Shit, man … do you think Eryndor is after you?" asked Kiplin.

"It would explain the attack. But what I am more interested in, is how in the hell did they even get past the wards that have been put up around the academy? I thought these wards were meant to be impenetrable?" said Hawk.

"Yeah, me too," said Kiplin, his brow furrowed. "Unless … unless they were already here."

"That doesn't make sense. How could they have already been here?" stated Sully, discarding the bloodied cloth in the bin across the room.

"Well, if they transformed into a bird, then they must be some sort of Supe. They could be hiding in plain sight, and we wouldn't even know it," said Kiplin.

"Humph … you might be right, Kiplin," said Sully, with a hint of contemplation in her voice.

"Do you guys think we should report this to the Head Chancellor?" asked Kiplin.

"NO!" stated Hawk, firmly.

"Then what would you like to do?" asked Kiplin.

"At this point, nothing. I will keep my ear to the ground to see if I hear anything. In the meantime, I will make sure that I am with others at all times. That way they can't attack me again," said Hawk. He pushed his legs over the side of the bed and placed his feet on the tiles. "I need to get cleaned up, so I'm going to have a shower." Standing, he walked over to the closet and pulled out a clean pair of denim jeans and a black T-shirt.

"Did you need some help?" asked Sully, standing.

"No. I'm fine, Sully," said Hawk, opening a drawer, which had clean underwear in.

"Okay. Well, if you're feeling better, I'll head back to my room and get some rest. I'm quite tired from all the healing I've done on you," Sully stated, making her way toward the door. "I'm sure Kiplin can take care of you in the meantime."

"Thank you, Sully," said Hawk, walking toward her. "I do appreciate everything you've done for me tonight." He leaned in and gave her a hug, feeling a sense of warmth and connection between them. "See you in the morning."

"You will," said Sully, her heart fluttering as she slowly pulled away. "Night, Kiplin. Catch you tomorrow." She opened the door, her mind filled with thoughts of Hawk, and the burgeoning emotions she couldn't quite explain.

"Yeah, night," said Kiplin, sitting back on his bed.

Don't worry, I will look after him, mind-thought Kiplin to Sully.

Thanks, Kiplin, mind-thought Sully, as she closed the door.

Sully glanced down at her clothes, now stained with Hawk's blood. *Great*, she thought, *looks like I'll need a shower—and these clothes are going straight in the wash.*

CHAPTER EIGHTEEN

"Sully was telling me about what happened last night. Are you all right, Hawk?" asked Elsie, as she watched Hawk and Kiplin sit at the table in front of her, with their breakfast trays.

"I'm fine. It seems my body has fully healed. Thanks for asking, Elsie," said Hawk, pulling his chair in closer to the table. He looked over at Sully and gave her a quick smile.

"That's good to hear. So … any idea who might have attacked you?" Elsie asked, her tone laced with curiosity and concern.

"No. And I would prefer if we didn't discuss this with anyone else. I don't want the Head Chancellor finding out," said Hawk, looking around the table at each of them.

Elsie pressed her index finger against her lips in a hushing motion and winked at Hawk.

"No problem, man," said Kiplin, picking up a piece of toast from his plate.

Sully nodded and continued to eat her breakfast.

"I hear there's some sort of graduation happening tonight?" queried Hawk, trying to change the topic of discussion.

"It's not really a graduation. It's actually a ceremony for any Supes that have been at the academy for a year or more. They present them with a weapon of their choosing and a medallion, that's all. Then once the ceremony is finished, the Head Chancellor has a dinner planned in the large hall for everyone," said Sully.

"Oh, right! Are any of you going to this tonight?" asked Hawk.

"Not me. I'm on guard duty at the ceremony, with Samuel and Chancellor Grayson," said Kiplin. He hadn't been at the academy for more than a year yet.

"Yes, I will be. My family are coming in from Zurich to help me celebrate the occasion," said Elsie. She was looking forward to seeing them, and celebrating with her adopted Griffin family.

"I'm on guard duty tonight, down by the river, so I won't be attending the ceremony," said Sully, placing her spoon in the empty cereal bowl.

"Aren't you meant to be getting your one-year medallion tonight too, Sully?" asked Elsie, her brow furrowed. She had been looking forward to celebrating the milestone with her roommate, and best friend.

"Umm … I'm not sure." She shrugged her shoulders. "I think William and Renee probably have more important things to worry about than my one-year graduation. Anyway, I'm not bothered with all the fuss."

"Oh, that's a shame," said Elsie.

"And you, what do you have planned tonight, Hawk?" asked Sully, trying to get the attention off her.

"Not sure yet. But don't worry, wherever I am, I won't be by myself. I don't want a repeat of last night, that's for sure," said Hawk, cutting into his sausage. "I may even attend the ceremony and dinner to see what all the fuss is about."

"If you're going to attend the dinner, you'll need a tuxedo. Apparently, the academy has spare ones in the bookshop; that's if you need one," said Kiplin, smirking.

"Oh, right!" said Hawk, who was not interested in getting dressed up for the occasion.

"I'm going to head off, guys," said Sully, standing with her tray in hand. "I'm meant to be meeting up with the chancellors who are on the committee for organizing tonight's ceremony and dinner."

"Oh, don't forget … I need you to help me with my outfit later," said Elsie, looking at Sully.

"I'll be there," said Sully, smiling. "See you guys later."

Both Kiplin and Hawk said, "Bye."

* * *

"Ah, there you are, Sully," said the Head Chancellor, Violette, looking up from her paperwork.

"Sorry I'm late," said Sully, looking around the room, and sitting at the long wooden table. "Got a bit caught up." She pulled her chair in and retrieved a notebook and pen from her bag.

"Tardiness is not tolerated. Please remember to be more punctual in the future, Sully," stated Violette, firmly.

"Yes, Head Chancellor." She gulped hard.

"Now that we are all here, down to business," said Violette. She looked at each of the sixteen Lepidoptera Vampires, who she had known for many years, sitting around the table. "We have a lot of dignitaries coming to the ceremony and the dinner tonight, so I have drawn up a plan for how we are going to keep them safe and guarded at all times." She passed a roster around the table. "Please make yourself familiar with this roster. It details who each of you will be guarding, and at what times of the day and night. Next on the agenda is guarding of the weapons that are to be handed out at the ceremony. Grayson, once these weapons have been given to the recipients at the ceremony, they are then to be returned to the weapons room for safe keeping. I don't want to see any Supes taking weapons home or to their rooms. Am I making myself clear?"

"Yes, Head Chancellor," said Grayson. He nodded once in her direction.

"Next on the agenda: the seating arrangement at the ceremony and the dinner. As per usual, there will be a seating plan for each family, which will be placed at the entrance to the grand hall for the ceremony, as well as at the entrance to the large dining room. I don't want to see any long lines of dignitaries. So, please make sure they are seated quickly and with no fuss."

Everyone nodded in agreement.

"Food and drinks … I have it on good authority from Lamiae, that the kitchen staff have everything in hand for tonight's service. Same with the bar staff; it's just a case of making sure the dignitaries don't have to wait too long for their refreshments. Lastly …" Violette sighed and looked around the table. "We had a security breach last night. It seems that the wards around the academy and its grounds were taken down, twice. At this stage we don't know who did it or why, but I want each of you to keep your wits about you tonight. Remember, communication and security at the facility is paramount. Understood?"

They all nodded in agreement.

When Sully heard Violette speak about the security breach, she felt her cheeks redden, and blocked everyone in the room from reading her thoughts. *Hmm, I wonder if the breach had anything to do with the attack on Hawk last night?*

"Okay, one last thing … the dignitaries will be arriving shortly, and before that happens, I need each one of you to review the security roster for tonight. Once you're done, please change into your security uniforms. It's crucial that we make all the Supe families feel welcome and reassured. We want them to know that they can trust us to not only protect their children, but also provide excellent care. So, let's ensure there are no unexpected situations tonight." Violette scanned the faces of those gathered around the table, seeking their attention and commitment.

They all nodded yes, and passed around the security roster for each dignitary family.

* * *

"Man, that was pretty intense in there," said Sully to Samuel, as they walked along the wide veranda that led into a courtyard. This had been the first year that Sully had sat in on the committee for the ceremony and dinner.

"Yeah, it's like that every year, and for good reason, too. Violette certainly knows her stuff when it comes to security or combat missions. We are fortunate to have her as not only our Head Chancellor, but also our Lepidoptera Princess," said Samuel. He knew firsthand what it had been like growing up in the Gramaze mansion, where Violette had resided for the last twenty years.

"Oh, definitely," said Sully, as she watched a couple of European Robins flit in and out of the plants, and recalled the events of the previous night. "I was a bit surprised, though, when Violette told us about the wards being taken down last night. I thought that once the wards are up, that they could only be taken down by Violette."

"Apparently not," said Samuel, shrugging his shoulders. "I believe from speaking with Father this morning, that the only other Supes that can take down the wards are Warlocks."

"Don't we have three here at the moment?" queried Sully.

"Yes, but I don't think they would be able to master that sort of power. They are only new to the academy and inexperienced, I believe."

"Hmm, maybe. I think we should keep an eye on them, Samuel. Especially as they can be masters of disguise," said Sully.

I remember hearing about three Warlocks that caused an argument with Hawk, when he first arrived. Maybe they are not who they say they are. It certainly would explain a lot about last night's attack on Hawk, thought Sully.

"What ...?" asked Samuel, who had heard Sully's thoughts. "Hawk was attacked last night. Where?"

Oh, shit. I forgot to hide my thoughts. Sully rolled her eyes and looked at Samuel sheepishly.

"It happened down by the pool area. Sorry I didn't tell you, Samuel. I know I should have, but …"

"Yes, you should have," interrupted Samuel. His brow furrowed. "Who attacked him?"

Sully recounted to Samuel some of the incident that had occurred the previous night.

"We need to report this to Violette … I can't believe you would keep something this important to yourself. Does anyone else know?"

"Only Elsie and Kiplin."

Samuel grabbed Sully by her arm and pulled her toward the Head Chancellor's office.

"Let go!" Sully's nostrils flared as she yanked her arm away from Samuel's grip. "I'm not going anywhere with you."

"Oh, yes you are. We are going to report this to the Head Chancellor, NOW. It's the right thing to do," said Samuel, his six-foot-tall body towering over her.

"You're always so focused on doing what's right, aren't you? HAVE YOU EVER stopped to consider the consequences of your constantly doing the right thing?" Sully exclaimed, her hands resting defiantly on her hips. She had endured Samuel's ways throughout her teenage years, and now that she was older, she no longer had the patience to listen to his perspective. "You're always so self-righteous!" She shook her head in frustration.

"Of all the people at this academy, I would have expected that you would agree with me. You know how important our safety is," said Samuel, his brow furrowed. "Why don't you think it's a good idea to let Violette know? We could be in danger. You realize that, don't you?"

Sully watched the leaves in the courtyard start to whirl around slowly, as Samuel got more and more agitated with her. Even though it was forbidden to use their Lepidoptera powers outside of the combat room, she could see Samuel was not able to fully control his powers yet. "Calm down, Samuel." She pointed to the wind and leaves.

"Shit!" He shook his head and sighed deeply, knowing he had lost control. The leaves slowly floated to the ground.

"Listen, I want to do the right thing, too," Sully expressed, her voice filled with empathy. "But we need to consider the potential consequences. If we disclose what has happened, Hawk might be forced to go back to Norway. Obviously, his parents believe he is safe here, and revealing the attack could jeopardize that. Besides, he's just beginning to find his place here, and we don't want to spoil that for him, do we?"

Sully had learned firsthand what it was like to fit into a new family - the Lepidoptera Vampire family, who had taken her in when she was a young girl living on the streets of Paris. The memories of her own journey shaped her understanding of the importance of stability, and a sense of belonging.

"What's going on here?" asked Chancellor Michael, hearing the heated argument as he walked toward them.

Oh, shit. Here we go, thought Sully, as she watched Michael come to stand in front of them both.

"Nothing!" said Samuel. He rolled his eyes.

"It didn't sound like nothing to me."

"It's okay, Michael. We were just having a discussion about the security for the dignitaries," said Sully.

"Right!" said Michael, who was dressed in his black leather battle gear. His nostrils flared as he looked from Sully to Samuel. "Well, keep your voices down."

"Sorry!" said Sully, smiling respectfully.

Chancellor Michael sighed and walked off without saying another word.

"Thank you for not saying anything about Hawk being attacked," Sully said quietly to Samuel, as she watched Michael, walk away.

"Don't thank me just yet. I am not totally convinced that it's the right thing to do. But I can see your point about Hawk being sent home; because I, too, have seen just how much Hawk has settled in at the academy," said Samuel quietly, as he also watched Michael, walk away. "But I do think that we had better keep an eye on these three Warlocks you mentioned. If I get a chance today, I'll try to get a look at their entrance paperwork that is kept in the academy front office."

"Great. Let me know if there's anything I can do to help."

"I will. But I'm sure you will have your hands full already with greeting the dignitaries," said Samuel. He took his mobile phone out of his jeans pocket and glanced at the time. "Shit, I need to get moving. Catch up with you later, Sis. Keep your phone on."

Sully nodded yes and watched him walk away.

CHAPTER NINETEEN

"Congratulations, Elsie," said Grayson, to the first-year graduate. He watched Elsie carefully place her weapon of choice into the locker provided backstage by the academy—a beautifully crafted piece made of Kashmir wood, with intricate hand-carved details and a sturdy steel lining.

"Thank you, Chancellor," replied Elsie, beaming with pride. The golden, full-length ball gown she wore glistened under the overhead lights.

Hearing more applause from another one of the graduate's families, Grayson watched the next graduate walk toward him, with their weapon in hand.

Kiplin, who was standing next to Grayson, had watched Elsie elegantly walk toward them, place her weapon in the locker and return to her family, who were seated in the large hall for the ceremony. Raking a hand through his blond hair, he thought, *wow ... she looks gorgeous*. Kiplin had only ever seen Elsie dressed in combat or training gear before this.

"Like what you see, soldier?" teased Grayson, smirking. He had heard Kiplin's thoughts.

"Yes, Sir ... I mean, no, Sir," said Kiplin, knowing it was forbidden by the academy to intimately fraternize with other Supes.

"Well, which one is it?" asked Grayson, who liked to tease the younger Supes.

"No, Sir."

Grayson placed a hand on Kiplin's shoulder. "Your secret is safe with me, Kiplin."

Kiplin grinned, rolled his eyes, and shook his head.

"How many first-year graduates are there tonight?" asked Samuel, who had been standing with Grayson and Kiplin to guard the weapons.

"Initially, there were twenty of them. However, we had three additional graduates, who decided last minute that they wanted to be part of the ceremonies," Grayson explained. "Head Chancellor Violette mentioned that these three Warlocks didn't have family members attending to celebrate with them, but that they had expressed their desire to take part. Hence, their inclusion." Grayson observed another weapon being placed into the locker; his attention momentarily diverted.

Those three Warlocks haven't been here for one year. How did they talk Violette into letting them take part in the ceremony? thought Samuel to himself.

Kiplin looked at Samuel and frowned. He too, knew the Warlocks hadn't been at the academy for one year.

Sully ... where are you? mind-thought Samuel.

I'm still down by the river. Guard duty; remember, mind-thought Sully.

Where's Hawk? asked Samuel.

Not sure ... why?

Can you just find him! Wait, don't worry ... I see him. He's at the back of the large hall. Humph, he has a black tuxedo on. Looks pretty swish too, mind-thought Samuel.

Sully grinned. *I had better go. I need to patrol the river banks. Chat to you later.*

Okay, Sis. Chat later.

Hawk ... mind-thought Samuel.

Man, get out of my head. You know I don't like the mind-chatter thing, Hawk responded, feeling a strong aversion to the sensation of someone intruding in his mind. Despite having spent a considerable amount of time at the academy, he still despised the feeling of having his mind accessed by others when he wasn't ready.

For fuck's sake ... thought Samuel, frustrated by Hawk's reaction to mind-chatter.

"I won't be a minute, Grayson. Just need to take a leak," lied Samuel.

Grayson nodded once, and continued to watch the ceremony.

Samuel ran toward Hawk at Vampire speed.

"Dude ... where did you come from?" asked Hawk, who was caught off guard by Samuel's sudden appearance beside him. He hadn't yet grown accustomed to the Lepidoptera Vampires' incredible speed, which allowed them to move swiftly and unexpectedly.

"Listen ... the three Warlocks that are now up on the stage, and ready to accept their weapons," Samuel pointed to the ceremonial stage. "I think they are up to no good."

"What gives you that idea?" asked Hawk, his brow furrowed and his body tense, as he watched the three Warlocks.

Samuel explained about how they were last-minute entrants in the ceremony.

"Right! Well, I gather Sully has told you about what we think about the Warlocks?" said Hawk.

"Yes, she did. I did some digging today in the academy's office, and found a lot of holes in their entrance paperwork; it just didn't add up," said Samuel, as he looked toward the stage, and watched the first Warlock, who was dressed in a crimson-and-black armor suit, accept his weapon of choice, which was an ornate engraved Eutregrul sword. The other two Warlocks, who wore black-and-silver armor suits, waited in the wings for their turn to accept their weapons and medallions.

"Really! That's not surprising." Hawk watched the first Warlock take the sword out of its black-and-golden carved sheath, and thrust the sword through the air, in front of the podium. With his fists clenched, Hawk edged slowly toward the stage, with Samuel. He leaned into Samuel, and softly whispered, "Who does that idiot think he is? Waving a sword of that caliber in front of everyone."

Samuel scowled and his nostrils flared, as he watched the second Warlock accept his weapon of choice, a Khopesh sword. The Egyptian sickle-shaped sword, which had evolved from battle blades, bore intricate engravings, hieroglyphs, and symbolic motifs. He then noticed the second Warlock join the first Warlock, who was still standing on the stage, with his sword drawn.

When the third Warlock accepted his weapon of choice, which was a straight, double-edged Roman Gladius sword, he shook the dean of administration's hand, and joined the two other Warlocks, who were standing to the left of him, with their weapons still in hand.

Grayson, who was standing backstage, could see that the three Warlocks were taking too long to bring their weapons to him for storage in the weapons locker.

You three ... bring those weapons here, NOW. Grayson mentally commanded the three Warlocks, his thoughts directed toward them with a firm tone.

The three Warlocks sneered at Grayson; their weapons trained on him.

You don't tell us what to do, Lepidoptera, mind-thought the first Warlock.

Grayson shook his head. *Who do these fuckers think they are talking to?* As he walked toward them, Grayson was stopped in his tracks when he noticed that the three Warlocks, who were in human form, had piercing white glowing eyes. Taking his sword from its sheath on his back, he waited for their first move.

Kiplin!

Yes, Sir, thought Kiplin, who was guarding the weapons locker backstage.

We have trouble. I need you to stay here and keep watch over the weapons. Grayson transmitted his message telepathically to Kiplin, emphasizing the urgency of the situation. Kiplin watched Grayson, walk toward the Warlocks.

Yes, Sir, replied Kiplin. When he spotted the three glazed-eyed Warlocks, he removed his sword from its sheath. With his stance firm, he waited for further instructions from Grayson.

Grayson! mind-thought Samuel, watching what was about to happen. *These three fuckers mean business.*

I realized they were up to no good when they didn't bring their weapons to me. But I want to get them away from the dignitaries first. Where are you? mind-thought Grayson to Samuel.

Hawk and I are at the front of the stage. To your right.

Grayson looked in their direction and then back at the three Warlocks. *What do they want?*

Me! mind-thought Hawk to Grayson and Samuel.

Grayson's brow furrowed, wondering why.

Hey ... fuckers, Hawk teased the three Warlocks. He waved his hands in the air at them. *Here I am ... come and get me.*

Samuel swiftly lifted Hawk into his arms, and ran faster than the eye could see, through the large hall and outside into the open courtyard, hoping that the three Warlocks would follow. As he placed Hawk on the ground, he quickly asked, "Do you have any weapons on you?"

"Only this small combat knife." He pulled the black knife out of the inside pocket of his tuxedo.

Samuel, who had previously been standing guard at the weapons locker alongside Grayson, had a sheathed sword strapped to his back. However, before he could retrieve it, the three Warlocks abruptly positioned themselves in front of him and Hawk. Recognizing that the situation had escalated beyond his control, Samuel swiftly lunged at the Warlocks, utilizing his Vampire speed in an attempt to regain control. With a fluid motion, he unsheathed his sword, aiming to halt their progress. Yet, despite his efforts, it proved futile as the Warlocks managed to evade his grasp.

The three Warlocks extended their hands, palms open and fingers spread wide, and as they exerted their magical influence over Hawk and Samuel, a visible aura of energy, glowing with a distinct ethereal light, emanated from their hands and surrounded their targets. With their commanding gestures, they forced both Hawk and Samuel's bodies to levitate and hang suspended in the air, completely under their control. The atmosphere felt charged with an otherworldly presence, indicating the strength and mastery of the Warlocks' magical abilities.

As Samuel's sword and Hawk's knife dropped to the ground, they were rendered defenseless.

"You will pay for this, Warlocks," said Samuel, who was treading air.

"Shut the fuck up, Lepidoptera," said the first Warlock. He picked up the sword Samuel had dropped and slashed it across his abdomen.

"Aww, shit. You fucker!" screamed Samuel, clutching his stomach.

The first Warlock hurled Samuel against the wall with brutal force, leaving him unconscious as his body crumpled to the ground.

Hawk gulped hard when he realized Samuel wasn't moving.

As the first Warlock loomed above Samuel's unconscious body, wielding the Eutregrul sword that had been bestowed on him during the graduation ceremony, his intent was clear—to sever the head of William Gramaze's son.

However, before he could carry out the intended execution, Grayson intervened. Employing his Lepidoptera power of illusion, he tricked the first Warlock into believing a bullet had penetrated his body, emanating from the gun he seemingly held. This ruse swiftly incapacitated the Warlock, securing Samuel's safety.

After rendering the first Warlock powerless on the ground, Grayson wasted no time. He seized the opportunity, swiftly retrieving the Eutregrul sword from the fallen Warlock's side. With a decisive motion, Grayson expertly beheaded the Warlock. Securing the newly claimed trophy, Grayson deftly sheathed the formidable weapon into a specially crafted pouch adorning his back.

"What the fuck is going on?" demanded the third Warlock, as he watched his comrade die. He turned to Grayson and commanded his body to rise and hang in the air, beside Hawk.

"Get the hell away from them." Sully's voice reverberated with authority as she approached the scene with steadfast resolve. Harnessing one of the formidable powers bestowed upon her as a Lepidoptera, she summoned her strength and propelled the two remaining Warlocks forcefully into a solid brick wall. The impact was powerful, causing their bodies to crumple and slump to the ground, defeated by the sheer force of her intervention. Sully's display of power served as a clear warning; she would protect those she held dear from any further harm.

Grayson and Hawk immediately dropped to the ground and got to their feet.

Sully ran over to them. "Are you both okay?"

"Yes, we are fine. But how did you know we needed help?" asked Grayson, his Croatian accent coming through.

"Samuel called to me. And I could feel he was hurt," said Sully. Looking around for Samuel, she spotted his unconscious body. "Samuel!" she screamed and ran over to him. Kneeling beside her brother, she placed him on his back and held her healing hands over him.

Within seconds, Samuel opened his eyes. He smiled and breathed a sigh of relief when he saw her face. "You came … thank you."

"What am I going to do with you?" said Sully. She shook her head and rolled her eyes. "You scared the hell out of me."

"Thank goodness you're okay, Samuel," said Grayson, as he came to stand next to them.

"Sully …," shouted a terrified Hawk.

Sully spun around and watched a struggling Hawk disappear with the two surviving Warlocks through a shimmering portal.

"No!" screamed Sully, as she got to her feet and ran toward the portal.

"Sully … stop," yelled Samuel. He got to his feet to stop her, but stumbled.

Without a second thought for Samuel's voice, or the potential repercussions, Sully seized the moment and leaped headfirst into the rapidly closing shimmering wall.

Grayson and Samuel were stunned beyond words as the portal closed in front of them. The abrupt departure of Sully, fearlessly plunging into the portal without hesitation, weighed heavily on them, and the gravity of the moment hung in the air as they grappled with the profound implications of what they had witnessed.

Fuck! William is going to have my head, thought Grayson. He raked a hand through his thick brown hair.

CHAPTER TWENTY

Sully emerged from the portal and found herself standing in a snow-covered field, surrounded by towering mountains that looked like ancient, majestic guardian sentinels, their peaks piercing the sky and their slopes blanketed in a pristine white. The air was crisp and cold, and a gentle breeze rustled through the evergreen trees that dotted the landscape. The snow beneath her boots crunched softly as she took in her new surroundings. "Where the fuck am I?" As the portal closed behind her, curiosity stirred within her to explore, and find Hawk.

As Sully ventured deeper into the snowy field, her gaze constantly shifting, she couldn't help but wonder what had prompted the two Warlocks to open a portal. Was it a hidden realm, accessible only through the portal? Or was it part of a remote and untouched corner of Earth, where they could hide? She wasn't sure.

"Hands up, and on your knees, bitch," said a voice behind her, as he pressed the tip of a sword into Sully's back.

Sully gasped, and her body tensed in uncertainty. Carefully, she turned her head, her eyes widening as she caught sight of a figure behind her. A cloaked individual stood there, his face obscured by a hood, and in his hand, a gleaming sword pressed against her.

Warlock ... thought Sully. She gulped hard.

"Where is Hawk?" demanded Sully. She knelt in the snow, and raised her hands in a gesture of surrender.

Suddenly, and without warning, the figure lunged forward, pushing her to the ground with a forceful shove.

Sully's head hit the hard, frozen ground, and everything went dark.

* * *

Ugh ... where am I? thought Sully. She rubbed her pounding head and tried to focus her blurred vision. Disoriented and confused, she lifted herself up onto her hands and knees, and saw the cloaked figure standing in front of her, his face still hidden in the shadows of the hood.

"What do you want from me?" asked Sully. Her voice was shaky with fear and confusion.

The figure remained silent, his hand reaching for the sword at his side.

Sully knew she was in danger, and her instincts sprang into action. She scrambled to her feet and tried to run, desperation fueling her every step, as she reached deep within for her Lepidoptera powers. Focusing, she willed her strength to surge—but nothing happened. A cold dread gripped her chest. *Why aren't my powers working?*

Panic flared as she tried again, but before she could make sense of her failure, the figure was upon her. He caught up with ease and struck her with the handle of his sword. Pain exploded in her skull, and she crumpled to the ground once again, her vision blurring. Her head spun violently, and as darkness closed in, she made one last effort to summon her power. Still, nothing. Her body refused to obey. As she slipped into unconsciousness once more, she could hear the figure's footsteps receding into the distance.

* * *

The next time Sully came to, she was lying in a cave that had cobble-stone walls, and the hooded figure was nowhere to be seen. Struggling to sit up, her body weak and unresponsive, she didn't know what had happened or why

122

she had been attacked. All she knew was that she was in a dangerous situation, and she needed to find a way out. With a mix of determination and fear, Sully pushed herself to her feet and began to explore the cave. She knew that she had to survive, escape the clutches of the Warlock that had attacked her, and find Hawk.

"Who's there?"

"Hawk?" called Sully, recognizing his voice.

"Sully? Is that you?" asked Hawk, surprised to hear her voice.

"Yes, it's me." As Sully's eyes adjusted to the dimness of the cave, she tapped into her Lepidoptera Vampire night vision, an ability that granted her enhanced sight in the darkness, and recognized Hawk sitting up against a wall, chained to the floor.

"Are you okay?" asked Sully, as she knelt in front of him.

"I'm okay. What are you doing here?" asked Hawk.

"I followed you through the portal. Where are the two Warlocks?" asked Sully. She attempted to release the firmly anchored chains securing Hawk to the cave floor, but they remained unyielding, resisting her efforts. They seemed to have been secured with a powerful enchantment, making them irremovable.

"I haven't seen the two Warlocks for days," stated Hawk.

"What do you mean, days? We only came through the portal today, didn't we?" questioned Sully. She looked into his eyes for confirmation.

Hawk looked into her confused eyes and said, "No, we didn't. I've been here for a few months. I'm not sure of the exact time frame, as I've lost count of the days, but I definitely know I have been here for at least three months."

"Shit, really?" stated Sully. Her brow furrowed. "So, if you have been here for three months, then where have I been? It doesn't make sense, Hawk."

"I don't know. This is the first time I have seen you since the ceremony." He looked at the confused expression on her face.

Concern and uncertainty coursed through Sully's veins as she considered the consequences of their prolonged absence from the academy. "I wonder if they're still searching for us?"

"I'm sure they are, Sully," reassured Hawk.

Sully sat on the ground, next to Hawk, leaned into his shoulder and sighed. "I hope you're right."

"Don't worry, they'll eventually find us. Hey ... if you've been here the same time as me, then don't you need some blood? Aren't you feeling weak?"

Sully nodded, yes.

"Would you like to feed from me?" asked Hawk. He was acutely aware of the vital role blood played in a Vampire's existence and the dire consequences that awaited them if they failed to consume enough over time.

"That's not even an option. But thank you for asking," said Sully, her voice steady despite the tension coiling inside her. She could hear his blood coursing through his veins, each pulse a steady, rhythmic drum in her ears.

"But ... why not?"

"Lepidopteras don't feed from humans," stated Sully.

"Technically, I'm not human. I am a Griffin." He gulped hard, and his heartbeat quickened, as he held his forearm out. "Take it ... please."

"No, I can't, Hawk. It wouldn't be right," said Sully. Her heartbeat quickened, not from fear, but from the weight of the moment, and the unspoken challenge between them.

"Let's not worry about what is right; drink." He placed his forearm closer to her mouth.

She looked into his earnest eyes. "Are you sure?"

He nodded. Despite his awareness that it would diminish his own strength, Hawk understood that harnessing Sully's Vampire powers was the key to their escape.

She took a deep breath, her gaze fixed on the pulsating vein on his forearm, a testament to the life force flowing within. With a mix of hesitation and hunger, she licked her lisp, and leaned in closer, her fangs descending. As her lips brushed against his skin, she pierced it with a swift and careful motion, drawing in the essence that sustained her Vampiric nature.

As Sully's fangs pierced Hawk's skin, a sharp gasp escaped his lips. When the discomfort subsided, Hawk observed intently as she drew blood from him, her actions both captivating and unsettling. As the crimson fluid flowed into her mouth, a range of emotions surged within Hawk, intertwining in a complex euphoria.

A mix of fascination and apprehension coursed through Sully's veins. She recognized the inherent power and primal satisfaction that came with the act of feeding, the intoxicating allure that pulsed through her Vampire being. Yet, beneath it all, a tinge of concern gnawed at her conscience.

As Sully reluctantly withdrew from their embrace, a bittersweet taste lingered on her lips. With a delicate touch, she ran her tongue over the bite marks, feeling a peculiar sensation coursing through her. To her amazement, the wounds began to close and heal at an accelerated rate, the regenerative power of her Vampiric nature taking effect. The skin knitted back together, leaving only faint traces of the once-pierced flesh. Sully had never drunk from a human before, only from bags of blood that were supplied to her from the morgue.

"Thank you," said Sully, her voice filled with genuine appreciation as she looked into his soulful eyes. Her words carried a sense of warmth and sincerity.

"You are most welcome," replied Hawk. Her sweet, alluring cinnamon scent wafted past his nostrils, igniting a surge of desire within him.

Leaning in, he pressed his lips against hers, their connection becoming a fervent and passionate exchange. In that moment, time seemed to stand still as their emotions merged, fueled by the intensity of their shared desire.

As their fervent kiss deepened, the world around them faded into insignificance. Their hearts beat in sync, the intensity of their shared passion enveloping them completely. It was a moment of profound connection, where the barriers between their beings dissolved, leaving only the raw and uninhibited expression of their desires.

Eventually, they pulled away, their lips lingering in a final, tender touch. Their eyes met, reflecting the love and understanding that had blossomed between them. In that single moment, they knew that their paths had merged, and their destinies were now intertwined in a way that neither of them could have anticipated.

"That was unexpected," said Sully, trying to settle her thoughts.

"Sorry, I shouldn't have …"

Sully held up her hand. "Don't be. I enjoyed every moment."

Hawk smiled warmly, a spark of affection shining in his eyes. With a gentle gesture, he draped his arm around Sully's shoulders, drawing her closer. They settled into a comfortable embrace, their connection radiating with a sense of ease and contentment.

"Well, well … what do we have here? You two look cozy," a Warlock remarked as he and another Warlock materialized out of thin air.

With a swift and determined motion, Sully rose from the cold, rocky floor of the cave, her senses heightened and her body primed for combat.

Struggling against the constraints of the chains that held him captive, a weakened Hawk, who hadn't eaten for a couple of days, exerted every ounce of his remaining strength in an attempt to break free.

With the agility and pace of a Vampire, Sully ran towards the two Warlocks, covering the distance in the blink of an eye.

Despite her impressive speed, Sully soon realized that the Warlocks' formidable powers far surpassed her own, because her body was still weakened from lack of blood and food. Helpless against their might, she was thrown through the air, crashing hard into the rough, cobblestone wall of the cave.

"Aww, fuck," cried Sully, as her body was held in place against the wall by one of the Warlocks. She watched on in horror as the other Warlock effortlessly tore the chains from Hawk, asserting his dominance over his weakened captive. With a firm grip, he forcibly marched Hawk toward a doorway situated at the far end of the dimly lit cave.

"Go get help," yelled Hawk to Sully. Casting a lingering glance over his shoulder, he watched her body hang from the wall, like a marionette puppet.

"I will come back for you," yelled Sully.

"We will see about that, Lepidoptera," said the Warlock, standing in front of her.

CHAPTER TWENTY-ONE

It had been four months since the first-years graduation ceremony, and a sense of unease gripped everyone, because they had neither seen nor heard from Sully or Hawk. Despite numerous reported sightings and leads, none had developed into a definite clue regarding their whereabouts.

"Why can't we reach her, Father?" Samuel asked, his voice tense as he stood at the head of the long oval table in the operations room of the Gramaze mansion. Dressed in black leather combat gear, he radiated an air of authority, with Kiplin standing steadfastly by his side.

William sighed, and shook his head in dismay. "There could be a few reasons, Son. She could be in another country or …" William looked away from Samuel and Kiplin and exhaled. He didn't want to even think about if Sully and Hawk had been tortured, or worse yet, murdered by the two Warlocks.

Samuel and Kiplin both knew from their training that the connection a Lepidoptera had to their coven never failed. But they had never come across this before; where a Lepidoptera couldn't be found or heard from, through mind-chatter.

"Is there anything I can do to help?" asked Kiplin.

"Not at this stage. But thank you for offering, Kiplin," said William.

"Sire … you need to look at this footage," Brock interrupted. He had been scouring the satellite feeds daily for months, watching for any sight of Sully or Hawk.

William turned to the large screen on the wall in the operations room.

Samuel and Kiplin walked over to the screen and watched the replay.

"What have you found?" queried William.

"It looks like Sully, but I can't be sure. Facial recognition confirms it's her, but Sire ... she ..." Brock trailed off. A mix of disbelief and determination flickered in his eyes as he fixed his gaze on the screen, deftly resizing the satellite image to zoom in for a closer look.

They witnessed a frail, red-haired woman, who was hunched over and dressed in rags, trying to walk with no shoes on, through the knee-deep snow.

"That couldn't be her," said Kiplin, as he watched the screen in disbelief.

"Wait, go back ... rewind that bit," said Samuel to Brock, as he pointed to the screen.

Brock replayed the footage again for a better look.

"There ... stop ... look at the face," said Samuel, when Sully looked up at them. "It's definitely Sully. I would know my sister's face anywhere."

"Fuck, it is her. Do you know where this is, Brock?" asked William.

"Looks like Stryn, Norway," said Brock, turning around.

Lepidopteras ... mind-thought William, to his family. *Get ready*. William's voice resonated with unyielding determination as he relayed the long-awaited news. *We have located Sully, and it's time to bring her home*. His words sparked a renewed sense of urgency within the coven. Without hesitation, he issued his directive to those not scheduled for patrol duty, commanding their presence in the backyard within ten minutes, fully prepared and dressed for the mission ahead.

William pulled his mobile phone out of his leather combat jacket and dialed Warlock Adrian Lachance's number.

"Hello, my friend," said Adrian, answering the call.

"We have found Sully. Can you come straight away and portal us to her?" said William.

"I am already here, my friend," said Adrian, as he walked into the operations room. He pressed end on his phone and walked toward William. "Emily and I have been in Bagnolet for a few days, visiting our beautiful daughters, Violette and Danielle." He placed a reassuring hand on William's shoulder.

"I didn't realize you were here. I have been so preoccupied with finding Sully. Can you create a portal to carry us to Stryn, in Norway?" asked William.

"Lead the way, my friend. Let's go bring your girl home," said Adrian.

* * *

"Must keep going!" Sully chanted over and over to herself. She was severely bruised and wounded from the many beatings she had endured before she escaped, and desperately needed blood. Her bare, frozen-black feet, which felt like lumps of lead, trudged through the knee-deep snow of Stryn with agonizing slowness. Since she had jumped through the portal to help Hawk, and was captured by the two Warlocks, Sully hadn't drunk any blood, other than Hawk's, to sate her Vampire cravings, and for the last three days, since she had escaped, she hadn't found anything to eat either. With cramps in her stomach from sucking on the snow, to keep herself hydrated, her Lepidoptera mind and body was starting to shut down, and if possible, feel weaker. With her healing powers failing her, she stumbled and fell onto the freezing cold snow and started to cry.

"Help … someone … please, help me." She lay in a fetal position and eventually fell unconscious, as the slow fall of snow began to get thicker, and the winter chill took over.

* * *

Sully's eyes opened slowly, and her blurred vision adjusted to the small bedside lamp, which dimly lit the darkened room. With a mixture of anxiety and her heightened awareness, she glanced around the room. *This looks like my old room, at the Gramaze mansion. Can't be.* She sat up quickly and noticed a familiar face looking back at her, from across the room.

"Welcome back!" said Samuel, hearing her thoughts. He smiled, walked over to her, and sat on the chair, which was next to her queen-size bed. "How are you feeling?" He leaned in to give her a hug.

She heaved a heavy sigh and hugged him tight. "I feel like I have been to hell and back." Pulling away from their embrace, she noticed the IV drip in her arm and the bag of blood attached to it. "I didn't think anyone was going to find me. I felt so alone …" Tears escaped her eyes, and she leaned in to Samuel for another comforting hug.

Sully had only ever felt like this once before, when she was twelve years old and had watched her parents being slaughtered by the Debauched Vampires. She remembered how alone she had felt on the streets of Paris, and how the Debauched hunted her for days, until William Gramaze came to her rescue. He killed the Debauched who hunted her for her blood, and took her into his home in Bagnolet. Since then, she had always felt safe; that was until the events of the past four months had occurred.

"Shh … you're home now, and that is all that matters." He rubbed her back in a soothing manner.

Pulling away from their embrace again, Sully asked, "Hawk … did you find him, too?"

Samuel shook his head. "No."

A deep sigh escaped her lips, and Sully's shoulders slumped forward.

"Do you know where Hawk was taken by the two Warlocks?" asked Samuel, as he looked into Sully's disheartened eyes.

Sully searched her memories. "It's the same place that you found me. You know the two Warlocks were working for Eryndor, right?"

"We figured as much," said Samuel, leaning back in the chair. He raked a hand through his dark brown hair.

"Yes, but what you don't know is that Eryndor is still in hell—or at least, he was when I escaped. Somehow, he managed to recruit the three Warlocks to do his bidding. Once they find the Twin Icefire Blades, Eryndor will be able to return topside." Sully shuddered, the memories of unrelenting torture and excruciating pain flooding back—torment inflicted by the two remaining Warlocks, desperate to find the Twin Icefire Blades for their master.

"Knock, knock," said Kiplin, standing in the doorway, with Elsie by his side.

Looking toward the doorway, Sully said, "Come in, guys. It's nice to see you both." Her smile beamed from ear to ear as Elsie and Kiplin walked into the room.

"How are you, roomie?" asked Elsie. She leaned in to give Sully a warm hug.

"I'm okay," said Sully, hugging her back. She kept her best poker face on.

"Good to see your beautiful smile again," said Kiplin, handing her a cup of blood.

"Thanks, Kiplin," replied Sully, taking the cup from him. She gulped down the contents. "Mmm, I have missed this."

"Well, I might go and let you catch up with your friends," said Samuel, standing. *I'll let Mother and Father know you're awake, Sis.*

"Okay, but you are going to come back later, aren't you?" asked Sully, her voice almost pleading with him.

"Of course! You can't get rid of me that easily, Sis" joked Samuel.

Sully smiled and watched her brother walk toward the doorway.

"So … where have you been for the past four months?" asked Kiplin, as he sat on the edge of the bed.

"Stryn, I believe." Sully explained to Kiplin and Elsie about the mysterious three-month gap in her memories, and the torture she had endured in the last month, and her daring escape one fateful night when a Warlock forgot to restrain her. "I hope Hawk is still alive. I really didn't want to leave him there by himself. Last time I saw Hawk he pleaded with me to go and get some help. I feel like I have abandoned him." A picture of Hawk's swollen face, and bloodied body, as one of the Warlocks took him away, entered her thoughts.

"I'm sure he wouldn't think that, Sully," Elsie said gently, now seated in the chair beside the bed, her expression soft with reassurance.

"I don't even know how long I was walking around for, before I was found. It's all a blur … but for some reason, I do remember where we were taken to in Stryn," Sully remarked, her brow creased in deep thought.

"Why did the two Warlocks take Hawk, anyway?" asked Elsie, her brow furrowed with curiosity and concern.

"They thought Hawk would know where the Twin Icefire Blades were hidden in Stryn. But according to Hawk, the Twin Icefire Blades aren't even in Stryn. I don't know why the two Warlocks assumed they were in that location." She shook her head. "Apparently, his mother, Elara, placed them somewhere else, and she didn't tell anyone where they are located," said Sully, as she vividly remembered the electric shock that surged through her while she was held captive. She could still feel the jolting current coursing through her body as she was submerged waist-deep in a barrel of water. The excruciating pain was etched into her consciousness.

Kiplin listened to her thoughts and gulped hard. As a young Lepidoptera, he hadn't felt or been through this sort of pain yet.

Sully heard a knock at the door. Looking up, she smiled when she realized it was Renee and William standing in the doorway. "Come in."

Kiplin and Elsie stood to attention as Renee and William Gramaze walked toward the bed. With their eyes averted, Kiplin and Elsie nodded once, to acknowledge the Lepidoptera Vampire leader and his life partner.

"Well, we might go," said Kiplin. He looked from Sully to Elsie.

"Yeah, we can come back later on," said Elsie. She smiled and gave Sully a hug.

"Thanks guys, and thanks for checking in on me," said Sully, pulling away from Elsie's hug. "Catch you later." She watched them walk toward the doorway.

Renee sat on the bed next to Sully, leaned in and gave her a comforting cuddle. "Don't worry, we will find him."

"How are you feeling, Sully?" asked William, standing next to the bed.

Sully pulled away from Renee's embrace, and looked up at William. "Much better. I wanted to ask …" She stopped mid-sentence because she heard his mind say, *NO*, to her question.

"But …" said Sully, her brow furrowed.

"There are no buts here. You are not fully recovered yet, and I don't see why we would take a liability with us to find Hawk. We only need you to pinpoint his location in Stryn," said William. He had already spoken with Samuel, and they had devised a plan to rescue Hawk.

"Please …" pleaded Sully. She had felt guilt-ridden since the day she had escaped.

William raked a hand through his brown hair, sighed and shook his head. "The answer is NO. Now, if you can tell me Hawk's location, the family and I can be on our way to rescue him."

Sully's soulful, dejected eyes welled up, and tears spilled onto her cheeks, as she recalled what she had told Hawk; that she would return and rescue him.

"He will understand, dear," said Renee, placing her hand on top of Sully's. "Our number-one priority is for you to get well."

"Yes, Ma'am." She looked up at William. "When are you leaving?"

"As I said, I need you to pinpoint the location, then we can portal to this place," said William, taking a map of out of his back pocket, and handing it to her.

Sully unfolded the map, revealing to William the precise spot where the house they had been taken to was located, as well as the lower dungeon where they had been kept in chains.

CHAPTER TWENTY-TWO

"Right … as we've previously discussed, we're all aware of our mission. It's time to move in and rescue Hawk," William declared, his gaze sweeping across the faces of his coven members.

Dressed in their black leather combat gear, with their weapons of choice already drawn, they all responded *yes* and walked toward the house that held Hawk.

Adrian, who had transported everyone via portal to the base of Stryn, hiked his way with William, Grayson and Michael toward their target, a red metal transportable home, perched precariously on stilts.

Looks like there is someone inside, mind-thought Grayson, as he watched two figures walk past the curtainless windows.

I see them. Let's go, mind-thought Michael. He threw a small grenade at the base of the tall stilts. When it exploded, he watched the house, with its billowing chimneys, slide down the slope to the snow-covered rocks below.

When the house came to a halt, Danielle, Christian, Kiplin and Brock bounded onto the roof, their muscles coiling like predators, ready to strike. The sound of their footsteps reverberated through the air, as they forcefully ripped off several metal sheets; the metallic screeches echoing in the surroundings.

As they descended to the wooden floor within the house, a powerful jolt propelled them against a timber-lined wall. Dropping their weapons, the four of them tried to struggle free from the force that held them in place, but it proved futile.

"You will pay for this intrusion, Lepidopteras," said a Warlock, as he held his hands out, holding them in place on the wall.

"It is you who will pay," said Adrian, crashing through the metal side door with William. Using his Warlock abilities, he held his hand out and tossed the young Warlock against the kitchen's metal bench. The inexperienced young Warlock was no match for Adrian, who was far wiser and more powerful.

As Adrian held him down on the floor with his celestial powers, William sliced the Warlock's head off with his sword.

Danielle, Christian, Kiplin and Brock dropped to the ground and collected their weapons.

"Stop!" shouted the second Warlock, who had witnessed his comrade's death. "Or I will kill him." He held a sharp knife against Hawk's throat, and pulled him backward toward another doorway, which led outside to a balcony.

"You are no match for me, fledgling," said Adrian, as he directed his index finger to pull the blade away from Hawk's throat.

"No ..." screamed the second Warlock, as the knife was knocked out of his hand, and he was tossed against a wall, eventually knocked unconscious.

Hawk's frail, bloodied body slumped to the ground like a rag doll.

"Danielle ... help Hawk, now!" yelled William, from across the room.

"Yes, Sire," said Danielle. She ran over to Hawk, knelt beside his battered body, and placed her healing hands over him.

"Kiplin, Brock ... I need you to check the house over. And once it's all clear, I want you to set up explosives and blow this dump sky high," commanded William.

"Yes, Sire," they both said together.

"Come with me, Kiplin. I will teach you how it's done," said Brock, who was happy to show the young Lepidoptera his trade.

"Yes, Sir," said Kiplin, eager to learn more about explosives and how to set them. He followed Brock into a hallway at the back of the house.

"Grayson, Michael, Christian, check outside. I want the house guarded until we are ready to go," said William.

"Yes, Sire," they said together, and ran toward the doorway.

William heard a muffled sound coming from a closed door, in the kitchen. Frowning, he followed his instinct, and walked over to the door. As he placed his hand on the doorknob, he heard the sound again. Swiftly, he opened the door and found a bound and gagged Elara, lying on the floor in a fetal position.

"Elara … shit!" said William. Bending down to her, he ripped off the ropes binding her. "Are you okay?" He peeled off the mouth gag.

Elara nodded weakly in agreement, before succumbing to unconsciousness.

William scooped Elara up in his muscular arms, and swiftly carried her over to Danielle. "Another one for you, Danielle."

"All good, Sire. Leave her with me," said Danielle, who had already healed all Hawk's physical wounds.

With a furrowed brow, William raked a hand through his hair. *How is this possible? I only saw Elara yesterday via Zoom conference call with Garrick.* William pulled his mobile phone from his pocket and dialed Garrick's number.

"Yes, William," said Garrick, swiftly answering the video call with a mixture of eagerness and apprehension, for any updates regarding his son, Hawk.

"Are you free to discuss something in private?" asked William.

"Sounds serious." Garrick walked toward his office door and closed it. "What is it, my friend?"

William turned his mobile phone around so that Garrick could see his partner, Elara, on the wooden floor, unconscious.

"Elara! How can it be? I saw only her a few minutes ago."

"Whoever is in your home is an imposter. The real Elara is here with us. Would you like me to send one of my family over to Olden, to help you eradicate that vermin from your kingdom, my friend?" said William, his nostrils flared.

"Humph … no. But thank you for the offer, William. I will deal with this bitch myself," said Garrick, sneering.

"Be careful, my friend. This could be one of Eryndor's Warlocks, and they have a lot of power," said William.

"This bitch is no match for me. Leave it with me," said Garrick, already planning in his mind what he would do with the imposter who dared to try and trick him. "Is Elara all right?"

"We think so," said William. He watched Danielle's healing hands wake Elara. "As soon as we are finished here, I will bring her back to you."

"Any word on Hawk?" asked Garrick, who hadn't realized his son was lying next to Elara.

William frowned. "He is next to Elara. He has been healed, but hasn't come round yet." He turned his mobile phone around to show Garrick Hawk's unconscious body.

"Shit!" Garrick raked a hand through his graying-blond hair. "Is he going to be, okay?"

"Yes, but he will need time to recover," said William, looking at Garrick's anxious face on the other end of the phone.

"Thank you, William. I am indebted to you and your family," said Garrick. "I suppose I had better go and deal with my vermin problem. Take care of my family, William. And I will see you soon."

"I will. Goodbye, my friend." William pressed end on the video call.

* * *

"Sire, we are ready to go," said Brock, with Kiplin standing beside him. "Everyone is out, oh … except for the two Warlocks. All the charges have been set."

"Great! Let's get the fuck out of here," said William. He walked over and picked up Elara, and carried her outside. "Danielle, can you carry Hawk outside?"

"Yes, Sire," said Danielle. She picked up the still unconscious Hawk and walked outside with him, alongside Brock and Kiplin.

A shimmering portal, meticulously crafted by Adrian, awaited them just a few hundred meters from the house.

"Would you like to do the honors, Kiplin?" asked Brock, as they neared the portal opening. He handed the detonator switch to Kiplin.

"It would be my pleasure," said Kiplin. A flicker of eager anticipation danced in his eyes, and a glimmer that spoke of uncontainable enthusiasm washed over Kiplin, as he pressed the button, and the red house flew off the snow, exploding into a fireball, sending debris everywhere. Some even landed meters from their feet.

"Good job, my friend. Let's go," said Brock, slapping Kiplin on his back. He grinned and continued on into the shimmering portal with Kiplin.

* * *

"No … no," shouted Hawk. Asleep, his body thrashed from side to side in the king-size bed, in a semi-lit bedroom in the Gramaze mansion. For the past few days, he had been reliving each and every detail of his kidnapping and torture in his dreams.

"Shh … you're safe," said Sully, her voice soothing, as she stood next to the bed, and tried to calm him with her healing hands.

"You won't be able to stop me, Warlock," shouted Hawk. In a dream-like state, with his eyes open, he pulled the saline drip out of his arm and pushed Sully away.

"Hawk … stop!" shouted Sully, as she backed away from him.

Hawk pushed the dark-colored quilt off his body and tried to get out of bed. However, his weakened legs betrayed him and he crumpled to the ground.

Sully rushed over to his motionless body. "It's okay … you're safe." She placed a healing hand on his forehead. "You're safe."

Hawk's terrified eyes quickly darted around the room. Adjusting to his surroundings, he looked up at Sully's concerned face. Blinking a few times, he shook his head. "Sully!" He sat up and hugged her. "Where are we?"

"My Father's … the Gramaze mansion." She slowly pulled away from him and smiled. "You are safe now."

Hawk sighed deeply. "Thank you for coming back for me."

"I didn't." She looked down at her hands. "I'm sorry." The tears welled in her eyes as she looked at Hawk. "Father wouldn't let me, because I wasn't fully recovered. He called me a liability." With her brow furrowed, she searched his soulful eyes for forgiveness.

"But they wouldn't have found me if it wasn't for you. So, thank you." He looked into her beautiful eyes and smiled, then leaned in to give her a tight hug.

"How are you feeling?" asked Sully, as she hugged him back.

"A bit foggy," said Hawk, pulling away from their embrace. He rubbed the side of his head. "I can't believe what we've been through, or that we even survived."

"Me neither … come on, let's get you back to bed," said Sully. She helped Hawk stand, and walked him over to the bed. "Are you sure you're, okay?"

He nodded yes and smiled.

Sully pulled the quilt over Hawk and fluffed up the pillows behind him. Sitting next to him on the bed, she asked, "Can I get you anything?"

"Nah … but I wanted to ask …" He gulped hard. "Did Eryndor get the Twin Icefire Blades?"

Sully smiled and said, "No … that fucker is still in hell, and I don't see him getting out of there any time soon."

"Thank the gods," said Hawk. He breathed a sigh of relief. "What happened to the two Warlocks?"

"You don't have to worry about them coming back to kidnap you again. They're dead." A mix of relief and reassurance washed over Sully's face as she conveyed the words.

"They got what they deserved. I don't think I will ever forget the torture they inflicted on me, let alone on you. I'm sure they enjoyed watching the pain on our faces. The fuckers!"

"Humph … you're right there. I still haven't fully recovered." Painful, unwelcome memories flooded Sully's consciousness, tormenting her with vivid recollections of the relentless beatings and the excruciating pain she had borne, leaving her with enduring emotional scars.

"I believe that the Head Chancellor is currently investigating how the three Warlocks managed to gain admission to the academy. Apparently, Violette suspects they might have employed their eldritch magic to manipulate her into believing that they had been enrolled for a year. She has also said her number-one priority is to keep everyone safe."

"This would explain how they were able to attend the ceremony," said Hawk.

"Sure would. Did you know that the two Warlocks had taken and tortured your mother?"

"What! How?"

"Apparently, they approached her through mind control. They told Elara, that if she didn't cooperate and tell them where the Twin Icefire Blades had been placed, they would torture and eventually kill you. Bloody fuckers …"

Hawk shook his head in disbelief. "Is she …?" He searched her face for answers.

"No …" stated Sully, when she realized that Hawk was asking if his mother was dead. "My Father took her back to Norway, and she is recuperating there."

"Thank the gods," said Hawk.

"Yeah, and I believe that when the two Warlocks coerced Elara into going with them, they also put another Warlock in her place, and the fucker pretended to be her, so that your father wouldn't notice she was gone."

"Unbelievable …" He shook his head. "So, what happened when my father found out that they had an imposter amongst them?"

"From what I hear, this Warlock was stripped of their powers and tortured by not only your father, but also the council, for the crimes that he had committed. But …" her voice quietened.

"But, what?" asked Hawk, searching her face for answers.

Sully sighed. "I'm afraid …" She paused. "Afraid of who Eryndor will use, or what he will do next, to get his hands on the Twin Icefire Blades. It's a pity we can't kill this asshole. I want to make him pay for what he did to us."

"Yeah, get in line. I'm sure there are others that feel the same way we do," said Hawk. "So … have my mother or father said anything about me going back to Norway?"

"From speaking with William, apparently your father said he feels sure that the academy is probably a safer place for you at the moment than your actual home."

"Right! I was sure he would have requested that I return home. Anyway, it's a relief." Hawk rubbed his right temple.

"Are you feeling, okay?" asked Sully.

"Yeah … I've got a bit of a headache, that's all. I'll be fine," said Hawk, not wanting to make a fuss.

Sully placed her healing hand on Hawk's forehead, and as she did this, a fleeting memory came back to her of how she had healed him a few times, when they were held captive and tortured. And of comforting times when they held hands and reassured each other.

Hawk leaned into her hand and closed his eyes. "Ah, that feels good. Thank you, Sully."

"You're welcome." After a few minutes, she watched Hawk relax, as his headache started to dissipate. "Well, I might go, and let you get some rest."

"Okay," said Hawk, taking his pillow out from behind him, and lying down. "Will you be coming back later?"

Sully smiled. "Of course, I will. You get some sleep." She leaned in and kissed his forehead, lingering for a moment to take in his scent. As she pulled away, their eyes locked and the memories came flooding back of how Hawk had given her his blood, and their intimate kiss. "See you later," her voice dipped low and alluring.

He nodded in agreement, as he looked into her mesmerizing eyes.

Sully gradually withdrew, her smile lingering, and she proceeded to walk toward the doorway.

Hawk watched as Sully gracefully made her way toward the doorway, his eyes fixed on her, silently witnessing her departure.

When she reached the open doorway, Sully paused, turned and gave a warm smile to Hawk. Their eyes briefly locked in a moment of connection, before she softly shut the door, leaving him alone with his thoughts.

As Hawk lay there, his gaze fixed on the closed door, fragments of the conversations he and Sully'd had, and the intimate contact they'd shared while held captive resurfaced in his mind, evoking a mixture of emotions and longing.

Her lips ... they were incredibly soft, thought Hawk, as he touched his own lips, and remembered the tender, velvety texture that lingered on his own.

When his eyes eventually closed, he dreamt not only of Sully, but also of the conversations he had overheard between the two Warlocks who had held them captive. He knew he had to somehow piece together their nefarious plans. Within his slumbering mind a sense of urgency grew, compelling him to unravel the sinister plot that had ensnared them both.

CHAPTER TWENTY-THREE

It had been two weeks since the return of Sully and Hawk. During this time, they effortlessly reintegrated themselves back into the academy, experiencing a remarkably smooth transition as they quickly settled into their routines once again.

"Do you believe they are prepared, Sire?" asked Michael, his mind flashing back to the harrowing debriefing they had attended just two weeks earlier, where the excruciating torment and anguish endured by Sully and Hawk had been recounted in detail.

"Hawk, definitely. He has already shown us his skills and dedication. Sully, I have no doubt in my mind. She is fully recovered and is ready. The other two … they have been at the academy for over a year now, and have had an abundant amount of training, so they should be ready," replied William. He had been observing the progress of Hawk, Sully, Kiplin and Elsie, and was eager to see what they would be capable of, as young Supes out on an assignment.

The glass doors slid open, and Hawk, Sully, Kiplin and Elsie walked side by side into the Gramaze operations room. Dressed in their battle gear, they came to a stop at the head of the long wooden table, each nodding once in William's direction, standing to attention.

"Do you know why you have been summoned?" asked William, as he looked each of them in the eye.

Silence filled the room, as the four stood in anticipation, their gazes fixed straight ahead, waiting to see what they have been called to the operations room for.

"Tonight, each of you will be going out on a mission. This assignment is for intel only, nothing else. Your job will be to mingle with the people at a party, and to find out as much information as possible," said William. He waited for a reaction from them; but there was nothing. "Questions?"

"Where is this party? And what intel are you seeking?" asked Hawk.

"You will be briefed on the assignment later. In the meantime, I need each of you to read over the information in this folder." He dropped a manila folder on the table in front of them. "This afternoon, I expect you all to get in some weapons training, and then I want you to help Danielle and Christian, who are going with you tonight, to get the weapons ready for this assignment. Are we clear?"

They all said, "Yes, Sir."

"What do we need weapons for if this assignment is for intel only?" asked Sully.

"Good question, Sully," said William. "We always take weapons and prepare for any potential challenges that might arise on every assignment."

"Right! So, you suspect we may come across these challenges tonight?" asked Sully.

"No, but it is always good to be prepared. Right, off you go. Danielle and Christian are waiting for you all in the combat room," said William. He watched Hawk pick up the manila folder from the table, and follow Sully, Kiplin and Elsie out through the glass sliding doors.

* * *

"Do you believe this? We have been given a new assignment," said Elsie, leaning into Sully, placing her arm around her best friend's shoulder.

"We've been on assignments before," stated Sully.

"Yeah, I know. This one feels different, though. Don't you think?" asked Elsie, taking her arm away from Sully's shoulder.

"Maybe," said Sully. She shrugged her shoulders. Sully was a little apprehensive about the assignment.

"I feel like this assignment could be a test," stated Hawk, who had been listening to their conversation.

"Yeah, you could be right," said Kiplin, as he walked beside Hawk.

"I don't think father would be testing us," said Sully, her brow furrowed. "Either way, I'm glad to be escaping the academy for the night, and finally being able to use some of my skills." Even though she loved her Lepidoptera family and everything the academy provided, Sully had grown weary of constantly being monitored, and she was determined to prove herself.

"Yeah, me too," said Elsie, her eyes fixed on the expansive combat room that gradually came into view.

* * *

"*Buon giorno*," said Christian, in an Italian accent, as he watched the four young Supes, whom he and Danielle had not worked with individually, except for Sully, walk down the stairs and into the combat room.

"Good morning, Christian. Ready to get your ass whipped?" Sully asked with a smirk. She had trained with Christian previously, when she lived in the Gramaze mansion, and liked to tease him.

"Bring it on, *senorita*," said Christian, gesturing with his hand toward himself.

"So … what's the 411?" asked Kiplin, as he came to stand in front of Christian and Danielle.

"411. I haven't heard that expression in a long time. Where are you from, Kiplin?" asked Danielle, listening to his American accent.

"Boise, Idaho. And you, where are you from?" asked Kiplin.

"Los Angeles, originally. But I have lived in Bagnolet for the past twenty years."

"Right. What about you, Christian. Where are you from?" asked Kiplin.

"Rome, but like Danielle, I have been in Bagnolet for about twenty years now," said Christian.

"Oh, wow, Rome … I would love to go there one day," said Elsie. "The architecture of the buildings, it's *bellissima*!"

"It sure is," said Danielle, remembering her first trip there, years previous, with Christian. "Well, guys and gals, we had better let you know a bit more about the assignment for tonight, and partake in some training."

"Sounds good to me," said Hawk, who wanted to know more about the mission.

"What do you know about tonight's assignment?" asked Christian.

"Not much. William gave us this manila folder, but we haven't had a chance to look it over yet," said Hawk, handing the folder to Christian.

"Right! Take a seat and I will explain," He took the folder from Hawk, and once they were all seated on the combat room floor, Christian continued. "According to the military intel we have been listening to in the last couple of days, Albinus Giordano, who works in the French government for the Ministry of Defense, and his daughter, Xanthia, are missing. Your assignment tonight will be to see if you can find out where they are being held, without raising suspicion. The extravagant gala that we will be attending is being hosted by none other than the French Debauched leader, Tassone Boardman. We are assuming there will be other Supes there, as well as humans." His brown eyes looked to each of their faces for acknowledgment.

"Now … don't worry about what to wear. I have already selected your clothing and shoes for this event, so that you will fit in perfectly," said Danielle, who normally was the one to select the dresses or suits and the shoes to match, for these types of occasions for the Gramaze Lepidoptera coven.

Elsie looked at Sully and smiled.

Christian opened the manila folder that Hawk had handed him, and said, "Take a good look at these photos of Tassone Boardman, Albinus Giordano, Xanthia, and the house interior layout. I want you to store them in your memory." He handed them around to everyone.

Hawk, Sully, Kiplin and Elsie took turns looking at each photo and the house plan.

"Any questions?" asked Christian, looking around at each of their faces.

"What can you tell us about Tassone Boardman?" asked Hawk.

"Not only does he hold the position of the French Debauched leader, but he is also a Vampire with a reputation for being untrustworthy. It is said that his wealth stems from illicit dealings in weapons and drugs. Rumor has it that he even has a number of brothels under his control," stated Christian.

"If he's truly as vile as you describe, why don't we simply eliminate the fucker?" queried Hawk, his voice laced with a hint of defiance. With arms crossed over his broad chest, he projected a stance of confidence and readiness to confront the perceived menace head-on.

"Believe me, we have tried. We can't seem to get close enough to take him out, yet," said Christian.

"Humph … right!" said Hawk.

"How are we getting there?" asked Kiplin.

"Danielle and I will drive you there in the Gramaze limousine. We won't be attending the gala; only you four are. We will stay with the car, but we are there for backup, just in case," said Christian.

"Remember, you are only there for intel. Nothing else," said Danielle, her blue eyes looking at each of their faces. "Do you have any other questions?"

They all shook their heads, and the room was filled with silence.

"Okay. So now you know what the assignment is, let's get on with some training for this mission," said Christian, standing.

* * *

"Woo-wee, woman, you look mighty fine," said Elsie to Sully. The floor-length, dark-green, one-shoulder dress with luxurious sequins and an open slit at the front, hugged every curve of her body. Sully twirled around to show Elsie the open back that had a looped top strap.

"Thanks. You don't look half bad yourself," said Sully, admiring Elsie's own floor-length dress, in raspberry-colored satin, with layers of black tulle, with a black satin V-neck and a fitted bodice, with a bell-shaped full skirt.

Elsie smiled and turned to show Sully the V-shaped back.

"Are you ready to go?" Sully placed the chain shoulder strap of her metallic clutch bag over her left shoulder.

"Nearly!" said Elsie. She picked up her black clutch bag and took one last look in the long mirror.

"Knock, knock," said Kiplin, who was standing on the other side of the closed door, with Hawk.

"Come in," Sully called out.

Dressed in a satin-lapelled black suit, with a black vest and white open-collar shirt, Kiplin swaggered into the bedroom. "Wow, you two scrub up well."

"You don't look too bad yourself, Kiplin," said Elsie, admiring the way the buttoned-up black suit hugged his muscular body.

Hawk raised his eyebrows and raked a hand through his golden-blond hair, when he walked into the bedroom. "Damn … you ladies look fine."

"Well, thank you, kind sir. You look handsome in your suit. Both of you do," said Sully, looking at Hawk's own satin-lapelled black suit, with a black open-collar shirt. "Umm … forget something?" She noticed his black dress shoes with no socks.

Hawk looked down at his shoes. "Apparently, and according to Christian, this is all the fashion, these days."

"Ah, right!" said Sully, smirking.

"You ladies ready to go?" asked Kiplin, as he looked from Elsie to Sully.

They both said yes.

Kiplin walked over to Elsie and held his arm out for her to take, and they walked side by side out of the room.

Sully walked over to Hawk and took his arm, and they followed Kiplin and Elsie.

"We have a car waiting for us outside," said Hawk. *Cinnamon, oh man, she smells good.*

Sully smirked when she heard his thoughts. "Thank you for the compliment."

Hawk rolled his eyes, grinned, and felt his cheeks heat up.

* * *

"Come!" said Tassone Boardman, his brown eyes momentarily glancing upward, when he heard a knock at the door.

"Sire … the car is ready for your trip home," said the soldier, as he walked into the Debauched Vampire leader's modern office and stood in front of the desk.

"I have one more phone call to make. Wait for me outside, soldier," ordered Tassone, his Irish accent lending a distinct charm to his commanding tone.

"Yes, Sire," said the soldier, his eyes averted. He walked toward the door and closed it on the way out.

Tassone activated the speaker function on his mobile phone, tapping the number to connect with his Russian counterpart. As he initiated the call, he patiently awaited the response on the other end, anticipating the conversation that lay ahead.

"*Dobri vecher*, my friend. What can I do for you?" asked the Russian Debauched leader.

"Good evening to you as well, Nikolai," said Tassone. "I have news that may be of some interest to you, my friend."

"And that is?"

"I have made significant progress in acquiring ammunition and weaponry. Are you interested in obtaining them?" said Tassone.

"I am always on the lookout to acquire these items. When will you have them ready to transport?" said Nikolai.

"In the next few days. I will send you the link that has been set up to bid on these items."

"Very well. I will await your contact, my friend. *Do svidaniya*," Nikolai uttered, with his distinct Russian accent.

"Bye, my friend," said Tassone. He tapped his fingers restlessly on the ornate wooden desk, a subtle sign of his impatience, as the line disconnected. Opening the lid to his laptop, he sent the bidding link off to Nikolai and a few other interested parties via Messenger.

Powerful, and rich. You won't be able to stop me then, Gramaze, thought Tassone. In his mind's eye, Tassone envisioned William Gramaze and his entire coven, yielding to his will. The image of their submission fueled his determination, amplifying his ambitions, as he painted a vivid picture of the power and dominance he sought to achieve, as the leader of all Vampires in France.

Tassone shut the lid of his laptop, rose from his seat and carried it across the room to a secure wall safe. With careful precision, he nestled the laptop inside. As he closed the door of the safe, he turned the handle, ensuring its complete security. With meticulous attention to detail, he returned the picture to its original position, cleverly obscuring the safe from any prying eyes that might be searching for it.

Making his way back to his desk, he retrieved his mobile phone and wallet, before swiftly proceeding toward the door. Stepping outside, he descended to the car park where his loyal security team of soldiers stood, prepared and awaiting his command.

As he stepped into the car, and became comfortable in his seat, Tassone addressed the driver with a firm yet familiar tone. "Home, soldier!"

The driver acknowledged the instruction with a nod, glancing at his leader in the rearview mirror.

* * *

"We are here, Sire," announced the driver, as he steered the limousine near the front entrance of the lavish homestead.

"Go around the back, you idiot." Tassone Boardman sighed, as his brown eyes looked through the tinted window. *Good help is hard to find these days.*

"Yes, Sire," said the driver, looking in the rearview mirror again. He quickly pulled away from the guarded front entrance, and drove the limousine around to the back of the property.

Waiting for them there were four tall, muscular Debauched Vampires, dressed in black leathers, with faded buzz-cut hairstyles.

As the car came to a stop, Tassone's door was opened by one of the guards, and he alighted from the vehicle.

"Good evening, Sire," said the guard. He averted his eyes and bowed his head to the seven-foot-tall leader.

Tassone marched past the guard with determined strides, his presence commanding and resolute.

Where is the girl? mind-thought Tassone to his guard, who was walking behind him.

She is upstairs, in your office, Sire, replied Shepherd.

Tassone took off his long black coat and threw it at a servant woman who was waiting at the doorway, as he continued to walk inside his home.

She gulped hard and averted her eyes, bowing her head as Tassone walked past before stealing a glance at the guard following their leader.

Not wanting any of the guests to see him, Tassone made his way to the back of the house, through the kitchen, to a secret stairway. Taking the steps two at a time, he quickly raced to the top and opened a doorway to the second floor of his home. With Vampire speed, he breezed down the hallway and opened the door to his office.

"Ah, there you are, my dear," said Tassone to Xanthia.

Gagged and bound to a wooden chair, Xanthia's blue eyes opened wide, and her heart raced when the Debauched leader approached her. The young teenage girl sobbed, struggling against the ropes as tears streamed down her face.

"There, there, my child. Don't fret, everything will be all right. As soon as Daddy does what is asked of him," said Tassone, sarcastically. He stroked her long strawberry-blonde hair, then pulled her head backward, so that Xanthia was looking up at him. "Well, he had better do as I have instructed. Otherwise, I'm afraid you will depart this life, my dear." He laughed and pushed her chair forward, making her fall to the ground.

Landing in a fetal position, still bound to the chair, Xanthia tried to scream with the gag in her mouth, but the sound came out muffled. Closing her eyes, she sobbed uncontrollably.

"Do something with that, will you," said Tassone, indicating for Shepherd to pick the young female up off the floor.

"Yes, Sire," said Shepherd. He knew better than to disagree with the Debauched leader, even if he didn't like what he had witnessed.

CHAPTER TWENTY-FOUR

Christian lowered the window of the limousine as he approached the guarded gates. Glancing at Danielle, who was seated beside him in the front passenger seat, he ran his fingers through his disheveled blond hair and muttered, "Here we go."

Danielle let out a weary sigh, as she reached into her backpack to retrieve the passports, and hand them to her life partner, Christian. Even though she had previously been on plenty of missions, she couldn't shake the familiar mix of anxiety and unease that always accompanied a new assignment. With her lustrous long blonde hair and captivating blue eyes, she stole a quick glance at herself in the rearview mirror, and noticed her flawless Lepidoptera Vampire reflection. Her eyes were vibrant and alluring, but held a hint of mischief, as she watched the guard approach the car, ensuring every detail of her supernatural allure was perfectly in place.

"Identification!" stated the broad-shouldered guard, who was posted outside the tall iron gates to Tassone Boardman's homestead.

Christian handed over the six passports to the guard, and watched him return to his shack to verify their IDs.

"What's taking so long?" Hawk asked from the back seat. It had only been five minutes since the guard took their passports, but the prolonged absence was making him uneasy. A knot tightened in his stomach as his imagination spiraled through a dozen possible scenarios.

"Relax. Everything is fine," said Christian, looking in the rearview mirror.

"I hope you're right," said Hawk. This was the first assignment that William had sent him on since he was offered the apprenticeship, and he was determined to execute it flawlessly. Failure was not an option, as far as he was concerned.

"Quiet, he's coming back," said Danielle, in a low voice.

The guard, who was returning with their IDs, bent to peer into the car. "Back window, down."

Christian did as he was instructed.

The guard walked to the back window and scrutinized the four young Supes seated in the back.

Sully and Elsie gave him a bland smile, while Hawk and Kiplin glared at the guard.

He glanced at their IDs once more, then gave a curt nod, and handed the passports back to Christian. "Everything seems in order. You are good to drive on in."

"Thank you," said Christian, looking up at the guard. He handed the passports back to Danielle, and drove through the open gates.

Hawk breathed a sigh of relief. "Thank the gods for that."

Christian watched the relief on Hawk's face in the rearview mirror and chuckled. "Brock is a magician when it comes to creating fake identities. You can be assured he would make you all look legit. The rest of the assignment tonight is going to be up to the four of you."

"Oh, no pressure there, man," scoffed Hawk.

They each had gone over the assignment several times on the drive from the Gramaze mansion to Boardman's estate, and hoped that they were prepared for any situation that might arise.

As Christian pulled the limousine around the back of the property, he noticed a security guard giving hand signals, directing him into an available parking space, which was in between two other limousines. Placing the car in park and turning the engine off, he pivoted around in his seat to address the four Supes. "Right … you all know how important this mission is." His deep brown Lepidoptera eyes looked at each of their faces and watched them nod in agreement. "Your assignment is to gain intel on Albinus Giordano and his daughter, Xanthia, and where they are being held in the building. That's all! Are we clear?"

They all said, "Yes", together.

"Remember … there will be others attending this party who can read minds. One of your parameters is to block them from reading you. Because we all know what will happen if they do read you.

They all nodded in agreement.

"Danielle and I will wait with the limousine. And if you run into any trouble while you're inside, you know that you only have to mind-talk to us, and we will come and help. Okay?" said Christian.

"Thanks, guys. But I'm sure we'll be fine," said Sully confidently, as she looked from Christian to Danielle. "Let's go and retrieve this intel." She was eager to put her Lepidoptera skills to the test tonight.

Christian got out and opened the back door, assisting the two girls to alight from the limousine, while Danielle opened the other back door for Hawk and Kiplin to quickly alight from the car.

* * *

Greeted by security at the front doors, Sully, Hawk, Kiplin and Elsie had their faces digitally scanned into the guard's iPad. Once cleared, the guard waved them all on inside.

"Stunning, isn't it?" asked Sully, leaning into Hawk, as they entered the house and walked toward the staircase, hand in hand.

Hawk nodded. "Yep … let's mingle." Coming from a wealthy family in Norway, Hawk was used to seeing mansions of this size and opulence.

"Look at this place," murmured Elsie, as she walked toward the ballroom, which was located at the back of the house. "Beautiful!"

"Just like you tonight, Elsie," said Kiplin, leaning in, and offering his arm.

"Why, thank you," said Elsie, taking his arm. When they came to a stop in the doorway of the long ballroom, Elsie was mesmerized by the two crystal chandeliers that hung from the high ornate ceilings, and the way the orchestra played. She recognized Dmitri Shostakovich's 'The Second Waltz'. The room was filled with men in tuxedos and ladies in evening gowns, some dancing on the hardwood and marble floor, and others chatting on the sidelines. The room was bursting with enjoyment.

"You ready?" asked Kiplin, gesturing to the dance floor.

"Sure. Let's do this," replied Elsie. She followed Kiplin, and they fitted in nicely with the other couples, who were twirling around the dance floor.

"Well, look who has joined us," whispered Kiplin to Elsie.

She turned to see Tassone Boardman and a woman settling in on the dance floor beside them.

Kiplin twirled Elsie around and tried to keep close to them, all the while, trying to read Tassone thoughts. But he had blocked anyone from reading his thoughts.

When the music stopped and everyone applauded, Elsie looked over at Tassone and smiled audaciously.

Tassone's eyebrows arched upward, and a mischievous smirk played on his lips as he gazed over at her. Leaning in closer, he posed the question, "May I cut in?" With the orchestra beginning to play a new tune, he turned his attention toward Kiplin, awaiting a response.

"Of course!" Kiplin stepped away from Elsie, and into the arms of the glamorous woman Tassone had previously been dancing with.

Elsie slipped her hand into Tassone's and placed her other on his shoulder. He steered her into the growing crowd, as the orchestra played Johann Strauss's 'Voices of Spring'.

"You're very good," said Tassone, as he looked into her hazel eyes.

"Thank you. You're too kind," said Elsie, smiling. "I would say that you have had a lot more practice than me. You are a really strong leader."

"I don't know about that," said Tassone, as he pulled her in closer and whispered, "Would you like me to tell you a secret?"

"Yes!" Elsie hoped her answer didn't sound too eager. In fact, she was intending to know all of this man's secrets before their dance was over.

"I don't really like dancing. I only partake for appearance's sake," said Tassone, as he moved in sync with her.

Elsie laughed in response to his admission. "Your secret is safe with me, Mr. Boardman."

"Tassone, please … call me, Tassone."

Elsie responded with a nod, accompanied by a polite smile. "So, Tassone … can I come by sometime? Maybe you can give me some dance lessons!" Elsie gently caressed her fingers down the side of his jawline.

"Usually I would love to, my dear. Regrettably … I am pretty busy at the moment, with a big shipment that is coming in, and I don't have much time to socialize," said Tassone. Even if she was beautiful, he didn't need any further distractions in his life.

Once I find out that security code to the ammunition building from Albinus Giordano, then I will have everything I need, for not only the rebellion in France with the Lepidopteras, but also to supply weapons of mass destruction to the Congo, and eventually the world, thought Tassone, as he gazed off into the distance and they continued to dance around the room. *Very soon, I am going to be one rich man, and no one will be able to stop me. But first, I need to see how my soldiers are doing down in my dungeon, with retrieving the code from Albinus Giordano. He had better come around soon, otherwise I will have to kill his only daughter.*

Elsie swallowed hard. She had anticipated the moment her Griffin power to siphon a person's thoughts by touching them would kick in, but when she heard Tassone Boardman's thoughts in her head for the first time, it came as a shock to her. It took some effort to pretend otherwise, while she continued to dance with him.

"Maybe another day … or night?" teased Elsie, as she raised her left eyebrow. She swallowed the bile that rose in her mouth.

"I am sure that can be arranged," said Tassone. His lips thinned in a chilling smile. When the orchestra stopped playing, Elsie and Tassone came to a standstill. "This has been—how do you say—*magnifique*. But I do believe that this is my cue to leave." He cast a glance across the room, locking eyes with Kiplin, and signaled for him to approach.

Every bone in Elsie's body prickled with disgust, and her skin crawled, as Tassone gave her a sly wink, and kissed her hand.

"Until we meet again, my dear," said Tassone, as he handed her back to Kiplin.

"I look forward to it." Elsie smiled briefly, and watched him walk away.

"Did you get what we came for?" whispered Kiplin.

"Yes, and more. Let's get the fuck out of here," whispered Elsie.

Kiplin and Elsie made a beeline for the ballroom doorway.

Sully, Hawk … we have what we need. Meet you at the car, mind-thought Kiplin, to only his team working the mission.

But there was no answer from Sully or Hawk.

Sully … Hawk … did you hear me?

Again, no answer.

Christian, have you seen or heard from Sully or Hawk? I can't seem to raise them, mind-thought Kiplin.

Not at all. Let me know if you don't hear from them, mind-thought Christian. He harnessed his Lepidoptera ability to create a mental shield around his thoughts, so that only his missions team members could hear his thoughts.

Christian noticed the concern etched on Danielle's face, and realized that she, too, had heard the mind-chatter from Kiplin, and was worried that the mission might have taken an unexpected turn.

* * *

At the top of the stairs, Sully and Hawk turned right and started to search each closed-door room in the hallway. As they neared a blind corner of the hallway, they overheard voices.

Hawk held his index finger up to his lips.

Sully nodded and peered around the corner. Her eyes widened in shock as she witnessed an unconscious Xanthia being transported by one of two soldiers toward the rear of the house. Reacting swiftly, she retreated behind the protective cover of the wall and whispered in a hushed tone, "There are two guards … they have Xanthia."

Hawk discreetly peered around the corner, and observed the two guards positioned in front of a closed elevator doorway. Meeting Sully's gaze, he swiftly unbuttoned his jacket and retrieved a sheathed knife from his pocket.

We should help her, mind-thought Hawk.

Yes, I agree. But remember, our mission directive was to gather intel. Shouldn't we request backup? mind-thought Sully.

Hawk rolled his eyes and shook his head. *Yes, but what if they hurt, or worse, kill her, and we have done nothing to help her. I couldn't live with myself.*

As the sound of the elevator's ping echoed through the hallway, Sully and Hawk waited for the doors to close and then ran toward them. Their hearts raced with anticipation as they reached the elevator, watching the number panel as they tracked the path taken by the two soldiers and Xanthia.

"You two … what are you doing up here?" asked a burly guard, who had quietly walked up behind them.

Sully and Hawk turned to see the seven-foot-tall guard coming toward them.

Hawk hid his blade in the back of his trousers.

"I was looking for the ladies, for my girlfriend," said Hawk, placing his arm around Sully's shoulder. "She isn't feeling too good.

"It's on the ground floor," stated the guard, coming to stand in front of them. As the guard delivered the information, his expression turned serious and focused.

"Thank you," said Hawk. He cast one final look at the number panel to see where the lift had stopped, then he walked with his arm around Sully toward the white marble stairs.

The guard followed them, and directed them to where the ladies' room was.

* * *

Sully, Hawk, where in the fuck are you both? mind-thought Christian.

In the ladies; we are both in here, mind-thought Sully, as she looked around at the lavish, modern room.

Why haven't you answered our calls? queried Christian.

When we heard Elsie's thoughts of where Xanthia was, we decided to go and find her, replied Sully.

For fuck's sake … you were instructed to find out the intel on her, nothing else, mind-thought Christian.

Yes, but … mind-thought Sully.

There are no buts. Get back to the car, NOW! ordered Christian, sighing deeply.

Hawk looked at Sully and shook his head. "There is no way in hell I could leave a defenseless girl and her father with these bastards. Are you with me?" asked Hawk.

"Yeah, I agree," said Sully, knowing that what they were about to do hadn't been approved by her coven, and was probably not safe. She opened the door of the ladies' toilets and looked for any sign of a guard. "He's gone. Let's go find them."

Hawk nodded and followed Sully out the door.

"Look!" Sully whispered, her voice filled with anticipation, as her eyes pointed toward an elevator doorway nestled beneath the staircase.

"Perhaps this could take us to the floor where they took Xanthia," Hawk whispered, his voice filled with hope. He gently tugged on Sully's hand, urging her toward the elevator.

As the elevator emitted its distinctive ping, signaling its arrival, Sully and Hawk stepped inside, and the doors smoothly closing behind them.

"Hopefully they haven't taken her to another location by now," expressed Sully, with a hint of concern, her finger confidently pressing the button for sublevel three. She took a deep breath to steady her nerves, as her gaze remained fixed on the numbers on the control panel, each increment signifying a floor drawing them closer to their intended destination.

When the elevator came to a halt on the third basement level and the doors slid open, Sully and Hawk were met with a tense and daunting sight. Standing before them were three formidable Debauched guards, each measuring a towering six feet or more in height. The guards had their sights fixed on the intruders, their muscular frames accompanied by menacing automatic rifles pointed directly at Sully and Hawk.

"Out!" said one of the guards, who was dressed in leather battle gear.

Sully's throat tightened, and she swallowed hard.

Hawk's eyes filled with dread as he exchanged a solemn glance with Sully. Resigned to their circumstances, they approached the three Debauched soldiers together, aware that arguing would be futile in the face of their superior firepower.

* * *

Christian shook his head in disbelief and let out a sigh, as a sense of unease crept over him. His Lepidoptera senses hinted that something had gone wrong with the mission. "Where are they?" queried Christian to Danielle.

"Hopefully, on their way back to the car," said Danielle.

Sully, Hawk … you had better be on your way back to the car, mind-thought Christian.

There was no answer from either of them.

Seething with frustration, Christian slammed his fist down on the trunk of the limousine. "Stupid idiots!"

"Calm down, Christian. We don't want to draw attention to ourselves," murmured Danielle. She placed her hand on his arm and looked into his eyes. "Let's go see if we can find them."

"I hope nothing has happened to them, because of their stupidity. William will have my balls for this," said Christian. He placed his hand in Danielle's and they walked toward the back of the house.

* * *

Suspended from the roof, his hands bound by chains and his bare feet left dangling, barely touching the ground, Albinus watched the guard place his beloved daughter, Xanthia, who was bound and gagged, in a barrel of water, and attach electrodes to her body.

"Please, don't hurt her. I beg you! She's just a child. She hasn't done anything wrong," pleaded Albinus, his voice laced with fear and desperation.

With a cold smug look, the Debauched guard turned the machine on. It hummed with the potential for suffering. "You know what is required of you, Giordano. Hand it over and this won't happen."

"What you seek is not something that I can give," stated Albinus. His gaze never wavered from Xanthia, who remained submerged in the barrel, her small form trembling. "Please, just let her go!"

No matter the consequences, Albinus couldn't betray his principles or endanger the lives of countless others by surrendering to the Debauched guard's demands of supplying the codes.

Xanthia's body convulsed, and her blue eyes rolled backward, when the muscular Debauched guard turned the machine up to a maximum setting, and electrocuted her.

"Please … don't hurt her any further," screamed Albinus. Tears welled in his blue eyes as he struggled against his restraints, his anguish intensifying with each passing moment. He yearned to protect his daughter and shield her from any harm. The sight of her in such a vulnerable state filled him with a sense of helplessness and despair.

"Get the fuck away from her, scumbag," yelled Christian, as he and Danielle burst through the door of the darkened room. Taking his short sword from its sheath, he swiftly decapitated the Debauched Vampire, and watched his body turn to ash. Turning the machine off, Christian quickly checked on Xanthia.

"Are you okay?" asked Danielle to Albinus Giordano, as she pulled him free from the chains, and placed him on the black sandy floor.

"Yes … don't worry about me, just check my Xanthia. She is all I have," said Albinus. He looked over at his daughter, and watched Christian retrieve her lifeless body from the barrel of water, and lay her flat on the sand.

"Danielle," shouted Christian. He looked over his shoulder in her direction.

Danielle ran over to Xanthia, and placed her healing Lepidoptera hands over Xanthia's wet clothed body. The room seemed to hold its breath as Danielle's healing abilities took effect. Soft tendrils of light emanated from her hands, caressing Xanthia's form.

Amazed by the sight, Albinus knelt beside his unconscious daughter and held her hand. "I am so sorry, my sweet Xanthia," Albinus whispered, his voice choked with grief. "I never wanted you to endure such pain and fear. Please forgive me, my darling. I will do everything in my power to keep you safe from now on." Albinus's heart pounded as he prayed that the healing touch would bring solace and relief to his precious daughter.

Danielle looked over at Christian, who was kneeling next to Albinus, and shook her head.

"I'm sorry, Albinus; she's gone," said Danielle, checking the pulse on Xanthia's wrist.

"No!" screamed Albinus. "Xanthia …" He laid his bloodied head on her chest and sobbed uncontrollably.

Christian placed a hand on Albinus's back. "I'm sorry for your loss, Sir."

"Ah, it looks like we have company, Shepherd," said Tassone Boardman sarcastically, as he walked into the dungeon, where Xanthia lay lifeless on the ground.

"You will pay for what you have done to my daughter, Boardman," said Albinus, as he got up off the floor and ran toward Tassone.

Tassone snickered and used his Debauched powers to stop Albinus in his tracks, holding him up against the dungeon wall by his throat. "I told you what would happen if you didn't cooperate."

Albinus tried to wriggle free from Tassone's hold, but it was useless.

"Let him go," ordered Christian.

With steely determination in their eyes, Danielle and Christian charged forward, confronting Tassone and his soldier. Their resolute expressions were hardened, revealing their determination and preparedness to face any obstacle in their path.

With a swift and powerful motion, Tassone ruthlessly propelled Christian and Danielle in the air, their bodies crashing against the unyielding wall, knocking them both unconscious.

"Get these pieces of Lepidoptera rubbish out of my sight, and dispose of them, Shepherd," said Tassone. His expression contorted into a disdainful sneer, revealing his contempt. His features twisted with a mixture of derision and disgust, emphasizing his dismissive attitude toward Danielle and Christian.

"Yes, Sire," replied Shepherd. He walked over to Christian and Danielle, effortlessly lifted their unconscious bodies from the ground, and tossed them over his broad shoulders.

Tassone watched Shepherd, walk toward the door and into the hallway, that had steep steps leading up to the back of the property. "Now …" he turned to Albinus, "You had better remember the code, Giordano, otherwise I will have no alternative but to kill some of your coworkers at the Ministry of Defense." He continued to hold Albinus up against the wall with his powers, and walked toward him. "Are we clear?"

Albinus looked Tassone in the eyes and said, "I don't care what you do with me, but if you hurt or kill anyone else, I know … I promise you; you will pay."

Tassone laughed loudly. "It is you who will pay … with your life, Albinus. But for now … what is the damn code?" He dropped Albinus's body to the ground.

A nervous Albinus glanced up at Tassone, and in that instant, a chilling realization washed over him. He understood that he had no choice other than to comply with Tassone's demands. Failure to do so would undoubtedly result in dire consequences for his coworkers. With a trembling voice, Albinus mustered the courage to speak, hoping to convince Tassone of his cooperation. "The code is computer generated."

"Right! Where is this computer?" asked Tassone. But before Albinus could answer, there was an explosion outside. "What the fuck was that?" Tassone rushed toward the doorway, closed the door behind him, locked it, and ran at Vampire speed up the concrete stairs, toward the back of the house.

His guests were screaming, running everywhere, some running toward their cars and some looking around in dismay. Then, Tassone spotted two familiar faces in the crowd. *Grayson, Kelan Gramaze!*

I'll go deal with this fucker, thought Grayson to Kelan, gesturing towards Tassone, as they stepped out of the portal onto the grass area. *And you see if you can find everyone else.*

On it. Try not to get yourself killed, thought Kelan as he ran towards the house.

Where are my family, Boardman? demanded Grayson, as he walked toward Tassone, with a flame thrower in hand.

Tassone snickered. *Hopefully, dead by now, Lepidoptera.*

Grayson ran toward Tassone at Vampire speed and knocked him off his feet. Pushing the hot nozzle of the flame thrower into Tassone's left cheek, Grayson placed his foot on Tassone's chest. "Where are they, fucker?"

But before Tassone could answer, Grayson was hit by a bullet to the chest, from one of Tassone's soldiers, leaving him vulnerable as he fell to the ground.

"Aww, fuck," cried Grayson, clutching his chest. Before he could regain his bearings, a sudden blow from the butt of Shepherd's rifle struck the side of his head. The world spun into a chaotic blur as darkness engulfed him, consciousness slipping away like sand through his fingers.

"Are you okay, Sire?" asked Shepherd, as he got to Tassone.

"Yes, yes!" stated Tassone, impatiently, as he stood up. "Did you dispose of those two Lepidopteras?"

"Yes, Sire. They're ash!" lied Shepherd, who feared the repercussion from his master. When the explosion happened, Shepherd didn't have time to dispose of Christian and Danielle; instead, he left their unconscious bodies down by the river for Tassone's pet alligators to eat.

"Good. Get Albinus and the other two, and let's get the hell out of here," said Tassone, as he surveyed the retreat of his guests, their red tail lights speeding away from his property, and disappearing into the distance.

"Yes, Sire," said Shepherd. He ran toward the house to secure his prisoners.

Sire, I have organized for a black four-wheel drive to be waiting for us around the front, mind-thought Shepherd.

Good man, mind-thought Tassone.

CHAPTER TWENTY-FIVE

Kiplin's heart raced as the sound of the explosion reverberated through the air. Panic surged within him, and he turned to Elsie, his eyes wide with urgency. "We can't sit here and do nothing," he said, his voice filled with determination. He turned to look through the back window of the limousine, and watched the guests scrambling away from the house, their faces etched with fear and confusion.

"Christian and Danielle told us to stay here in the car, no matter what happens," said Elsie, her brow furrowed.

"Listen, Elsie, I can't seem to raise Christian or Danielle, so I think they may be in trouble," said Kiplin. He opened the car door. "Come on, let's go."

"No, Kiplin. We will be in big trouble if we leave the car. You know that," said Elsie, as she grabbed his arm, stopping him from exiting the car.

"Look …" he turned to her. "I know we were told to wait. But I feel we are needed. I can't explain it … please, Elsie, I don't want to leave you here by yourself," said Kiplin.

Elsie looked into his pleading eyes and sighed. "Okay. But I am blaming you if we get into trouble with Christian."

He rolled his eyes and shook his head at her. "I think we need to get changed first, though," said Kiplin, looking at her gown. "I remember Christian mentioning that there are combat clothes and weapons in the boot."

"Yeah, good call," said Elsie, as she exited the car with Kiplin.

* * *

"Grayson … wake up, man," said Kelan, his voice filled with concern. Kneeling beside Grayson, he shook his shoulder, hoping to rouse him from unconsciousness. As Kelan's brown eyes scanned Grayson's still form, a wave of alarm washed over him. His gaze fixed on the bullet hole in Grayson's shirt.

Grayson opened his eyes wide and he sat up quickly. "What happened?

"You were shot," said Kelan, as he raked a hand through his short blond hair.

Grayson pulled his shirt up, and watched the bullet start to expel from his chest. "One of the many things I love about being a Lepidoptera; we self-heal from wounds like these."

"Man, I should never have listened to you. This would never have happened if we didn't split up," said Kelan, standing and holding his hand out to Grayson.

"All good, man. Don't fret. Have you seen anyone yet?"

"No. And I can't seem to raise them through mind-chatter either," said Kelan. He handed Grayson the flamethrower he had dropped earlier.

"Right! Let's check the back of the property first. Then we can check the house," said Grayson, taking the weapon from Kelan.

As Kelan and Grayson ran toward the back of the house, they spotted Elsie and Kiplin in the distance, walking toward the creek.

Kiplin, stop. Wait for us, mind-thought Grayson.

Kiplin stopped in his tracks when he heard the voice in his head. He grabbed Elsie's arm and said, "Wait. Someone is calling us." Looking around he spotted Grayson and Kelan, whom he knew from the Gramaze coven, running toward them.

Within seconds Grayson and Kelan were standing in front of Elsie and Kiplin.

"Grayson ... we are so glad to see you," said Kiplin, relieved to be standing with his Lepidoptera family.

"Where is Sully, Hawk, Christian and Danielle?" asked Grayson.

"We don't know," said Kiplin. He looked at Grayson and gulped. "All Christian and Danielle told us was they were going to find Sully and Hawk, and that we were to stay in the car until they returned."

"Right! Looks to me like you didn't listen ..." said Grayson, looking from Kiplin to Elsie.

"No, we didn't," said Elsie, averting her eyes. "But with good reason." She looked up at Grayson and Kelan and gulped hard. "Sorry."

"Don't be sorry. Be proud of yourselves, that you actually took the initiative to look for them," said Grayson, who had been listening to their nervous thoughts, and knew where they had already searched the property for Sully, Hawk, Christian and Danielle.

"So ... how did you know we needed help, or that the mission had failed?" asked Elsie.

"Christian had informed William of how the mission was going and what was happening. William sent Kelan and I, via a portal, to assist, if needed. But we haven't been able to reach anyone," said Grayson.

"Guys, enough of the chitchat," said Kelan, looking at each of them. He raked a hand through his blond hair and sighed. "Let's go find our family."

Family ... thought Kiplin. He had been in a lot of foster homes since he was a child, and never had a real family. He liked boarding at the Legacies Academy but had hoped one day to be a part of the Gramaze coven, and to become an explosives expert.

"We have searched most of the property, and were just about to look down by the creek," said Elsie, pointing to the back of the property. She extended her Griffin wings.

"Wow … they're huge," said Kelan, his brown eyes looking at her two-meter wide wing span. "We'll meet you at the creek."

Elsie nodded and flew off toward the back of the property.

With Vampire speed, Kelan, Grayson and Kiplin were at the edge of the creek in no time.

Guys … I've found them. Go to your right. They're near the jetty, mind-thought Elsie, hovering above them.

"Christian! Danielle!" Elsie called out from above. She retracted her wings as she landed on the grass area and ran toward them.

"Christian! Danielle!" Grayson knelt beside their unconscious bodies to see if they had any injuries, and tried to wake them.

Kiplin knelt beside Danielle's body and placed his hand on her abdomen. Because he had the Vampire power of mimicry, he was able to copy Danielle's power of healing and could start the healing process on both Danielle and Christian.

Within seconds both Danielle and Christian were awakened and healed.

"Thank you, Kiplin," said Danielle, as she sat up.

"You're welcome."

"Have you found Sully and Hawk?" asked Danielle.

"No. We were hoping you might be able to shed some light on that," Grayson said, extending his hand toward her.

"Let's split up, and see if we can find them," Christian suggested, clasping Kelan's outstretched hand.

"We are better off in numbers. I think we should check the inside of the house first. Elsie and Kiplin have already checked the outside, and they are not out here," said Grayson, who had now taken charge of the mission.

They all nodded in agreement, and followed Grayson toward the house.

* * *

As he cautiously entered the darkened lower-level room, Kiplin's heart pounded with anticipation, but then he stumbled upon a sight that sent shockwaves through his being. There, lying motionless on the cold dungeon floor, was Xanthia's body. The realization of her passing struck him like a thunderbolt, leaving him breathless and overwhelmed with regret. His mind raced back to the photographs he had seen, etching her face into his memory.

"Fuck, Xanthia!" Kiplin's voice cracked as he rushed to her side, his hands trembled as he knelt beside her lifeless form. Desperation filled his eyes as he instinctively reached out, his palms hovering over her. A flicker of hope surged within him, fueled by the dormant power of healing he had absorbed from Danielle. Summoning every ounce of his will, Kiplin closed his eyes, concentrating on the pulsating energy coursing through his veins. With a mixture of determination and uncertainty, he gently placed his hands upon Xanthia's body, willing the healing power within him. The room fell silent as Kiplin poured his energy into his efforts, desperately hoping for a miracle, his heart aching with the desire to bring her back.

"It's no good. I already tried," said Danielle, her voice tinged with a mix of resignation and sympathy, as she walked into the room. She understood the depths of Kiplin's sorrow, having attempted her own healing before.

Kiplin looked up at Danielle, his gaze pleading. His belief in the possibility of a different outcome lingered in his eyes. Resolute, he replied, "I would still like to try."

Danielle nodded and knelt beside Xanthia. Placing both hands over the body, she chanted *Ong Ma Lee Bae Mae Hong.*

"What is that?"

"It's a healing ritual," said Danielle. She had been taught this ritual by Talitha, the Lepidoptera Vampire Queen, many years previous.

Kiplin decided he would try this too.

After a few exhausting minutes, Danielle looked at Kiplin and said, "I don't think this is going to work."

"I think we should at least keep trying, don't you?" said Kiplin. He placed one of his hands on Danielle, and the other one on Xanthia and chanted louder. The weight of expectation hung heavy on his shoulders, and the thought of disappointing the Gramaze coven leader was an unbearable burden he couldn't shake.

Christian, Elsie, Grayson, and Kelan stepped into the dimly lit room; their footsteps hushed by the weight of the somber atmosphere. As they entered, they saw Kiplin and Danielle, with hands gently placed over Xanthia's lifeless body, their expressions a blend of hope and determination. A sense of anticipation filled the room.

Let's form a circle and chant for Xanthia, mind-thought Elsie.

As Kiplin and Danielle held their healing hands over Xanthia's body, Christian, Elsie, Grayson and Kelan formed a circle around the three of them and helped to chant the ritual out loud.

The more they all chanted, the more the room started to glow white, eventually lifting Xanthia's body off the ground. When they were all standing and had finally finished, and Xanthia's body was firmly on the floor again, they all realized that it was too late. She had definitely passed over.

"What are we going to do with her body?" Elsie asked, her voice trembling as she stared at Xanthia's lifeless form, her hands clenched tightly at her sides. The weight of the moment pressed down on her, leaving her breath shallow and her heart heavy.

"For now, we'll take her back to the Gramaze mansion and give her the dignity she deserves—at least until we can find her father," Grayson said, his tone steady but laced with sadness.

"Can I help with this?" Elsie asked softly, her eyes pleading as she stepped closer.

"Yes … actually, do you think you could fly her back to the Gramaze mansion?" asked Grayson.

"Sure. It will be my honor," said Elsie. With a solemn nod, Elsie took a deep breath, and gently cradled Xanthia in her arms. The weight of their collective sorrow seemed to rest upon her shoulders, but she remained resolute. Determination shone in her eyes as she accepted the responsibility of carrying Xanthia, a final act of care and reverence.

They all gathered around Elsie, forming a protective circle as they began to make their way out of the lower-level room and back outside.

* * *

"It's still crazy out here," said Kiplin, watching the last of the guests quickly drive away, some scrambling to work out what had happened.

"The humans are scared, understandably," said Grayson.

"Would you like me to return, once I have dropped Xanthia's body off at the Gramaze mansion?" asked Elsie, as she extended her Griffin wings.

"No. Could I ask you to stay with Xanthia's body?" asked Grayson. He placed a white sheet over Xanthia, and neatly wrapped her body, to show respect for the deceased.

"Yes, Sir. I am only too happy to do what I can to help."

"Thank you. I will be in touch when we return to the mansion," said Grayson.

As Elsie's delicate feathers caught the gentle breeze, she ascended into the air, cradling Xanthia's lifeless form against her chest. Despite knowing that Xanthia had passed, Elsie's Griffin instinct to protect and care for Xanthia remained strong. With every beat of her wings, Elsie ensured that Xanthia was shielded from the cold night air.

She held her close, as if embracing her could somehow provide comfort, even in death.

The others watched from below, their gazes lifted toward the heavens, their hearts filled with a mixture of sadness and awe.

"Right … I want each of you to start having a good look around for Sully, Hawk and Albinus. Then, I want this place cleaned up before we leave," said Grayson, looking around. "Stay together at all times."

They each nodded and walked toward the house.

* * *

With her eagle-like feet securely cradling Xanthia's body, Elsie's Griffin wings continued to beat rhythmically against the night sky. As they soared closer to their destination, the backyard of the Gramaze mansion came into view. Elsie hoped that someone would be waiting at the mansion to help with Xanthia's body.

"You're safe with me, Xanthia," said Elsie.

As Elsie's feet touched the ground, near the backyard swimming pool, a voice in her head grew clearer, whispering into her consciousness. Its muffled words carried a sense of urgency and guidance, causing her to pause and search her surroundings for the source. Her eyes scanned the area, but she couldn't identify the origin of the voice.

Retracting her wings into her back, Elsie heard the muffled voice again and looked around, but dismissed it when she saw the Head Chancellor.

"Hello, Elsie," said Violette, as she walked toward her.

Elsie stood tall and bowed her head. "Head Chancellor."

"Can I take Xanthia from you?" asked Violette, as she held her arms out.

Elsie placed Xanthia's body gently into Violette's arms.

"Would you like to help me get Xanthia ready, for when her father returns?" asked Violette, watching the gloomy look on Elsie's face.

Elsie nodded in agreement. "I would be honored to assist you."

Violette's offer struck a chord within Elsie, reminding her of the importance of honoring Xanthia's memory, and providing closure for her loved ones.

"Come this way," said Violette, as she held Xanthia's body close to hers, and walked toward the back of the mansion. "What did you say?" She turned to Elsie, as they walked up the steps.

Elsie shook her head and frowned. "Nothing."

Violette paused at the top of the limestone stairs, her eyes scanning the surroundings. It was only then that she recognized the voice calling for help—it was Xanthia.

Help ... Xanthia's muffled voice said.

Xanthia ... Violette quickly unwrapped her body and placed her on the outdoor lounge. *What the hell ...*

Elsie gasped when she realized what was happening, and saw Xanthia's eyes open. She looked to Violette for answers.

"Xanthia ... we thought you were ... well, dead," said Violette, watching the frightened look on Xanthia's face.

Xanthia's gaze darted between Violette and Elsie before she sat up abruptly, curling her legs tightly to her chest. "Where am I?" she asked, her voice tinged with panic.

"You're at my home," Violette said gently, noting the nervous flicker in Xanthia's eyes and the whirlwind of frightened thoughts swirling in her mind. She lowered herself onto the seat beside Xanthia, her tone calm and reassuring. "It's okay. You're safe here with us." After a pause, she added, "Do you remember what happened?"

With a furrowed brow, Xanthia nodded, yes. "That man, Mr. Boardman, he had me tied up and tortured, at his mansion. My father, where is he?" asked Xanthia, the concern on her face apparent.

"We don't know," said Violette.

The tears welled in Xanthia's eyes.

"Tassone Boardman and his men escaped with your father earlier this evening," said Elsie, kneeling in front of Xanthia. "Don't worry, I am sure the Gramaze family will find him and bring him safely home." She placed her hand over Xanthia's.

Xanthia looked into Elsie's eyes and frowned. "Who are the Gramaze family?" Her breathing became rapid. "Once my father gives that man the code, he will have no further need for him, and …" Xanthia's tears spilled over onto her cheeks, her emotions overwhelming her as she succumbed to deep sobs. The young teenager's shoulders shook with each heaving breath, her cries echoing the depth of her pain and anguish.

"Try not to worry. Come on, let's get you inside and cleaned up," said Violette, standing. She held her hand out for Xanthia to take.

Xanthia wiped her tearstained face and tried to stand, but her body was weak from the electric shock she had endured earlier that evening. "I don't think I can stand."

"That's okay. I can help you," said Violette. She scooped Xanthia up in her arms.

As soon as Violette scooped her up, Xanthia's body went limp—she had fainted, overwhelmed by everything crashing down on her young mind.

"Is she going to be, okay?" Elsie asked anxiously, her voice barely above a whisper.

"She will be," Violette assured her, her tone steady yet gentle. "Come on, follow me."

Elsie followed Violette into the Gramaze mansion.

CHAPTER TWENTY-SIX

Sully's eyes opened slowly and adjusted to the darkness as she activated her Lepidoptera vision, a unique ability that granted her enhanced perception. The room's features began to come into focus, revealing a cold, dimly lit space. Her heart raced with a mix of confusion and apprehension, as she sat up quickly.

Surveying her surroundings, Sully noticed the dull gleam of metal sheet walls surrounding her, creating an enclosure that felt oppressive. The air carried a faint musty odor, and an eerie silence seemed to permeate the room. Every instinct within her screamed that she was somewhere that could be dangerous.

Where am I? Sully wondered.

"I think we are in a shipping container," came the response from Hawk. He had heard a ship's horn blast earlier, when he woke. Leaning back against the wall of the container, with his hands bound behind his back, he tried to break the steel chains, but to no avail.

"Hawk!" whispered Sully. She used her Lepidoptera abilities to break the chains that held her wrists and rushed over to him.

"Yep, one and only," whispered Hawk.

"How did we get here?" She knelt in front of him and ripped the chains off his wrists.

"I'm not too sure. I remember coming out of the lift, but after that, nothing," said Hawk, rubbing his wrists. "Thanks, that feels better."

"Yeah, me too." Sully got to her feet and walked over to a small bolt-sized hole on the wall of the container.

Peering through the hole, she noticed it was daytime outside, and rows upon rows of shipping containers crowded the deck. "Fuck … we are out at sea."

"What!" Hawk walked over and pushed her aside, to look through the small hole. "How in the hell did we get here?"

"Aww, my head."

Sully turned around, and spotted Albinus in the corner, sitting on the floor, rubbing his head. She remembered his face from the paperwork they had looked at, prior to going on the mission the previous night.

"Albinus!"

"Yes," said Albinus, anxiously looking around, trying to focus. "Who's there?"

Sully walked over to Albinus and knelt in front of him. She introduced herself and explained to him about her and Hawk's mission, and the events that took place on the previous night.

"Xanthia!" moaned Albinus. He remembered seeing her lifeless body lying on the cold sandy floor of Tassone's place.

"Do you know where she is?" asked Hawk, as he sat next to Albinus.

"Dead … Boardman's henchman killed her," said Albinus, his eyes looking off into the darkened container. "He told me if I didn't give him the code to the ammunition factory, then he would kill some of my coworkers as well."

"Oh, shit! I'm so sorry. My deepest condolences," said Hawk. He placed his arm around Albinus's shoulder in support.

"That fucker is going to pay … believe me," said Sully, as she sat on the other side of Albinus.

"What is that smell?" asked Hawk, noticing a metallic taste in his mouth.

Sully sniffed the air. "It's a sort of sweet smell, isn't it?"

"Its nitrous oxide. I would know that smell anywhere," said Albinus. *My years as a chemist have taught me well.*

Within seconds, the three of them were rendered unconscious from the nitrous oxide that had been pumped into the shipping container to keep them quiet.

* * *

"For fuck's sake, William, why does this keep happening?" asked Garrick, who was standing in the operations room of the Gramaze coven.

"I think you know the answer to that, my friend," stated William.

"Yes, but Eryndor hasn't returned topside, so I am surmising their disappearance has nothing to do with him and the Twin Icefire Blades. And who is this Tassone Boardman?" He paced the room back and forth. "You assured me that Hawk would be safe here. What am I going to tell Elara? She will be furious." *As if I didn't have enough to worry about.*

William stood in Garrick's worn pathway, halting him mid-stride. Meeting his distressed gaze, he rested a steady hand on Garrick's shoulder. "We will find them, my friend. But first, you need to focus."

"This Boardman, you said from speaking with Elsie, that he wants a code for the ammunition factory. I think we should start there, don't you?" said Garrick.

"Yes. But I don't think that is all he wants. According to the intel that Elsie received, Boardman wants to annihilate my coven, as well. So, I am surmising that once he tries to obtain the ammunition, we will be seeing him here, soon enough."

"Right! So, what … we just wait?" He looked into William's eyes. "Fuck that! I am out of here." Garrick walked toward the glass sliding doors. "I need to get back to Olden and figure out how I am going to get my son back, alive," said Garrick.

"Wait! Garrick, we're better off working together on this," said William, watching Garrick, walk toward the doorway.

"No, William." Garrick stopped in his tracks and turned to face him. "I will do this my way. And when Hawk returns, he will no longer be attending the academy. I want him home where he will be safe," stated Garrick. He continued on through the sliding glass doors. Preoccupied by the disappearance of his son, Garrick hadn't even realized how ungrateful he had come across to William.

"Fuck!" said William, with his fists clenched by his side, as he watched the glass doors close.

Humph ... and here I was thinking you would help me, especially after my family and I saved your family, and your kingdom, thought William shaking his head in disbelief.

"Brock ... anything yet?" snapped William.

"No, there's nothing on the CCTV footage yet, Sire" replied Brock, turning around in his chair. "Boardman and his men haven't even turned up, nor Albinus."

"Is everyone in place at the ammunition warehouse, if they do turn up?" asked William, facing Brock.

"Yes, Sire."

"Good! Let me know the minute you see or hear anything." He walked toward the sliding doors.

"Yes, Sire."

You will pay dearly, Boardman, if you have in any way hurt my daughter, thought William.

* * *

"Keep an eye on them, Shepherd. They will be needed later," instructed Tassone. He glanced at the gagged and bound unconscious bodies of Sully and Hawk as he stepped out of the black van, which was parked in the underground garage at the Ministry of Defense in Paris.

"Yes, Sire." He understood that Sully and Hawk would likely be exploited as pawns in some future scheme.

Tassone pulled Albinus out of the black van, untied his hands, and pulled a pistol out of his business suit jacket. Pointing it at Albinus, he used his jacket to conceal it. "Don't try any funny business Giordano, otherwise some of your coworkers will die."

With a furrowed brow, Albinus rubbed his wrists and said, "Leave them out of this."

Tassone pushed Albinus toward the elevator door, which was in front of them. "As long as you do what is asked of you, they will be safe."

Albinus stood in front of the elevator door with Tassone and pressed the blue down arrow button. When the elevator pinged and the doors finally opened, they walked inside, and the doors closed.

"Well, what are you waiting for?" Tassone wondered why the lift hadn't moved yet.

"Nothing," said Albinus, who was hoping that the security guards in the control room hadn't seen them. His hand shook as he pressed the floor number and inserted his card, so that the elevator would move down the shaft.

When the doors opened to the floor that Albinus's office was on, he was relieved to see that no one was standing there waiting for them.

Tassone pushed Albinus out of the lift and into a vast concrete-lined warehouse, which gave a sense of security and seclusion. "Lead the way, Giordano."

Albinus nodded and walked toward the row upon row of black racks that were in front of them. Stopping in front of what looked like a multi-level black rack, which had lots of cardboard boxes stacked on it, Albinus inserted his card into a slot on the side of the rack. As the ground rumbled under their feet, and the rack parted, a secret concrete-lined room appeared. Inside was a lonely computer sitting on a white desk, with a black chair neatly pushed under the desk.

Tassone pushed his pistol into Albinus's back and asked, "What trickery is this?"

"This is my office," said Albinus, glancing over his shoulder at Tassone.

"Right!" said Tassone, looking at the cold room in front of him. "Get moving."

"Wait!" Albinus exclaimed, his voice quivering. The urgency in his tone was evident, as his voice wavered with a mixture of fear and desperation. A panel opened on the wall next to them, which displayed a keypad and retina scanner. Albinus reached over to the keypad and entered a six-digit code, then placed his eyeball up against the scanner.

"Good evening, Albinus Giordano. You may enter," a female recorded voice said.

Albinus walked slowly into the small room with Tassone, pulled the chair out from under the desk and sat down. His computer screen came to life as he moved the mouse.

"Good evening, Albinus Giordano. Please enter your password," the same recorded voice said.

He did as the machine instructed and entered the code on the keyboard.

"The Ministry of Defense sure has a lot of protocols to go through, before you can do anything," said Tassone, still pointing the pistol at Albinus. "What happens now?"

"When I ask for it, the computer will generate a code, so that I can gain access to the ammunition warehouse," said Albinus.

"Well, what are you waiting for? Get the code," demanded Tassone, pushing the pistol into the back of Albinus's neck.

"Yes, Sir." Albinus's hands trembled, in fear of what would happen once he received the computer-generated code. Clicking on the app for the generation of a code, he entered his name and then the alphabetical, numerical code appeared on the screen. Albinus wrote the code on a bit of paper and begrudgingly handed it to Tassone.

Tassone smirked. "Where to from here?

"The factory is around the other side of the facility. The Ministry of Defense has a small railcar that can take us there," said Albinus, pushing his chair back, and standing. "Follow me!"

* * *

When the railcar came to a stop, Albinus could see from Tassone's jittery knee that he was anxious to get this over with. Standing, he climbed out of the railcar and headed toward a steel doorway. But before he got to the doorway, two guards dressed in military-style uniforms and armed with rifles approached them.

"State your business," said the first guard, his finger on the trigger of his rifle.

"Umm … I am here to look over the inventory," said Albinus.

"Your identification, please," requested the first guard.

Albinus handed the guard his card and watched him scrutinize the information on it.

"You are free to enter, Albinus Giordano." He turned to Tassone and said, "Your identification, Sir."

"For fuck's sake … I don't have time for this bullshit," said Tassone, as he hurled the two guards, using his Vampire powers, up against the steel wall, knocking them unconscious.

Albinus gulped hard as he witnessed the two guards colliding with the unforgiving steel wall, unsure of their fate. A mixture of fear and concern coursed through his veins, compelling him to rush toward them and assess their condition. However, before he could reach them, Tassone unleashed his Debauched powers, freezing Albinus in his tracks, preventing any further movement.

"Where do you think you're going, Giordano?" said Tassone, holding him by his throat, in the air.

The more Albinus tried to wriggle free from Tassone's hold, the more his airflow was restricted, and soon enough, he too, was rendered unconscious.

Throwing Albinus's body to one side, Tassone retrieved the piece of paper with the code on it and walked over to the keypad, which was beside the steel door to the ammunitions factory, and punched in the code. As the door slid open, Tassone eyes lit up with amazement, at all the firearms and weaponry that was now available to him, right before his eyes.

You won't be able to stop me now, Lepidopteras. All mine for the taking, thought Tassone, as he walked into the large warehouse, rubbing his hands together. He opened each crate before him to check its contents, and reveled in delight at how rich he was about to become. Taking his mobile phone out of his jacket pocket, Tassone dialed the number for his head soldier, who was waiting in the back streets of Paris, along with others, ready to collect the weapons and ammunition, with trucks they had stolen earlier that evening.

* * *

Brock's eyes remained fixed on his computer screen in the operations room as he painstakingly combed through the vast array of CCTV images and camera recordings, searching relentlessly for any trace of Tassone Boardman. Suddenly, a flicker of intrigue danced across Brock's face as his brow furrowed. He had stumbled upon a significant breakthrough, a recording that revealed a sleek black van tucked away in the depths of the Ministry of Defense's underground garage.

Swiftly, he accessed the French police database, and entered the vehicle's number plate, and waited with anticipation for it to retrieve the owner's name. A wave of realization washed over Brock as the information unfolded before him. The van belonged to none other than Tassone Boardman, the very person they were pursuing.

Sire ... I've found something. Can you come to the operations room? mind-thought Brock to William.

Within seconds, the glass doors to the operations room slid open, and Brock watched William, walk toward him, exuding confidence and authority.

"Sire, this is live feed from the garage at the Ministry of Defense." Brock showed the footage from the underground garage to William. "This vehicle is registered to Boardman. I've been closely monitoring this van for the past few minutes, and I've observed intermittent movement within it. An individual appears to be shifting between the driver's seat and the rear of the van."

"Right! Is there any footage for around the back of the van?" asked William, as he watched the screen.

"Unfortunately, no," replied Brock. "I wonder if Boardman has Albinus with him, and they have already breached the secured weaponries?" The uncertainty hung in the air, leaving them both with a sense of unease as they contemplated the potential consequences of such a breach.

"You could be right, Brock. Good work!" said William. He pulled his mobile phone out of his top pocket, and dialed Grayson's number.

"Yes, Sire," said Grayson, answering the call.

"I want you to check out the first level of the garage at the Ministry of Defense. There's a black van parked there that belongs to Boardman, and there seems to be one male sitting in the driver's seat. Let me know what you find," said William, as he continued to watch the CCTV footage.

"Yes, Sire. Michael and I will have a look now," said Grayson. He turned to see where Michael was standing. "I'll get back to you, Sire." He pressed end on his phone and returned the phone to his jacket pocket.

"Let's get this fucker, Michael," said Grayson.

Michael nodded in agreeance, as he had been listening, with his Vampire ability, to the conversation with William.

Grayson and Michael ran at Vampire speed toward the entrance of the underground garage. When they spotted the black van, Grayson signaled to Michael to go around one side of the vehicle, while he would stay at the rear of the van.

Aware that there was an occupant inside the vehicle, Michael proceeded to approach the van from the driver's side in an attempt to attract their attention. Suddenly, the driver's door swung open forcefully, striking Michael in the chest and sending him sprawling to the ground. For a brief moment, he felt disoriented, unable to react. His vision cleared just in time for him to see a disheveled Debauched soldier with dark, curly hair looming over him, brandishing a drawn sword.

"State your business," said Shepherd Mornington, pointing his sword toward Michael's chest.

"I don't answer to you, Debauched," stated Michael.

"Drop your weapon, soldier," said Grayson, as he pressed the tip of his sword into Shepherd's back.

Shepherd gulped, lowered his sword, and discarded it onto the concrete floor.

Michael quickly regained his feet and picked up Shepherd's sword.

"What are you doing down here?" asked Grayson, as he came to stand in front of Shepherd.

"None of your business, Lepidoptera."

"That's where you have it wrong. This is our city, and our business," said Grayson.

"Humph!"

"I don't want to waste any more time on this idiot, Grayson. Let's ash the bastard," said Michael, his nostrils flaring.

"Wait!" said Shepherd. He looked from Michael to Grayson. "I haven't done anything wrong. I'm just waiting here for my boss."

"What a load of fucking bullshit. Let's not forget how you shot me, and knocked me unconscious. What else aren't you telling us?" said Grayson, remembering what happened at Tassone Boardman's residence.

"I swear, nothing!" stated Shepherd.

"Check the vehicle, Michael," instructed Grayson.

Michael walked around to the back of the vehicle and opened the rear doors. To his surprise, Sully and Hawk were lying unconscious in the back of the vehicle. "What the fuck!"

"What is it?" asked Grayson, as he walked around to the back of the van with Shepherd, who now had his hands bound mystically behind his back.

Michael jumped inside the van and tried to wake Sully and Hawk. "What have you done to them?" asked Michael.

"Boardman gave them something to keep them quiet," said Shepherd. A wave of apprehension washed over him, causing his brow to crease while he swallowed anxiously, fully aware of the impending threat that could reduce him to mere specks of dust scattered along the pavement.

"Boardman … So, you're just another one of his lackeys?" stated Grayson, heatedly.

Shepherd nodded, yes, and gulped hard.

"Just ash him, Grayson. He's not worth our time," said Michael, who was gently shaking Sully, trying to wake her.

"No … please," pleaded Shepherd. "I will do anything." He tried to wriggle free from Grayson's hold on him.

Michael … said a faint voice inside Michael's head.

Michael's brow furrowed, and he scanned his surroundings upon hearing the voice.

Don't hurt Shepherd. Sully opened her eyes and looked up at Michael. "Don't kill him."

"Sully … are you alright?" asked Michael. He smiled at her and helped her sit up.

Sully nodded yes. "Don't kill him." She looked from Michael to Grayson. "He's been good to us, since we were taken."

"What! This piece of shit, *good*. I find that hard to believe," said Grayson. "No Debauched is good."

Usually, I'd agree with you. But believe me, I know— I've been reading his thoughts, thought Sully to Grayson.

Hawk's eyes fluttered open, showing disorientation at first. His gaze darted around, taking in his surroundings before he shot upright. A wave of relief washed over him as he exhaled deeply, leaning back against the inside of the vehicle. "Michael … Grayson … thank the gods," he murmured, his voice filled with gratitude.

"Glad you could join us in the land of the living, Hawk. How are you feeling?" asked Michael.

"A bit groggy, but I'm fine. Where are we?" replied Hawk.

"The French Ministry of Defense building," said Michael.

"France?" questioned Hawk, his brow furrowed.

Michael nodded, yes.

"The last time we were conscious, we found ourselves confined in a shipping container adrift at sea," said Sully.

"How did you find us?" asked Hawk, as he looked from Michael to Grayson.

"Brock found you on CCTV footage. Actually, he found the van, and we came to investigate what it was doing parked here. Then we came across this fuckhead." Grayson indicated to Shepherd.

"You know Shepherd saved our butts, don't you, and more than once," said Hawk, looking from Grayson to Shepherd. "If Boardman had his way, we would be dead by now,"

"Yeah, I don't think we would be alive, if it wasn't for, Shepherd," added Sully.

Grayson looked from Hawk to Sully and frowned. "Is that right?"

"He was only doing Boardman's bidding because he fears for his life," said Sully.

"Explain yourself, Debauched," demanded Grayson, who was now holding a small knife to Shepherd's throat.

Shepherd's Adam's apple bobbed, as he gulped hard. "I haven't been a Vampire very long, or with Boardman that long, either. He treats me and others like shit, but beggars can't be choosers, can they?" He shrugged his shoulders.

"Right! How long has it been since you were turned?" asked Grayson, taking the knife away from Shepherd's throat.

"About four months, I think," said Shepherd, remembering the first day he'd drunk human blood, at the morgue.

"Have you drunk from a human?" asked Michael, knowing full well that if Shepherd's answer was yes, he would have to ash him.

"Hell no! That's disgusting. Plus, I've been warned about the consequences of consuming blood directly from a human, and I definitely don't want to become a Debauched Vampire." Shepherd's brow furrowed and he shook his head. "I've only ever relied on bagged blood, the kind you find in hospitals," he added.

"Right! Where's Boardman?" asked Grayson.

"Inside," said Shepherd, indicating to the building. "With Albinus Giordano."

"Shit!" Grayson took his mobile phone from his pocket and rang William.

"Yes!" said William.

"Good news … we've found Sully and Hawk. They were in the back of the van," said Grayson.

"Thank fuck for that!" William exhaled sharply, relief flooding his voice. "Are they okay?" he asked, his eyes wide with concern.

"They're a bit groggy, but they both seem to be okay. Sire, we need more Lepidopteras down here at the Ministry of Defense building. One of Boardman's soldiers has told us that Boardman is inside with Albinus Giordano. And that can mean only one thing," said Grayson.

"Give us a few minutes, and we'll be there," William said firmly before hanging up. Without wasting a moment, he reached out telepathically to his coven, sharing the details of their new mission through their mental link.

CHAPTER TWENTY-SEVEN

With the help of his Debauched coven soldiers, Tassone Boardman loaded the last of the weapons and ammunition he required into the truck and pulled the roller door closed. "Let's get the fuck out of here," said Tassone, walking toward the driver's door.

"Sire … what about these two wooden boxes? Are we taking them, too?" asked one soldier, as he carried them toward Tassone.

"What's inside them," asked Tassone.

The soldier carefully placed them on the ground and unlatched the catch of each lid, allowing them to peer inside.

"Hmm … I think I could get a pretty penny for these two beautiful pieces of steel," said Tassone. He bent over and brushed his fingers over their medieval gold handles, and their sharp blades. "Good find, soldier. Place them in the truck."

As the soldier closed the lids of both wooden boxes, his attention was drawn to the intricate patterns that had been engraved into the lid of each wooden box. Tracing his fingers over the pattern, the soldier thought, *I wonder how old these are, and where they originated?*

* * *

As the large steel door of the Ministry of Defense warehouse slid open, William and his coven stood with their weapons drawn, ready for whatever they might find on the other side of the door.

"Sire!" exclaimed Christian to William, as he stood in front of an empty warehouse, with a stunned expression on his face. "Looks like we're too late."

"Fuck!" William walked further into the warehouse. He couldn't believe what he was seeing. "How in the hell did they get everything out of here so fast?" Taking his mobile phone out of his jacket pocket, he rang Brock, who was in the Gramaze coven operations room.

"Yes, Sire," said Brock.

"The warehouse is empty. I need you to have a look at the CCTV footage for the ammunition warehouse for say, the last five minutes. Tell me what you see," said William.

"I'll call you right back," Brock stated before ending the call. As he meticulously scanned through the images, a frown formed on his face. The trucks had entered the area, but there was no trace of them leaving, and everything seemed undisturbed. "Hmm ..." Brock pressed the number one button on the desk phone in the operations room, initiating a call back to William.

"What did you find?" asked William, abruptly.

"I have scoured over the footage, and well ... trucks came in, but they haven't left yet. So, they should still be inside," said Brock. He continued to watch the footage as he spoke with William.

"Well, they're not here. How in the fuck did they get out of here?" said William. He raked a hand through his hair.

"Wait, what is that?" said Brock, as he replayed the footage. "Sire, there was a bright light under the doorway." He replayed the footage again. "Yep, there it is again. I think they used a portal. Now I know why I didn't see the trucks leaving the warehouse."

"Shit! Thanks, Brock," said William. He pressed end on his phone and placed it back in his jacket pocket.

"Where to now, Sire?" asked Christian, overhearing the conversation.

"Boardman's residence."

Grayson, Michael, I want you to take Sully and Hawk back home, and ask Violette to look after them. Then I want you both to join us at Boardman's place, mind-thought William.

Yes, Sire. What would you like us to do with this Debauched scum? mind-thought Grayson. He looked over at Shepherd, who was sitting on the ground, his hands still bound, next to the black van in the underground parking lot.

Until I can interrogate him, place him in the cells at home, mind-thought William.

Yes, Sire, replied Grayson.

* * *

Two Debauched security guards stood in front of the closed wrought-iron gates at Tassone Boardman's residence. Heavily armed, with their automatic assault rifles drawn, they watched as the black SUV pulled up in front of them.

"What do these fuckers want?" asked the first soldier, as he watched the van come to a stop. He looked from the van to his comrade, and gulped hard. Walking around to the driver's door, he motioned for the driver to lower the window.

Christian pressed the button on his electric window, and watched the Debauched soldier point the tip of the automatic rifle toward him.

"State your business here," said the first soldier.

"We're here to see Tassone Boardman," said Christian, indicating to Danielle in the passenger seat.

"You're not welcome here, Lepidopteras. Leave … before there's trouble," said the first soldier, looking from Christian to Danielle.

With his nostrils flared, the second soldier walked closer to the van and pointed his rifle toward Christian and Danielle.

"We're not looking for trouble," said Christian, as he slowly reached for his loaded gun, which was down beside the seat.

Before the soldier could say another word, William jumped out of the back of the SUV with a blow torch in his hands, and set both Debauched guards on fire.

As the two soldiers fell to the ground and screamed in pain, William pulled his sword from its sheath on his back, cut both of their heads off, and watched them turn to ash.

"Right … now that is sorted, let's find out where these weapons are," said William. He walked over to the guards' hut and pressed the button to open the gates.

As the gates opened, there was a huge fireball explosion that shook the ground, which came from an area at the back of the house.

William sprinted around the side of the house with Vampire speed, coming to a sudden halt as he reached the back of the property. His eyes widened in disbelief at the massive crater before him, steam rising from the ground as if the earth itself were still burning. "Bloody hell! What the fuck happened here?" he muttered, his voice thick with astonishment.

Christian sped through the now-open gates, toward the house and pulled the van to a sudden stop at the edge of the crater. "Fuck!" He jumped out of the car with Danielle, and they ran to William's side.

"What do you think happened?" Danielle asked William, as she came to stand next to him.

William shook his head. "Not sure."

With his brow creased, Christian stood at the edge of the crater, next to William and Danielle. "Sire … there are a lot of dead Debauched here, and humans too," said Christian, looking for any sign of life. "Do you think Albinus is down there?"

"Well, he wasn't at the ammunition warehouse, so I am surmising that his body is amongst those down in this crater," said William, looking for any sign that he might be down there.

"Sire!" said Grayson, who had joined them, and was now standing next to William. "Would you like me to organize a cleanup crew?" Considering that humans were oblivious to the existence of Vampires and other supernatural beings, and based on his past experiences, he understood that the sight of this chaotic scene and the numerous lifeless bodies could raise countless queries from humans.

"Yes!" William walked down the side of the crater to the bottom, and picked up a piece of melted steel, which was one of many items lying at the bottom. *Weaponry?* William then spotted an identification tag lying on the ground. Picking it up, he wiped the dirt from it and read the name: *Albinus Giordano! Shit* ... He placed the tag in his jacket pocket and thought, *I will deal with this later*.

Michael, who had just arrived, walked down the side of the crater, and pushed a sheet of metal over in the black sand, with his foot. "What the hell happened here, Sire?"

William didn't answer; instead, he pulled his mobile phone out of his jacket pocket and dialed the Gramaze operations room. "Brock ... there's been an explosion at Boardman's house. Can you pull up footage and see what happened here?"

"Yes, Sire," said Brock, entering a code on his computer to search the footage. A few minutes later, "Fucken hell ..."

"What did you find?" asked William.

"Boardman and his henchman arrived via a portal at the edge of his property. The trucks were driven into a large shed at the back of the property, and then all of a sudden there was an almighty explosion," said Brock, watching the bright light from the explosion on his computer screen. "It looks like they were wiped off the face of the earth."

"Thanks, Brock," said William. He pressed end on his phone, and leapt to the top of the crater. Placing his phone in his jacket pocket, he used his Vampire vision to search the grounds.

Fuck! thought William, as he spotted a familiar face. *Eryndor ...*

What is that fucker doing here? mind-thought Grayson, as he came to stand next to William.

Not sure. Looks like he is carrying something, mind-thought William. He ran at Vampire speed toward Eryndor, and Grayson followed.

I can't be sure, but I think Eryndor is holding the Twin Icefire Blades, mind-thought William to Grayson, as he positioned himself across from Eryndor. *How in the fuck did he acquire them?* His mind raced, attempting to comprehend how Eryndor had come into possession of the two formidable blades, let alone that he was topside again.

"Eryndor, stop," demanded Grayson, as he came to stand across from Eryndor, his sword drawn.

"Ah … I wondered how long it would be before you lot turned up," stated Eryndor, sarcastically. He waved his deep purple feathered hand, creating a shimmering clear portal.

"Where do you think you're going?" asked Grayson, as he ran towards the unsettling shadowy aura of Eryndor, and watched the portal wall open.

Eryndor extended his sharp, elongated claws, the dark, blood-red talons fanning outward, before slowly curling them back into his palm.

Grayson came to an abrupt halt. A sudden jolt coursed through his body as his windpipe was mercilessly constricted. Desperately clutching at his throat, he collapsed to the ground, his gasps for breath echoing in the air.

"Eryndor!" shouted William. "You will desist with this torture. Get the fuck away from him." With a burst of Vampire speed, he closed the distance in an instant, sword in hand. Before Eryndor could react, William drove his blade straight into his chest, the steel sinking deep. The force sent the menacing Harbinger of Shadows staggering backwards, and his eyes flashed with shock and fury.

"Ah, shit! You will pay for that, Gramaze," said Eryndor, pulling William's sword slowly from his chest, discarding it to the ground. His malevolent face contorted when he tried to stand.

"It is you who will pay," said William, as he kicked Eryndor in the head, knocking him flat on his back. William stood over Eryndor's soulless body, with his boot planted firmly on his neck, and his sword pointed at one of Eryndor's green piercing eyes.

Michael walked over to the two wooden boxes, which lay in front of the shimmering portal. As he bent down to open them, both boxes glided in the air toward the portal. "What the fuck!" said Michael, as he watched them float toward the portal, eventually entering the shimmering wall and gliding through.

"Well … it looks like you won't be seeing them too soon, will you?" said William to Eryndor, watching the two boxes enter the portal.

With a contemptuous snort, Eryndor's voice dripped with arrogance as he addressed William. "Humph! Do you honestly believe you have what it takes to stop me, Vampire?" His words oozed with disdain, laced with a superiority that aimed to belittle William's abilities. A smug grin tugged at the corner of Eryndor's lips.

"Moot point, don't you think? I have already stopped you, you fucking sadistic bastard," said William, his nostrils flared. He pushed the tip of his blade into Eryndor's cheek. "You will pay for all you have done."

As William spoke, Eryndor's body disappeared, and the end of his sword dug into the ground. Adjusting his stance, he looked over at the portal, and saw Eryndor floating toward it.

"Stop him, Michael," shouted William.

By the time Michael realized what was happening, it was too late. Eryndor held the portal open just long enough to glide through, then closed it behind him, before anyone could stop him.

"Fuck! That bastard sure has nine lives," said William, as he came to stand next to Michael.

"What's our next move?" asked Grayson, picking himself up off the ground.

"Get everyone together. This mess needs to be cleaned up. NOW! Before any humans see what has occurred here tonight," demanded William. He raked a hand through his hair and sighed. "Once we are back at the Gramaze mansion, I will be calling a meeting in the operations room, to discuss what our plan of attack will be."

"Yes, Sire," said Grayson. *Let's go, Michael.*

Michael nodded once and followed Grayson toward the house.

William pulled his mobile phone from his jacket pocket, took a deep breath in, then out, and dialed Garrick Ironclaw's number.

CHAPTER TWENTY-EIGHT

"Thank you for the call, William. Rest assured, the moment we receive any updates regarding the whereabouts of the Twin Icefire Blades or Eryndor, you will be the first to be informed. And I appreciate the assistance you and your family will be able to provide to us and our city," said Garrick. He looked over at Elara, who had been sitting across the room, looking out at the waters of Olden Fjord, and watched her reaction, as she listened to the phone call on speaker.

"You are welcome, my friend. Well, I will bid you goodbye for now. Ring when you need us," said William.

Garrick placed his mobile phone on the desk and walked over to Elara. "At least Hawk is safe." He sat next to Elara on the couch.

"Yes, but for how long?" stated Elara, her brow furrowed with concern.

Garrick shrugged his shoulders and shook his head.

"Why did William think that it would be all right to send Hawk out on a mission? Clearly, he was not ready," said Elara, shaking her head. She took a deep breath and sighed. "I want the boy home with us, Garrick. He is not safe in Bagnolet."

"I agree, my love. But what are we to do with Hawk when he returns to Olden?" He looked into Elara's jade-green eyes, raked a hand through his hair, and sighed. "We had pinned our hopes on the academy, and now that has failed. What are we to do with this insolent, arrogant boy who, by the way, is meant to be next in line to the throne."

"I don't have all the answers, Garrick." Elara stood up and walked over to the window. "Maybe we can speak with William Gramaze about what he has been teaching the boy."

Garrick and Elara hadn't even realized yet how far Hawk had come or what he had achieved at the academy. But what they did know was the training he was receiving was teaching him more than they could prepare him for.

Garrick followed Elara over to the window. "Yes, maybe. But that is the least of our problems, at the moment."

"Eryndor!"

Garrick's nostrils flared at the sound of his name. "Yes. We will need to go and speak with our soldiers and our family about how we are going to stop him," said Garrick.

"I agree. Let's go," said Elara. She walked toward the wooden doors with Garrick.

"Do you feel his presence yet?" asked Garrick, as he walked beside Elara.

"No, not yet. I think it's only a matter of time, though," said Elara. She shook her head as she opened the wooden door. "I knew it was a bad idea placing both blades together. I just knew it … I should have gone with my gut feeling, as I usually do, and placed them in two different countries. At least then we wouldn't be having this problem or conversation." She turned to Garrick. "We are strong, Garrick, but we won't be able to defeat Eryndor, not this time."

"Maybe not, but we will give it a good go, my love," said Garrick, trying to reassure her.

"I am not ready to give our land or our kingdom up," stated Elara, her brow furrowed.

"Nor I, *min elskling*," said Garrick. "It will surely be a fight to the death."

* * *

"What do you have for me, Brock?" asked William, as he strode into the operations room.

"Not a lot at this stage. I've set up a facial-recognition program to look for any sign of Eryndor worldwide, but there's nothing yet," said Brock, looking up from his computer screen to William. "I've also been over the footage from before and after the explosion at Tassone Boardman's place, and it was as we suspected. Eryndor lay in wait for Boardman and his soldiers to return, caused the explosion, then escaped with the Twin Icefire Blades. Has Garrick heard anything from Eryndor yet?"

"Nothing … which is a bit of a concern, especially as Eryndor will have all the power he needs, now he has the Twin Icefire Blades. He is up to something, but we don't know what yet," said William, rubbing his chin as he watched the screen display all sorts of satellite pictures from around the world. "Let me know when you find something, Brock." William walked toward the glass sliding doors.

"Yes, Sire," replied Brock. He watched the sliding doors close, then continued with his search for Eryndor and the Twin Icefire Blades.

* * *

Shepherd's bloodshot eyes opened wide, and he sat up quickly, when he heard the door to his cell unlock, and then watched it open. Looking over to see who had unlocked the door, he stood up rapidly when he noticed a brown-haired, seven-foot-tall, broad-shouldered male Lepidoptera Vampire walking toward him.

"State your name, soldier," commanded William, his voice laced with authority. Every inch of his demeanor exuded confidence and a no-nonsense approach, leaving no doubt about his position of leadership and the expectation of respect and compliance.

"Shepherd Mornington, Sir." His Adam's apple bobbed up and down when he gulped hard.

"I am William Gramaze; the leader of this coven. Where are you from, Shepherd?

"Orlando, Florida," replied Shepherd, the realization of the person he was speaking to dawning upon him.

"How long have you been in France?" asked William.

"About four months."

William scrutinized Shepherd as he listened to his thoughts. "So … tell me, how did you get from Florida to France?"

"Well, that's a bit of a long story," said Shepherd.

"Spit it out, boy. I don't have all day."

Shepherd swallowed hard, a nervous tremor running through his body. "Yes, Sir. Umm, it all started around four months ago when I turned seventeen," he began, his voice filled with a mix of trepidation and vulnerability. "At first, I started to see humans' veins pulsating, and it felt like their blood was calling to me. The thirst for their blood consumed my thoughts, although I couldn't understand why. However, I managed to resist the urge; I never acted upon it."

He paused for a moment, gathering his thoughts before continuing. "But as time went on, my sanity started slipping away. I could hear people's thoughts, as if their innermost secrets were laid bare before me. My skin was in a constant state of restlessness, and anxiety plagued my every waking moment. And then … my fangs descended."

"It was then that I met Mr. Boardman. He explained to me that when our kind turn seventeen, we turn into a Vampire. I didn't believe him at first, until he gave me a bag of blood to drink. It was then that I realized he was telling me the truth. Mr. Boardman said that I could come and live with him, and in return I would have to work for him. So, after much consideration, I left my family and friends and came here to France," said Shepherd.

"Since you have been in France, have you drunk from a human?" asked William.

Shepherd's face contorted with a mix of revulsion and discomfort. "Oh, God, no. That doesn't seem right to me. I mean, I have watched other vamps do it, and it looks disgusting," said Shepherd, his body shuddering at the thought of it. "I've been getting all the blood I need from Mr. Boardman's back kitchen fridge and the hospital." Shepherd's gaze dropped, his internal struggle evident as he grappled with his Vampiric nature and the choices he had made.

"Right! So, were you adopted?"

"How did you know that?" asked Shepherd.

"It's common among Vampires. Actually, you are very special to our kind. You are called a Lepidoptera Vampire, and were born from our Queen. Can I have a look at the back of your neck?"

"Queen …?" queried Shepherd, his brow furrowed.

"I will explain in a minute," said William.

Shepherd frowned and asked, "Why do you need to look at the back of my neck?"

"Just turn around, boy," commanded William.

Shepherd did as he was instructed.

Red … very interesting, thought William.

"What is red?" asked Shepherd, who had heard William's thoughts.

"You have a red butterfly on the back of your neck. It means you have the strength and the power to shift others' thoughts."

Shepherd traced his fingers over the butterfly on the back of his neck. "I didn't even know it was there."

"Yes, that is quite common. Only other Vampires can see it."

"What is going to happen to me?" asked Shepherd. He looked into William's eyes and gulped.

"It will depend on how much you cooperate. What do you know about Tassone Boardman and his operation?"

"Umm … not a lot. I know where most of his businesses are, and where he stores firearms, drugs, that sort of thing. But not a lot else," said Shepherd. "I think he kept me in the dark because I was new to the house and operations. I didn't feel like he fully trusted me yet."

"Right!" William knew Shepherd was telling the truth from listening to his thoughts.

"How would you feel about going back home to Florida?" asked William.

"I don't know. Is that possible?" asked Shepherd, with a hint of curiosity mixed with a touch of concern in his voice, as if he was genuinely pondering the possibility of what was being discussed.

"Of course. I personally know the Florida Lepidoptera leader, and I am sure he would be grateful to have you join his family. I can call him if you're willing," said William.

"Umm … you mean, I can go back to live with my parents?" asked Shepherd.

"I'm afraid not," said William, placing a hand on Shepherd's shoulder. "They wouldn't understand, and I am sure it would be hard for you to live with humans, considering you are a new Lepidoptera Vampire."

Shepherd nodded and lowered his eyes. "I suppose so." He looked up at William and said, "Would it be possible for me to stay here, with your family? I'm willing to learn and do whatever you need."

"I would welcome that, Shepherd. But I do have reservations. Why do you want to join my family, instead of the Florida Lepidopteras?"

"This is going to sound strange, but here goes." He took a deep breath and continued. "Even though I worked for Mr. Boardman, I had always thought that he was out for himself, and I didn't like how he used and treated everyone, let alone how he conducted his business. If you can call it a business. So, while I worked for him, I tried to find out if there were any other Vampires in France. That is when I heard about the Gramaze coven and what you all stood for.

I have longed to make myself known to your coven for months, but have never had the opportunity. This would be the reason why I would like, if you will allow it, for me to stay with your coven here in France, instead of moving back to Florida."

William held his hand out to shake Shepherd's. "Welcome aboard."

Shepherd shook William's hand and smiled. For the first time in months, he actually believed that he had made the right decision. "Thank you. Thank you. You won't be disappointed, Sir."

"Follow me, and I will introduce you to my family and our Queen," said William, who was always eager to have another Lepidoptera join his coven.

CHAPTER TWENTY-NINE

"Knock, knock," said Sully, as she opened the door to Hawk's room.

Hawk smiled when he saw her standing in his doorway. "Come in, Sully."

"Looks like you're all packed and ready to go," said Sully, noticing the empty tallboy drawers and the packed bags lying on his bed.

He nodded and sat on the edge of his bed. "You know, even though I'm looking forward to going home tonight, I'll miss this place. But I think what I'll miss most of all is you, Sully." He patted the bed for her to come and sit beside him.

"Yeah, I'll miss you too, Hawk," said Sully, sitting on the bed. "Do you reckon if you asked your parents, that they would let you stay longer?" She looked into his soulful eyes.

"I tried, but they want me home. Something about keeping me safe. As if I can't look after myself, anyway. How ridiculous."

"Yeah, I know, right? I get the same from William and Renee. I wish there was a way of leaving, and finding a place of our own, together," said Sully. She leaned in and kissed his lips, ever so softly.

Since their first abduction, and their return to the academy, Sully and Hawk had grown even closer, and their attraction for one another had been strengthened. They didn't relish the thought of being apart.

As Hawk kissed her soft lips, he felt her sorrow. Slowly pulling away, he said, "We could leave our families, and go out on our own, you know."

His eager demeanor sent waves of excitement through her body. "You would do that? Leave, I mean?"

"If that's what you want," said Hawk, searching her face for answers.

"I do have friends that could help us, and I'm sure we would be able to find jobs to support ourselves," said Sully. She was excited at the prospect of leaving the life she currently had at the academy. All she had to look forward to here was training for combat missions. Even though she was grateful to William and Renee for saving her life when she was younger, and taking her in, Sully still wanted a life of her own. A life away from the wars between good and evil. "What time are your parents coming to take you back to Olden?"

"I'm told we will be departing Bagnolet at about ten o'clock. Apparently, my mother and father are coming for dinner, which will be held at the Gramaze mansion. After that, I believe the Warlock, Adrian, is creating a portal to take us back home," said Hawk.

"Oh, right!"

"About leaving … even if we wanted to, it won't be possible. The wards are still up, remember?"

"You're right," said Sully. She leaned in and placed her head on Hawk's shoulder.

"As much as I would love to run away with you, Sully, I fear the consequences from my mother and father."

"I think William and Renee would be angry with me, too. Maybe it's not a good idea, hey?" She placed her arm around Hawk's back. "I really don't want to be apart from you. What are we going to do?" said Sully.

"We'll figure something out. Don't worry," said Hawk. He placed his arm around her shoulder and kissed the side of her head. "At least we have a few more hours together, before my parents get here and I have to leave."

* * *

Curled up in a fetal position, on a queen-size, four-poster bed at the Gramaze mansion, Xanthia wiped her tear-stained face with the back of her hand. In the darkened room, which at this point in time was a place of solace for her, she thought about her father, Albinus Giordano, whom she'd been told had departed this world, at the hands of Eryndor, and the explosion at Tassone Boardman's residence.

"Oh, Father … I wish you were here," sobbed Xanthia. "What am I going to do without you?" She heard a knock at the door and watched it open. As the light hit her red, swollen eyes, she squinted and tried to focus on who was entering the room.

"Are you all right, Xanthia?" asked Elsie, as she walked toward the bed.

"I want my daddy …" sobbed Xanthia. Tears flowed freely down the teenager's cheeks.

Elsie sat on the bed next to Xanthia and rubbed her arm for comfort. "Shhh. Is there anything I can get you? Food, water …?" asked Elsie.

"No …" Even though she was hungry, the thought of food made Xanthia's stomach churn. "Maybe some water."

Elsie turned the bedside lamp on and spotted a jug of water and an empty glass. She poured water into the glass and handed it to Xanthia.

"Thank you," said Xanthia, sitting up against the headboard and taking the glass from her. Sniffing back her tears, she took a sip.

"I wanted to say … I'm sorry about your father. It must have been a shock when you were told of his death," said Elsie.

"He was all I had."

Elsie's shoulders slumped forward and her brow furrowed. "I'm sorry, Xanthia. I know how you feel. I lost my parents at an early age, too," said Elsie, remembering the death of her parents and how alone she'd felt, until her Griffin aunt and human uncle adopted her.

Xanthia wiped her eyes and patted the bed. "Can you sit with me for a while?" She placed her glass of water on the bedside table.

"I sure can," said Elsie. She moved closer, to sit next to Xanthia, and leant back on the headboard. "You're not alone."

"Thank you, Elsie. I just … I can't believe he's gone. Ever since my mother passed away when I was three, Father and I have always been a team, been there for each other. And now … well, I don't have anyone." She leaned into Elsie's shoulder and started to cry again.

Elsie placed her arm around Xanthia's shoulder. "You know, you can always count on me. And I'm sure that the Gramaze family will look after you."

"What do you mean, they'll look after me?" asked Xanthia. Her blue eyes searched Elsie's face for answers.

"She means that, if you are willing, we can take you in," interrupted Renee, as she and William walked through the open doorway and into the room.

"I don't understand … why would you do this?" questioned Xanthia. She clutched her legs to her chest and started to rock.

"We are offering you a home to live in," said William, standing at the end of the bed.

"Thank you for offering, but I'm sure I'll be all right. I think Daddy would have left me some sort of money, or insurance policy, so that I would be taken care of. Wouldn't he?" asked Xanthia, looking from William to Renee, then to Elsie.

William searched the young teenager's cluttered mind.

"I wish, for your sake, that was true, Xanthia," William began, his voice laced with sympathy and regret. He took a moment to gather himself before continuing. "I've conducted a thorough investigation into your father's affairs, and I hate to be the bearer of bad news, but there is no money left, nor any insurance policy to rely on. In fact, he was burdened with debts. I fear that once the bank learns of his passing, they will proceed to foreclose on your beautiful home and seize everything inside." William's words hung heavily in the air, weighed down by the sorrowful truth he had uncovered. The sincerity in his tone echoed his genuine remorse as he concluded, "I'm truly sorry, Xanthia."

"I know it's a lot to think about Xanthia, but you are welcome to live with us," said Renee, standing next to William.

Xanthia took a deep breath and shook her head. "Why is this happening?" sobbed Xanthia. She pressed her head into her knees, and the tears flowed freely.

Elsie pulled her in close and said, "Let it out ... don't worry, everything will be all right, you'll see."

"Thank you, but you can't promise that, can you, Elsie?" said Xanthia, through muffled tears.

Elsie looked at Renee and William with sadness in her eyes.

"Xanthia." William waited for her to look at him.

"Yes," said Xanthia, wiping her tearstained face.

"I know it's a lot to take in, especially as your father only passed away yesterday. But do think about what Renee and I are offering. We're willing to take you in, so that you don't become a ward of the state, and we can look after you," said William.

"Thank you ... and I do appreciate what you're offering. But I am not sure ... it's just ..." Xanthia didn't finish her sentence for fear of what would happen.

William and Renee heard her thoughts, and looked at each other briefly.

"It's all right, Xanthia. We understand," said Renee. She walked over to Xanthia and sat on the bed. "I can assure you that you will be safe here." She placed her hand on Xanthia's.

"After what I have witnessed over the past week … I'm scared. What are you people? Or should I say *creatures*?" asked Xanthia, looking into Renee's eyes.

"I am sure you already know the answer to that question," stated William.

Xanthia gulped hard.

"We are Vampire, dear. But I'm sure you have already, as my partner, William, said, worked it out by now," said Renee.

Xanthia pulled her hand away from Renee's, and jumped out of bed. As she ran toward the doorway, Renee ran at Vampire speed, and stood in front of her, preventing her from leaving.

"I assure you, we are not here to hurt you," said Renee, sincerely.

"I don't believe …" But she didn't finish her sentence. The room started to spin and darken, as her young mind tried to process what she was being told, and she fainted.

Renee swiftly caught Xanthia's unconscious body, her arms instinctively wrapping around her to prevent her from crashing to the floor. With utmost care, she lifted her fragile form and carried her back to the bed, laying her down gently on the soft mattress. Tenderly tucking the blankets around her, Renee uttered, "Poor girl," her voice filled with empathy and sorrow.

"It's a lot to take in," said Elsie, standing.

"Would you be willing to take her under your wings?" asked Renee, looking at Elsie. "She seems to trust you."

"I would love to help her fit in, but … well, she's not a Supe. So how am I going to do this?" asked Elsie, looking from Renee to William.

Renee shrugged her shoulders and sighed. "Just being a good friend to her will help."

"Let her get some rest now, and we can come back later to discuss with Xanthia what she would like to do. Okay?" said William.

"Yes, Sir," said Elsie.

William took his mobile phone from his pocket and glanced at the time. "We have some business to attend to with Garrick and Elara," said William, walking toward the door. "Renee and I will check in with Xanthia later."

"Okay," said Elsie, watching Renee and William, walk away. "Call me, if you need me," she called out as they walked through the doorway and into the passage.

CHAPTER THIRTY

"Ah, Hawk and Sully, there you are, finally gracing us with your presence," exclaimed William, his eyes fixed on the duo as they made their grand entrance into the lavishly adorned dining room. With graceful strides, they approached the impressive long wooden table, resplendent in its full regalia—a white woven-cotton tablecloth, delicate bone china plates that gleamed in the soft light, polished silver cutlery arranged meticulously, and glistening crystal glassware. Along the center of the table a magnificent floral masterpiece stretched its vibrant blooms, a testament to the grandeur of the occasion, and a warm welcome to their esteemed guests.

"Sorry we're late," said Hawk, looking at William. He bowed his head once and pulled a wooden chair out for Sully to sit at the table, next to Samuel.

"Have you finished packing?" asked Elara, looking across the table at Hawk, as she watched him take his seat.

"Yes, Mother," said Hawk, nodding, the sadness in his eyes apparent, as he sat next to Sully.

Samuel's brow furrowed, as he watched Hawk reach beneath the tablecloth, to place his hand in Sully's. Their intertwined hands formed a hidden connection, a silent understanding that seemed to speak volumes. Samuel's contemplative gaze lingered, intrigued by the unspoken bond that existed between them, wondering what secrets might lie veiled beneath the surface of their seemingly ordinary interaction.

Sully looked from Hawk to his parents and asked, "I was wondering ... well ... is it possible for Hawk to stay longer at the academy?"

"Sully, we have been over this previously. Elara and Garrick want Hawk to return home," said William, who was sitting at the head of the table, with Renee.

"Yes, but ..." said Sully, looking at William, then Renee.

"There are no buts. Can we just enjoy this evening?" William declared firmly, his voice leaving no room for argument. He let out a deep, exasperated sigh, his frustration palpable. His lips formed a tight line, a visual representation of his resolve to put an end to any further discussion or disagreement.

Sully sighed and her shoulders slumped forward. "Yes, Sir."

"Ah, it looks like dinner is being served," said Renee, noticing Lamiae and some helpers enter the dining room with trays of food. She was glad of the distraction from the conversation at hand.

"Mmm, smells divine," said Elara. She watched as Lamiae placed a plate in front of her and Garrick.

Once everyone's food had been delivered, Lamiae closed the ornate double doors to the dining room, and left them to enjoy their meals.

"Is there any news on Eryndor?" asked William. He looked down the table to Garrick, as he cut into his food.

"Nothing. Which is a bit disconcerting," said Garrick, placing his knife and fork on the edge of the plate.

"What have you put in place if he returns to Norway?" asked William.

"My soldiers and my family are ready and willing to fight Eryndor and his army, but it will all depend on whether Eryndor has taken the power from *Eisvarda* and *Blaznira*. Once he has their power, he will be unbeatable," said Garrick.

"I hope you know that my family and I are always here, if you need help to destroy Eryndor," said William.

"Thank you, my friend. I appreciate the offer, especially after our heated words the other day," said Garrick.

"Yes, thank you, William," said Elara, looking down the table to William. "We may have to take you up on that offer."

"If we know Eryndor is going to return to Norway, then why am I returning home? Wouldn't it be safer for me to stay at the academy, where he can't penetrate the wards and get to me?" asked Hawk, looking from his father to his mother, then William.

"Hold your tongue, boy. This is not for you to negotiate," said Garrick, his nostrils flared.

"I won't be silenced, Father. This has been happening for far too long," said Hawk, pushing his chair back and standing.

"You will do as you are told, boy, or else," said Garrick, also standing, looking him in the eyes. His chair fell backward with force.

"Or else what?" challenged Hawk, narrowing his eyes.

Hawk, calm down, thought Sully. Looking up at him, she grabbed his hand.

"Come on, Sully, let's get out of here," said Hawk, pulling her out of her seat to a standing position.

Sully looked down the table to William and Renee, seeking their permission to leave the room with Hawk.

William nodded once in her direction. *Be cautious, child.*

Sully chose to ignore William's comment.

"Where do you think you're going?" asked Garrick, as he crossed his arms over his broad chest.

"Somewhere you're not!" replied Hawk, as he walked toward the closed door, holding Sully's hand.

"What is going on here?" asked Chancellor Michael, who had heard them arguing. His voice carried a mix of authority and curiosity, as he demanded an explanation.

Now look what you've done, thought Sully to Samuel.

"Nothing, Michael," said Sully.

"It didn't sound like nothing to me," said Michael, now standing in front of the three of them.

"We were just having a disagreement, that's all, Michael. Nothing for you to worry about," said Hawk.

"About what?" asked Michael, looking each of them in the eyes.

No one answered.

"Samuel …?" questioned Michael.

Samuel gulped hard and looked from Michael to Hawk and Sully.

Don't you dare, thought Sully to Samuel.

"Really … it's like Hawk said, it's nothing to worry about. We were just disagreeing about how Hawk has to return home. That's all … honestly," said Samuel.

"Right … well keep it down, will you?" demanded Michael.

"Okay," said Samuel.

Hawk and Sully nodded yes.

"Actually, Samuel, are you able to fill in for me, in the training room at the academy?" asked Michael.

"Sure. When?" asked Samuel.

"Now, if you're free," said Michael.

"I can be there in say, ten minutes. I just need to get changed," said Samuel.

"That will be perfect. It's just basic one-on-one training for a new female Supe," stated Michael.

"Right," said Samuel.

Michael took his mobile out of his pocket and looked at the time. "Shit, I need to get going. Thanks for your help, Samuel. Catch you all later," said Michael, as he walked away from them.

"So, what are you going to do?" asked Samuel to Hawk.

"Go back to the academy, of course," lied Hawk. He blocked Samuel from reading his thoughts.

"But you're meant to be leaving, aren't you?" asked Samuel.

"Yeah … my parents can wait. I'm in no rush to leave. And it seems they have a lot to talk about with your parents," said Hawk.

"You sure know how to push their buttons, Hawk," stated Samuel.

Hawk shrugged his shoulders.

"Well, we'll see you later, Samuel," said Sully.

"Catch you later, man," said Hawk. He walked away hand in hand with Sully.

"Bye, guys," said Samuel. He walked away from them, and toward his room to get changed. Taking his mobile out of his jacket pocket, he glanced at the time. *I wonder what they are up to, really. When I finish this training, I will follow up on them.*

* * *

"Where are we going?" asked Sully, as Hawk pulled her toward the Seine River at the back of the Gramaze property.

"Anyplace other than here," said Hawk. As they reached the water, Hawk took his shirt off.

"What are you doing?" asked Sully, watching him discard his clothes and shoes onto the ground.

"I'm going for a swim. You want to come?" asked Hawk, who now only had his boxer briefs on.

Sully frowned. "I don't have anything to wear. It's all back at the academy."

"Why can't you wear your underwear?" He smirked and raised his left eyebrow.

"Funny, aren't you? Not!" said Sully, her sarcasm showing.

"I thought so." He grinned and watched her squirm. "But seriously, once I'm in the water, I'm actually not intending on coming back."

"Oh, right! Where are you thinking about going?"

"At this stage, I'm not sure. I do have a few places I would like to check out, though." He looked deeply into her jade-green eyes. "Will you come with me?"

"I'm not sure. And what if they reinstate the wards? We won't be able to bypass them," Sully expressed with concern.

Hawk shrugged his shoulders and grinned sheepishly, then pulled her in close, and kissed her soft lips.

As she returned his affection, Sully thought, *Should I go with him ... what will William and Renee think? I will be in big trouble for disobeying them. But I do love Hawk.* She slowly pulled away from their embrace, and looked into his soulful eyes. *Fuck it ...*

"Okay ...," said Sully.

CHAPTER THIRTY-ONE

In their human forms, Sully had enjoyed the deep swim with Hawk, gliding effortlessly through the water's depths. As the shoreline came into view, she turned to him and asked, "Where are we?"

"The lights over there," Hawk pointed toward the night lights of the city in the distance. "That's Castries. It's the capital city of Saint Lucia."

Sully observed the distant city lights sparkling like jewels and remarked, "We've been swimming for quite a while, and I'm aware we crossed the Atlantic Ocean, but I've never come across Saint Lucia before."

"It's a little island in the West Indies. Actually, we're currently on the eastern edge of the Caribbean Sea, where it meets the Atlantic Ocean."

Sully's brow furrowed, as she tried to comprehend why Hawk would bring her here. Especially this far from her family and their protection.

"Don't look so worried … my family have a place here, which is located just outside of the Castries city center. We'll be safe there," said Hawk, listening to Sully's thoughts.

"Oh, right!" said Sully, nodding, though a trace of uncertainty lingered in her voice.

"Let's go … we can *samtale* later. See that cruise ship over there?" Hawk pointed toward the harbor, where the ship was docked.

Sully looked toward the harbor and then back at Hawk and nodded.

"We'll head toward the cruise ship. I'm confident we can find some clothing on board. Sound good?" suggested Hawk.

"But how will we pay for the clothes? I don't have any money," said Sully, remembering how they both had stripped their clothes off before they entered the Seine River at the back of the Gramaze mansion. "Oh, and … I'm sure as hell not getting out of the water naked." Her stubborn facial expression toward Hawk said it all.

"It's fine … I'll board the ship and get some clothes for both of us."

Sully gulped. "You mean steal them from the passengers?"

"Yup!"

"You can't do that, Hawk. And what if you get caught?"

"Don't stress … leave it to me. Come on …" Hawk swam toward the harbor, and Sully hesitantly followed.

* * *

"Samuel … have you seen Hawk?" asked William, as he walked down the stairs and into the combat room at the academy.

"No. The last time I saw him and Sully was after Hawk argued with Garrick, at dinner tonight," said Samuel, hanging his sword on the wall. "They might have gone back to Hawk's room. I can't be sure, though."

"Hmm … I have checked there. He has definitely packed his room up at the academy, and his bags are still there, but we can't seem to locate him. Did he say anything to you this evening about going back to Norway?" asked William. He placed his hands on his hips.

"No, Father. Well, that is besides the fact that he didn't want to return home with his family. You know he wanted to stay at the academy, don't you?"

"Yes. It's a pity Garrick and Elara don't trust us enough to let him stay. Hawk is doing so well here, too."

"And I am sure Sully would have liked him to stay," said Samuel, raising his eyebrows.

"Don't even go there, Samuel. That is not something I'm happy about. Your sister is way too young and naïve, and I think she would be better suited to our kind," said William, his nostrils flared. He walked back toward the combat room stairs.

"Hang on … I'll come with you, and help you find Hawk," said Samuel, as he followed. "Have you been able to connect with Sully?"

"No, which is concerning me. I would have expected Sully to answer my mental communication with her at least, but she hasn't," said William, turning to Samuel. "Follow me, I think we will head to the mansion and check out the CCTV footage for the academy and our coven's home, just in case something has happened to them both."

"Good idea," said Samuel, remembering what had happened previously at the graduation.

* * *

"Sire … I was just about to call you," said Brock, as he watched William and Samuel, walk into the command center. He had heard via the Lepidoptera chatter that Hawk and Sully were missing.

"What is it?" asked William, coming to stand next to Brock, in front of a large screen.

"Watch!" said Brock, as he replayed the CCTV footage of Hawk and Sully leaving the Gramaze mansion and then swimming out into the river.

Samuel gulped hard and he felt his cheeks redden when he realized that he should have stopped Sully and Hawk, or even told someone about what he thought they may have planned. But he wasn't about to let his father know this, for fear of reprisal. "Far out!"

"Fuck!" William raked a hand through his hair. "Fast forward it a bit, Brock. I want to see if they return."

"Yes, Sire," said Brock, pressing the button on his mouse to increase the speed on the footage.

William, Samuel and Brock waited in anticipation, but didn't see Hawk or Sully return.

"Bring up footage from the satellite, to see if we can track their movements further," said William.

Brock did as he was instructed. The three Lepidopteras watched Hawk and Sully swim from the Seine River, then out to the English Channel, and on to the North Atlantic Ocean.

"Have you found them, William?" asked Garrick, as the glass sliding doors slid open.

"Yes and no!" William turned and watched Garrick and Elara, walk into the command center. "Brock, show them the footage."

"Yes, Sire."

Garrick and Elara watched the replay.

Elara nostrils flared and she sighed heavily.

Garrick turned to William and said, "How in the hell was this even allowed to happen? Don't you have some sort of alarms in place for when this type of behavior occurs?"

"Normally, yes," said William, abruptly. "However, the wards around the Gramaze property, except for the academy, were deactivated to allow both of you to visit via a portal. Unfortunately, they haven't been reactivated since then."

"This is the exact reason why we don't want Hawk at the academy. You can't even look after your own daughter, let alone our son! If anything happens to Hawk, you will be to blame, William," stated Elara, shaking her head.

"I don't think we have time here for a blame game, do you?" William looked from Elara to Garrick. "Do you have any idea where they may be going?"

"None," said Garrick, shaking his head.

"They could be heading anywhere. Maybe one of our properties that we have. Most of which don't have anyone living in them," said Elara. She pulled her mobile phone out of her long jacket pocket. "I will make some phone calls, and ask our people to keep an eye out for them."

"Thank you, Elara. In the meantime, Brock, I want you to follow them via satellite, to see where they end up," said William.

"Yes, Sire," said Brock, knowing it would be difficult to track them if they had shielded their movements to avoid satellite detection.

CHAPTER THIRTY-TWO

"How much further, Hawk?" Sully asked, stepping off the free ferry onto the vibrant shores of Marigot Bay. She paused, taking in the lush, tropical surroundings, and the scent of saltwater mingling with the fragrant greenery.

"It's just up ahead," Hawk remarked, gesturing toward a captivating four-level villa nestled into the hillside. It boasted a stunning view of the bay, and was enveloped by lush gardens. "It's about ten minutes away, on foot."

Sully's gaze fell on the breathtaking infinity pool nestled at the base of the white Tuscany-style house that Hawk had indicated to. Astonished, she turned to Hawk and said, "Wow … that's beautiful."

"Sure is. Wait until you see inside. Come on." He took her hand in his and pulled her toward the steps that led up to the villa.

"How are we going to get in?" asked Sully, when they were standing at the front door of the villa, a beautiful timber door with leadlight glass.

"I think there's a spare key here, somewhere." Hawk lifted up a few pot plants located near the front window. "Here it is." Inserting the key in the lock, he opened the front door and gestured for Sully to walk inside.

Standing on the cream-colored travertine floor entry landing, Sully noticed the open design main living area, with vaulted ceilings, and tall bay windows framing a breathtaking ocean view as far as the eye could see. Walking in and down a few steps, she noted a contemporary kitchen with stainless-steel appliances and wrap around black marble countertops to her left, and a glass-topped dining setting, with brown rattan chairs, and matching lounges to her right. Opening the glass sliding door, she stepped out onto a large balcony. *Wow ... look at that view of the ocean and the steep, forested hills ... magnificent.*

"What do you think?" asked Hawk, now standing beside her.

"Breathtaking." She turned to him and said, "Are you sure it's okay for us to stay here?"

"No, it's probably not. But they won't know we're here, anyway."

Sully shook her head and sighed. "You don't know my father ... he won't stop until he finds us."

"Well at least we'll have some alone time together. I really didn't want to return to Olden," said Hawk. He held her hands and pulled her in close.

"Yeah, I'm glad we're here. But I am worried about how we're going to look after ourselves. We don't have any money, so ..." said Sully, looking into his mesmerizing eyes.

"Don't worry ..." interrupted Hawk. He stepped closer and placed his arms around Sully for a hug. "I know some places we could get work, so that should solve the money situation."

"Where?"

"There are restaurants and shops nearby; we should be able to find work there. And if worse comes to worst, we could always find work at the fish markets. I'm sure we'll get something," said Hawk. He pulled away slowly and looked into her jade-green eyes, pushing a strand of her deep-red hair behind her ear. "We could go and check these places out now, if you like, after we have a shower and get something a bit more conservative on, of course. There should be some clothing in the villa somewhere. My family always leave clothing here for emergencies."

"Sounds like a plan. Can you show me the rest of the house first, though?" asked Sully.

"Sure. Come on," replied Hawk, taking her by the hand.

* * *

"Thank you for coming in to see us about some work. With COVID around, it's really hard to find staff these days," said the manager of the Marigot Bay Resort. He extended his hand for Sully and Hawk to shake and smiled.

"Thank you for the opportunity," said Sully, shaking his hand.

"Yes, thank you," said Hawk, as he shook the manager's hand. "We'll see you tomorrow."

"Bright and early, as discussed," said the resort manager.

With smiles on their faces, Hawk and Sully nodded and proceeded toward the front gates of the lavish five-star resort.

"Well, that was easy. I really didn't think we had a chance of getting any work," said Sully, walking beside Hawk.

"And we start tomorrow. How good is that?" said Hawk, smiling as he took her hand in his.

"I'm looking forward to working at the resort. The manager seems nice, and it's not too far for us to walk to work each day or night," said Sully. She was stopped in her tracks when she noticed the sun setting, and how the magnificent colors of a pale-orange-and-pink sky, over a deep-blue, pink-stained ocean made her feel calm. "Oh, wow ... so pretty."

"Sure is," said Hawk, noticing it too. "You're probably wondering what we're going to do for food tonight."

"Yeah, it did cross my mind. I will also need some blood. Do they have a hospital here?" stated Sully.

"Not on Marigot there isn't. But from memory, there are a couple of hospitals in Castries. We should be able to get some blood for you there. And the food, well, I teed it up with the resort manager. I told him if he had any leftover food tonight, we would be interested in eating it, instead of them throwing it out," said Hawk.

"Thank you, Hawk."

"I explained to him in the interview that we didn't have any money left from our trip here. He was happy to help us out," said Hawk, as they walked through the open wrought-iron gates to the villa.

"That was nice of him," said Sully, looking at the gates as they walked down the paved driveway toward the villa. "Hey … do you think we should close these gates?"

Hawk turned to look back at the gates. "Yeah, not a bad idea. That way, no one will suspect we're here," said Hawk. He walked back to the double gates and closed them.

* * *

It had been four weeks since Hawk and Sully had left Bagnolet and their families behind. In that time things had certainly fallen into place for them. They were no longer looking over their shoulders for supernatural creatures, and there were no missions to go on, no having to try and prove themselves to their families. Their new jobs had worked out well, and they had settled into life together as a couple without the interference from their families.

With Hawk asleep, and the sun rising for the day, Sully enjoyed the quiet serenity of the morning, overlooking the smooth ocean, while she sipped a cup of blood that she had obtained from the Castries hospital morgue. In the distance, she could see small yachts moored around Marigot Bay, and two majestic dolphins swimming and breaching out of the water every now and then.

Life sure is grand at the moment, thought Sully, as she sat on the balcony deck chair, and remembered all the things she had done with Hawk since leaving Bagnolet. The long beach walks, kayaking, swimming, cooking dinner together, cuddling up on the sofa, and watching their favorite programs together, playing board games, shopping. She couldn't resist his charm, or the way he made her feel safe.

* * *

Hawk woke, startled, and his eyes darted everywhere as he quickly sat up straight in the bed. Wiping the sleep from his eyes, he realized he'd been dreaming of Eryndor and the Twin Icefire Blades. *Why in the hell was I dreaming of that evil bastard?* Hawk raked a hand through his hair, and breathed a sigh of relief. Pulling the heated sheet from his sweaty body, he moved to the edge of the bed and placed his feet on the ground. *Might have a shower, and see what Sully is up to.* Standing, he glanced at the digital clock beside his bed and noticed it was only six o'clock, then continued into the bathroom.

* * *

With her back to the house, looking out to sea, Sully thought she heard someone call out her name from behind her. But when she turned around there was not a soul in sight, even though her Lepidoptera Vampire senses were telling her differently. With her heart beating fast, she felt uneasy, and decided to go and see if Hawk was awake yet. As she walked toward the closed sliding door, she thought she saw a reflection in the glass of someone behind her. Turning quickly, with her fists clenched ready to fight, she soon realized that no one was there. Frowning, she thought, *I must be seeing things. Why am I feeling this scared? Humph, maybe it's because Samuel has always told me that I needed to stay where we are protected by family.* She continued on inside, and tried to shake her thoughts off.

"There you are," said Hawk, who was making a cup of Milo. "Enjoying the view?"

"Yeah, it's beautiful. I don't think I'll ever tire of it," said Sully, sitting on a breakfast bar stool. "Did you sleep well?"

"I think so. But I had the strangest dream. It was about Eryndor and the Twin Icefire Blades," said Hawk, sitting next to Sully.

"Oh, no!" She watched the terror appear on his face. "Are you okay?"

"I'm not sure. I can't explain it. Ever since my dream, I've been feeling anxious, and my Griffin instincts are telling me that we're being watched," said Hawk, his brow furrowed.

"Shit, really? Now you're making me feel scared," said Sully. She walked over to the sliding door and closed it.

"Sorry, but …" Hawk didn't finish his sentence, when he saw who was standing on the other side of the glass door.

Eryndor!

"Sully … run," yelled Hawk.

Sully turned to see Eryndor float through the glass panel of the door and appear before her eyes. "Shit!" She ran at Vampire speed toward the front door.

As Sully tried to make a run for it, Eryndor extended his claws and channeled his powers malevolently, and then screwed his talons into the ball of his palm, which stopped Sully in her tracks, and made her start to gasp for air. She dropped to the ground clutching her throat, and was eventually rendered unconscious. Eryndor raised his sword to slice Sully's head off, but was stopped mid-strike by Hawk's voice.

"Don't kill her … Eryndor! … PLEASE," shouted Hawk, as he ran toward them.

Eryndor placed his right claw out, and with a flick of his wrist, stopped Hawk in his tracks and flung him hard against a wall. "You're no match for me, brother."

"Don't kill Sully ... that is all I ask," begged Hawk, trying to recover, and wriggle free from Eryndor's predatory hold on him.

"Ah ... does one detect feelings for this worthless Vampire?" said Eryndor, sarcastically.

"Please ... I beg of you. I will do anything; just don't kill ..." pleaded Hawk, his sentence interrupted by Eryndor who had now zipped Hawk's mouth closed.

"Yes, yes, I get it," said Eryndor, as he lowered Hawk to eye height. "You will do anything to save her life?"

Hawk's brow furrowed, and a perplexed expression overtook his face. With his body pressed against the wall, he found himself suspended a few inches above the ground, unable to make contact with it no matter how hard he tried.

"Humph!" Eryndor's menacing facial features sneered, when he thought of how this could play out, and what information he could acquire from Hawk. Stripped of what he thought was his rightful claim to the throne and cast into the depths of hell, this opportunity seemed like the closest he could get to reclaiming his power. Placing a hand on Hawk's forehead, he watched Hawk's eyes roll back in his head and glaze over, turning completely white. "You will do my bidding, brother."

Eryndor released Hawk to a standing position and unzipped his lips. "Yes, Sir," said Hawk, in a trancelike state, his voice monotone.

"Get the Lepidoptera bitch, and let's blow this joint," said Eryndor, as he commanded a portal to open.

An obedient Hawk did as he was instructed by his master.

CHAPTER THIRTY-THREE

The ground beneath Garrick's feet vibrated violently, accompanied by a deafening explosion. The force sent dust and loose papers flying from his desk, and his breath hitched. "What the fuck is going on?" he growled, his heart pounding in his chest. He rushed toward the expansive window, which commanded a sweeping view of the Olden Fjord shoreline, and watched a colossal fireball illuminate the night sky, descending upon the homes of his citizens with devastating force.

As the fireball tore through the darkness, its fiery glow reflected off the inky waters, and plummeted toward the village below. In an instant, an eruption of flame engulfed the homes of his people, and distant screams of his citizens echoed through the air. The acrid scent of smoke and burning wood seeped through the walls of his castle and clawed at Garrick's senses.

Before he could fully process the devastation unfolding before him, the large ornate wooden doors to his office burst open with a crash.

"What the hell was that, Garrick?" Elara's voice was sharp with urgency, her eyes flicking from him to the flames outside.

Garrick barely turned. "Look for yourself."

Before she could step forward, an eerie, wailing sound cut through the chaos—the Olden Fjord civil defense siren. The mournful cry sent a chilling realization through them both.

Then, a second explosion rocked the ground.

Elara gasped, and her head snapped toward Garrick, just as his arm shot out, pointing to the creature hovering over the dark waters.

"There's your answer," Garrick muttered, his voice filled with grim finality. "Eryndor."

Elara sucked in a sharp breath, her wide eyes locking onto their adopted son. The glow of the flames reflected off his dark form as he loomed over the destruction, and his body pulsed with an unnatural energy. "We don't stand a chance against him, Garrick," she whispered, fear lacing her words. "What are we to do?"

Garrick's jaw tightened, and his fingers curled into fists at his sides. "I know ..." he admitted, his voice barely audible over the distant cries. "And I don't think we will be able to reason with him, either."

As he watched Eryndor's form pulsed brighter each time another life was lost, the truth hit Garrick like a hammer to the chest—his adopted son was feeding off their suffering, growing stronger with every death. "Now that Eryndor, has the Twin Icefire Blades, he will be unstoppable."

The civil defense siren wailed again, this time long and piercing; a warning of total annihilation.

Elara turned to Garrick, her face pale. "We need to get out of here," she said, her voice steady but filled with urgency.

From reading her thoughts, Garrick knew what she was thinking—this was their home. They had fought for it, ruled it, bled for it. But staying meant death.

And right now, survival was the only option.

Outside, chaos reigned. People fled their homes in frantic waves, their shadows stretching wildly against the inferno. Fireballs rained down like the wrath of a vengeful Warlock.

Above them, Eryndor tilted his head slightly, as if sensing his adoptive parent's presence. His glowing eyes, which were full of malice, locked onto the castle.

He knew exactly where they were.

Then, the next fireball came hurtling straight toward them.

Run and hide, my family and friends, mind-thought Garrick to his loyal citizens.

The small community of Olden listened to their leader, and fled their homes and businesses.

"Let's go, Elara," said Garrick. He pulled Elara by the arm toward a secret entrance in the floor, which led them down to the waters of Olden Fjord.

Knowing their fate if they didn't flee, Elara followed her partner to a small submarine, which was moored under the castle.

"Where are we going, Garrick?" asked Elara, as she stepped into the sub, and watched him fasten the submersible hatch.

"Loen. We should be safe there," said Garrick, as he sat in the driver's seat, and steered the submarine deep into the waters of Olden Fjord, away from their home.

Garrick knew—this was only the beginning.

* * *

William stood at the edge of the Seine River, shaking his head. *Where are you, Sully? I hope you haven't been killed.* Looking out across the darkened smooth waters, he raked a hand through his hair, and remembered the night he had first met a frightened young teenage girl, who had watched her parents die a few weeks previous, and how she had bravely handled herself, when the Debauched confronted her in the Paris city center alleyway.

"William!" called Renee, coming to stand beside him. She had been listening to his thoughts. Renee placed her hand in his. "Sully will be okay. You taught her well."

"Hmm, I hope so. I can't believe I let this happen," said William, turning to Renee.

"No matter what you did, she would have run away with Hawk anyway. You know how the Lepidoptera attraction works," said Renee.

"Yes, but Hawk is not Lepidoptera," said William, frowning.

"But they are both Griffin, and that is where their connection is. And you know that for a Lepidoptera the attraction is heightened because of our powers," said Renee, remembering how she first met William, and the instant attraction they'd had to one another.

William felt his phone vibrate, before it actually rang. Taking it out of his jacket pocket, he looked at the screen. "It's Garrick. What does he want now?"

"You won't know unless you answer."

"Yes," said William, pressing the screen to connect the call.

"William!"

"What can I do for you, Elara?" He was surprised to hear her voice.

"We are under attack. It's Eryndor … can you come and help?" pleaded Elara.

"Shit! Give me ten minutes." He shook his head and rolled his eyes.

"Thank you, William. You'll need to come to Loen, as Eryndor has taken over our home and village in Olden. Come quickly …" said Elara, the urgency in her voice apparent. The phone then went silent.

"Elara … are you still there?" asked William, looking at Renee, then the screen on his phone. "Fuck! She hung up. Let's go."

Lepidopteras … heads up. I want everyone who isn't on a mission geared up and weapons ready in five minutes. Adrian … I need you to create a portal that will carry each and every one of us to Loen, Norway. They are under attack from Eryndor, and are in need of our help.

William heard each Lepidoptera and his Warlock friend, Adrian, acknowledge his order, as he and Renee ran at Vampire speed from the river back toward the Gramaze house.

"Renee, I need you to go and get some of the experienced Supes from the academy. We're going to need as many Supes as possible to help with this mission," said William.

"No problem. I'll gather everyone and meet you at the portal behind our house," said Renee. She sprinted toward the academy with lightning speed.

* * *

Eryndor, who now had taken over Garrick and Elara's castle, overlooking the Olden Fjord, watched his minions do his bidding in the castle grounds below. With the knowledge inside Hawk's head of how the country was run and its weaponry and other assets, Eryndor was able to gain full control of Olden, the village and its people.

"Come," said Eryndor, hearing a knock at the large wooden door. He watched a glazed-eyed Hawk open the door and walk toward him.

"Master … we have executed your plan," said Hawk, as he came to stand in front of Eryndor. "What's next?" He noticed Eryndor's Warlock body was glowing from all the new souls he had taken, as each villager died.

"Have you found Garrick and Elara?"

"No, Master," said Hawk.

"You had damn well better find them, or else you and your Lepidoptera girlfriend will be next on my kill list," said Eryndor, viciously.

Hawk noticed the Twin Icefire Blades glowing in their wooden boxes next to Eryndor, and gulped hard. He knew that whoever had control over the Twin Icefire Blades would have a power that he could never beat on his own. "Yes, Master." He turned and walked quickly out of the room.

Sully! Hawk thought, desperately struggling to regain control of his mind. Stepping outside and witnessing his village engulfed in flames, he shook his head vigorously, attempting to break free from the grip Eryndor had on him. However, his efforts proved futile as an overpowering voice within his mind pushed him down and took control once again.

"You … soldier, how many prisoners do we have?" demanded Hawk.

"Quite a few," said the soldier.

"I want each and every one of them tortured, until one of them tells us where Garrick and Elara are," said Hawk, authoritatively.

"Yes, Sir," said the soldier, ready and willing to serve Hawk, whom Eryndor had placed in control of his army. The soldier walked toward the dungeon at the back of the castle, with his sword drawn, ready to do his master's bidding.

Hawk! Sully's mind cried out. It had been two grueling weeks since she had been taken captive by Eryndor. In this time, she had been deprived of blood and was growing increasingly weak as a result.

Get the fuck out of my head, bitch, thought a glazed-eyed Hawk.

Sully … I'm trapped, thought Hawk, as he looked around at the black abyss in front of him, trying to escape the hold Eryndor had on him. *Help!*

I wish my family were here, thought Sully.

* * *

Did you hear that, Father? mind-thought Samuel, as he stepped out of the portal with Elsie and Kiplin, in Loen.

Yes, faintly. It sounded like, Sully. Keep an eye out for her, mind-thought William.

"I heard her, too," said Kiplin, looking all around, as he stepped out of the portal. "How in the hell did she get here?"

"Good question!" said Samuel.

"Who?" asked Elsie, as she stood next to Kiplin and Samuel.

"Sully … I heard her voice," said Samuel. looking around at his surroundings.

"Where is she?" asked Elsie, as she readied her Griffin wings.

"I am not sure. Give me a minute, and I'll see if I can find out," said Samuel.

Sully! mind-thought Samuel.

But there was no answer.

Where the fuck are you, Sis? thought Samuel telepathically.

Samuel? mind-thought Sully. Her eyes opened, and she looked around the darkened room with her Lepidoptera vision.

Yes, it's me. Where the hell are you?

I don't know where … some sort of castle, by the looks of this brickwork. Eryndor has me chained up in a dark room. Samuel … the tears formed in her eyes. *Help me, please*, sobbed Sully.

I will find you, Sis. Don't worry, we're on our way, mind-thought Samuel, with resolute determination and unwavering loyalty to his sister.

Weak and exhausted, Sully fell unconscious.

Samuel turned to Kiplin and Elsie and said, "Guys … Sully said she doesn't know where she is. How are we going to find her?"

"Well, if you can hear her, doesn't that mean that she would be in Norway somewhere?" asked Elsie, her Griffin wings spread.

"Yes, you are correct; but where?" asked Kiplin.

"She did say that she thought she might be inside a castle," said Samuel, looking from Kiplin to Elsie. "Is there a castle here in Loen?"

"Yes, but she wouldn't be here in Loen. Garrick and Elara are still in control of this village at the moment. Think about it. Eryndor has taken control over Olden, and if he has Sully and Hawk, he would keep them close by for leverage. I would think that they are both in Olden, wouldn't you?" said Kiplin.

"I would say you are correct, Kiplin," said William, overhearing their conversation, as he came to stand next to the three of them. "Can I trust you all to go and rescue Sully, and Hawk, if he is there? I have my hands full here."

"Yes, Sir," said Elsie and Kiplin together.

"You can count on us, Father, but …," said Samuel.

"But, what?" asked William.

"I would like to take one or two more with us, just in case we run into trouble," said Samuel.

"I agree." *Christian, Danielle*, mind-thought William.

Yes, Sire, replied Christian, as he and Danielle, ran at Vampire speed, to come and stand in front of William.

"I need you both to go with these three to Olden. When you reach Garrick and Elara's home, I need you all to search for Sully and Hawk. Once you find them, I want you to bring them here, to Loen. Nothing else," commanded William, his unwavering gaze fixed on each of them. "I expect you to maintain constant communication with me regarding your progress and remain vigilant for any signs of Eryndor."

"Yes, Sire," they all replied together.

Adrian … portal these five to Olden, mind-thought William.

Yes, my friend, replied Adrian, looking in their direction.

CHAPTER THIRTY-FOUR

Eryndor took a seat on the second marble step, his feathered claws gently tracing over the carved wooden boxes that held the Twin Icefire Blades. "I treasure every moment with you, my beauties." His menacing smile beamed from ear to ear, as he continued to collect their eternal powers through touch.

We are not safe here, Eryndor. When are you going to find a resting place for us? thought the *Blaznira* blade.

"Soon, my beauties … soon," replied Eryndor, as he continued to stroke the boxes.

Eryndor wanted to enjoy what time he had with *Blaznira* and *Eisvarda*, and not only store their eternal powers, but also learn from their wealth of knowledge. As he continued to stroke the boxes, he remembered how he'd initially felt their presence, when they were opened at the ammunition factory, a few weeks earlier, and how he had followed Tassone Boardman to his mansion.

Stupid, blood-sucking Vampire thought he could win the fight with me … but he soon realized he was mistaken, when I killed him and his soldiers, thought Eryndor.

Eryndor picked up the wooden boxes and carried them toward a hidden doorway in the wall, where he placed the Twin Icefire Blades in a concealed vault and locked it with his mind. *You will be safe here, my beauties.*

"Come," said Eryndor, hearing a knock at the door, just as the hidden doorway closed tight behind him.

"Master …," said Hawk. He bowed his head slightly to Eryndor, as he walked toward him. "We have a lead on where Garrick and Elara are."

"Well …" said Eryndor, his nostrils flaring, as he waited for a glazed-eyed Hawk to answer.

"They are in Loen," said Hawk. He gulped hard.

"Loen! Smart move on their part. I would never have guessed that they would be so close by." Eryndor's eyes narrowed as he concocted a plan of attack. "You will come with me, Hawk, and I will show you what I do with Griffin vermin. Get the soldiers together and meet me near the drawbridge in five minutes."

"Yes, Master," said Hawk. He turned and walked toward the doorway. The longer Eryndor had him under his mind control, the more obedient Hawk became.

* * *

Crouched behind the lush bushes and trees that lined the grounds of Garrick and Elara's property, Samuel, Kiplin, Elsie, Danielle and Christian huddled together to watch the goings-on, and to make a plan of attack.

"Look … there's Eryndor, and he has created a portal. I wonder where that fucker is off to?" said Christian, his nostrils flared.

"Is that Hawk?" asked Elsie, as she watched him interact with Eryndor and the soldiers, standing near the drawbridge.

"Yeah," said Christian, frowning. "And he doesn't look like someone who has been kidnapped. In fact, it looks like he's doing Eryndor's bidding."

"What the hell …?" said Kiplin, his voice trembled with disbelief. Being Hawk's roommate and close friend, he struggled to comprehend the scene unfolding before his eyes. It shattered his perception of Hawk. He looked from Christian to Samuel and frowned.

"Let's not worry about that now. Our top priority is to find Sully. We can deal with Hawk later," said Christian.

Fucking traitor, thought Christian, as he watched Hawk, walk through the portal alongside Eryndor, with Eryndor's soldiers following behind.

"How are we going to get past those two guards?" asked Elsie, pointing toward the drawbridge, which was still open.

"Easy, they won't see us coming," said Danielle.

"Ahh," said Elsie, nodding, knowing that a Lepidoptera Vampire had speed on their side.

"Watch," said Christian. He ran at Vampire speed and stood in front of the two soldiers. Before they could register his presence, Christian snapped their necks.

Within seconds Samuel, Kiplin, and Danielle joined Christian on the bridge.

As Elsie landed on the bridge and was about to retract her wings, she dropped to the ground in pain. "Ugh … shit, I've been hit." She looked at her left wing, where an arrow protruded from it.

"Elsie," yelled Kiplin. He ran over to her, inspected the wound and pulled the arrow out.

"Aww, fuck, that hurts," said Elsie, clutching her wing.

Danielle rushed over to her side. "Keep still, I'll heal you." As Danielle kneeled next to Elsie to heal her, she heard a gunshot. Looking up, she noticed that Christian, her Lepidoptera life partner, had been shot.

"Christian!" Danielle screamed.

"I'm okay, my love," Christian called out, as he watched the bullet expel from his upper torso. "One of the things I like about being a Lepidoptera is the abilities we have."

Danielle breathed a heavy sigh of relief and smiled at Christian. "Yeah, me too."

The bullets continued to fly in the air past them, some missing by inches. Utilizing their Vampire speed to rush toward Eryndor's soldiers, Kiplin and Samuel swiftly put an end to the gunfire.

Samuel, who had captured one of Eryndor's guards, held him immobile with a knife to his throat. "Where's the girl?"

"What girl?" the guard questioned, as he tried to break free.

"Don't play games, or I will slice you open, you bastard. Where is she?" Samuel's voice dripped with menace as he applied pressure with the sharp blade, piercing the guard's neck slightly.

"I don't know," said the guard, his tone abrupt.

Samuel snapped his neck, and let him drop to the ground.

Sully! mind-thought Samuel.

There was no answer.

Sully ... Sis, where are you? mind-thought Samuel, standing in the open courtyard.

There was nothing but silence in his mind.

"Is everyone all right?" asked Samuel, as he came to stand with Kiplin, in front of Danielle, Elsie and Christian.

They all nodded, yes.

"How's the wing, Elsie?" asked Kiplin.

Elsie flexed her wing in, then out again. "Yep, all good. Thanks to Danielle." She looked at Danielle and smiled.

"You're welcome," said Danielle. She smiled back at Elsie.

"Let's head into the castle, and see if we can find Sully," said Samuel.

"Keep your wits about you, everyone. I'm sure there will be other soldiers guarding this castle," said Christian, whose wound had fully healed. "Let's not get separated, either."

They continued into the castle with their swords drawn, ready for anything or anyone that would try to stop them.

Sully ... where are you? mind-thought Samuel again, as he continued searching each room which was situated under the main floor of the castle.

Sully ... mind-thought Danielle. She looked at Christian and asked, "Where is she?"

"Good question," said Christian, as he continued to open each door, and check inside each room.

But there was only silence.

I hope she's all right, thought Elsie to herself.

"I hope so, too," said Kiplin, who had heard her thoughts, as he walked next to her.

Samuel tried the door knob of the next room, but it was locked. Using his Lepidoptera strength, he pushed hard with his shoulder against the steel door and stumbled into the room. As he looked around the darkened room with his Vampire night vision, he spotted the battered, limp body of Sully, who had been chained to a brick wall by her hands and feet.

Sully!

Running over to her, he snapped the chains, and Sully's limp body fell into his arms. Samuel placed her unconscious body on the ground. "Sully, come on, wake up." He gently shook her.

Guys, she's in here, mind-thought Samuel.

Danielle, Christian, Elsie and Kiplin, ran into the darkened room.

"Sully ... Sully!" said Samuel, as he tried to rouse her.

But she didn't awaken.

"Move over, and I'll try to heal her," said Danielle. Kneeling beside her, Danielle ran her Lepidoptera healing hands over Sully's body, and watched the bruising disappear from her face.

"Sully ..." said Samuel, his brow furrowed.

Sully sat up quickly and clutched at her stomach. "Aww, shit, that hurts!" She looked at Samuel, and noticed the worry on his face. "You came." Sully smiled and leaned in to hug her brother.

"Always!" said Samuel, engulfing her in his arms.

"Lie back down," instructed Danielle. "I'll be able to heal you some more."

Sully pulled away from Samuel's strong hold on her and lay on the cobble stone floor of the room, then watched the light from Danielle's hands move from her head to her feet, healing and soothing her pain. Looking up at Danielle, she said, "Thank you."

"You're welcome. Is that starting to feel better?" asked Danielle, indicating to Sully's stomach, and pulling her hands away from her body.

Sully nodded in agreement.

"Let's get you up off the floor," said Danielle, standing, holding her hand out for Sully to take.

Taking her hand, Sully once again said, "Thank you."

"How are you feeling?" asked Samuel, who was hovering.

Cricking her neck, left then right, she said, "Better! But I will need some sustenance. I haven't fed for a while."

"Right! Let's get going," said Christian, hearing the urgency in her voice, knowing from experience that a young Lepidoptera Vampire could turn rogue at any time if they didn't get enough blood.

Hawk ... Sully remembered the last time she saw him was in the Marigot Bay villa. "Did you find Hawk?"

"He was with Eryndor, last we saw him," said Samuel, picturing how Hawk seemed to be helping Eryndor.

"We need to find him," pleaded Sully.

"Our instructions are to find you and take you to William. Nothing else!" stated Christian.

"But ..." said Sully, looking at Christian.

"We have our instructions. Now, let's get moving," said Christian, firmly. "Are you okay to walk, Sully?"

"Yes!" She sighed heavily and followed Christian out the room.

"Are you okay, my love?" asked Christian to Danielle, concern etched across his face, as he came to stand next to her. He had sensed from their connection the weight of exhaustion emanating from her, recognizing the toll her healing efforts had taken on her.

"A bit fatigued. I'll need some blood to replenish my energy," said Danielle, her tone carried a hint of weariness. "I'll be fine, though."

Christian intertwined his fingers with Danielle's, providing her with a reassuring touch. She leaned into him, finding solace in their connection. Looking around the room, he said, "We need to get going." Christian knew how important it was for Sully, and now Danielle, to feed. They were all now vulnerable without a healer.

Christian pulled his mobile phone from his pocket and called William, so that they could portal back to Loen.

CHAPTER THIRTY-FIVE

"Here you go," said Renee, offering bags of blood to Sully and Danielle as they walked out of the portal.

"Thank you, Renee. You're a lifesaver," said Danielle, taking one bag of blood from her.

"You're welcome, dear," said Renee.

Within seconds of drinking the crimson fluid, Danielle felt her Lepidoptera strength and abilities return.

"Thanks, Renee," said Sully, as she took the other bag from Renee, and gulped the contents down fast. "I haven't had any blood for a few weeks."

"I guessed as much. How are you feeling?"

"Better now! What is going on over there?" asked Sully, hearing the explosions and watching the smoke rising up into the air.

"Eryndor is trying to take over Loen," said Renee, as she watched Sully's eyes dart toward the war zone that Eryndor had created. "Garrick and Elara, along with our Lepidoptera family, and a few of our academy graduates are trying to stop him."

"How did this happen?" asked Sully, as she discarded the empty blood bag on the ground.

"Now that Eryndor has access to the power of the Twin Icefire Blades, he seems to be unbeatable. First, he took over Olden and now he's trying to take Loen. Garrick and Elara asked our family to come and help. But I don't know how we're going to be able to beat him and his army of soldiers," said Renee, looking in the direction of the war zone ahead of them.

"What can I do to help?" asked Sully.

"Nothing … William has instructed me to take you back home," said Renee, handing Sully another bag of blood.

"Like hell I'll be returning home. This is my fight, too. And …" she swallowed hard. "I need to find Hawk." Taking the bag of blood from Renee, Sully swiftly consumed its contents, allowing the crimson liquid to cascade down her throat. A sense of revitalization surged through her as the nourishing essence reached her stomach, initiating a remarkable rejuvenation process that commenced the repair of her fatigued Vampire form.

"You won't like what you find," said Christian, as he walked over to Sully and Renee from the portal, along with Elsie, Kiplin and Samuel.

With a questioning look, Sully asked, "Why? What has happened to Hawk?"

"We can't figure the why or how, but he is now Eryndor's little puppet. Maybe he's the reason Eryndor has been able to conquer Olden so swiftly," said Christian.

"No … you're lying. Hawk would never betray his family. He hates what Eryndor stands for, and his beliefs," said Sully. Her nostrils flared with rage, at the thought of this even being considered a possibility. She may not have known Hawk long, but she knew he would never betray his family, country or her.

"Christian is right, Sully. We watched it happen," said Samuel, placing a hand on her shoulder.

"Enough of this talk. William instructed me to take Sully home. So, we will be leaving," said Renee. She grabbed hold of Sully's arm and pulled her toward Adrian, who had created another portal to take them back to the Gramaze mansion.

Sully yanked her arm from Renee's hold and stood her ground. "I told you; I'm not returning home." She turned to Christian and Samuel and said, "Show me proof. I want to see it with my own eyes."

Renee rolled her eyes. *Stubborn as ever.*

Sully ... you will do as you are told. I don't want another liability here. We have enough problems as it is, without your presence, thought William to Sully. Renee had relayed the problem to him via mind-thought.

I am not leaving without Hawk, mind-thought Sully to William.

You will do as you are told, young lady. Am I making myself clear? asked William, authoritatively.

Sully's throat tightened as she swallowed hard, a sinking realization washing over her. She knew she was not going to be able to win this battle with William. *Please help Hawk.*

I will do what I can, but I can't promise you anything at all, at the moment, mind-thought William.

Thank you. That is all I can ask, mind-thought Sully.

"Let's get moving," said Renee, who had been listening to their conversation. She walked toward the portal with Sully. "Elsie, I want you to join us."

"Yes, Ma'am," said Elsie, following them.

* * *

In their mountain cabin, Garrick and Elara observed with heavy hearts the devastation of Loen unfolding in front of them. The once-serene town was now engulfed in chaos, leaving its inhabitants in distress.

"Zephyrion ... you can put out some of these fires that Eryndor has triggered with his lightning strikes," instructed Garrick to his son, as he looked from the rugged mountains toward the shoreline of Loen, and watched everything in the path of the fires burn out of control.

"Yes, Father," said Zephyrion.

"Drakon ... you will need to work with Zephyrion," said Garrick.

"Yes, Father," said Drakon.

"Well, what are you waiting for?" yelled Garrick.

Zephyrion and Drakon nodded once to their father, and ran toward the Loen shoreline.

Garrick and Elara stood side by side, their eyes fixed on the twin forces of nature before them. Zephyrion, his presence as unyielding as the tides, raised his arms, and commanded the ocean to surge forward. The water obeyed, rising in a towering swell at his call. Beside him, Drakon unleashed his dominion over the wind, summoning powerful gusts that drove the cascading waves toward the blazing inferno. The rushing water met the fire with a fierce hiss, steam rising in thick, twisting plumes. As the last embers drowned beneath the flood, dense gray smoke billowed skyward, drifting toward them in slow, ghostly tendrils.

Where did we go wrong with this one, Elara? mind-thought Garrick. A profound sense of anguish gripped his heart, as he gazed upon the devastating aftermath brought on by Eryndor and his soldiers.

I wish I knew, Garrick, mind-thought Elara. The weight of responsibility bore down on her, as she contemplated the choices and actions that had led to this moment of destruction by their adopted son.

"I have rounded up some of the human soldiers that Eryndor has had under mind-control, and I have placed them in a metal cage, near the city center, until we can deal with them later," said Rimmer, who was now standing next to Garrick and Elara. "Speaking of Eryndor; I haven't seen him for a while."

"Good work, son," said Elara. "As for Eryndor, I think you spoke too soon. There he is." She pointed to Eryndor, who was hovering over the water of Loen.

Eryndor ... you will halt this destruction of Loen, thought Garrick, as he looked down to where Elara was pointing.

Ah, there you are, Mother ... Father. Oh, and little bro, thought Eryndor. He appeared in front of them, before they could blink.

"You will cease your reign of terror on this village and its people, Eryndor," said Garrick, authoritatively.

"Humph! Is that so …? What do I get if I agree to your crazy ideas, Father?" asked Eryndor. He sneered, as he looked from Garrick to Elara.

"Nothing! You sick moron," said Rimmer. He placed his hand out, and commanded Eryndor to move toward him. As he grabbed Eryndor by the throat, Rimmer was electrocuted by him and thrown into the air. "Aww, fuck!"

"Eryndor, stop!" shouted Elara, as she watched Rimmer's body shake violently in the air.

Eryndor dropped Rimmer's unconscious body to the ground and sneered.

"Perhaps if you had shown me this sort of affection, I could have been your favorite child too, rather than … this," said Eryndor, mockingly. He gestured with a sweeping motion of his feathered hand toward his shadowed form, which was the embodiment of his otherworldly existence. His bitter words hung in the air, laced with a mixture of resentment and longing.

"How dare you accuse me; your mother, of not showing you affection! Our relationship was not based on favoritism, but rather on mutual respect and understanding. I believe you had your chance at redemption, but you chose your own path, Eryndor," stated Elara.

Eryndor chose to dismiss Elara's comments. "Humph! What a crock of shit. Anyway, enough of this chitchat. Who am I going to torture next?" pondered Eryndor. He looked at Garrick and Elara and smirked. "Eeny, meeny, miny, moe."

"It is you who will be next, Eryndor," said William, who was now standing behind him.

He turned to see who dared threaten him. "Humph, you are no match for me, Lepidoptera," stated Eryndor.

"Maybe not by myself, but I am sure all of us together can and will defeat you," stated William, confidently.

Eryndor's eyes darted past William, catching sight of eight Lepidopteras, each possessing unique Vampire powers, accompanied by a powerful Warlock, steadily making their way toward him. Gathering his courage, he prepared to face this formidable assembly head-on, knowing that the clash between their extraordinary abilities would determine a fate that awaited them all.

"One last chance, Eryndor," stated Garrick.

"Chance … humph. It is you who will need the chance, Father," said Eryndor, sarcastically. His nostrils flared in frustration, as he raised his right hand in the air to defeat them all. *What the fuck!* thought Eryndor, when he realized that he couldn't move his fingers to use the powers he had acquired from the Twin Icefire Blades. His eyes flew immediately to Elara, when he heard her command the gods to stop him.

With their strength in numbers, and the confidence that this was going to be the only way to stop Eryndor, Danielle thrust her ability to change others' thoughts at Eryndor, and watched his face contort, as he became confused about his surroundings. Drakon, Zephyrion, and Rhydian then used their combined strengths, to overpower Eryndor, and brought him to his knees.

"You will pay … all of you. I don't forget faces," shouted Eryndor, as he tried to block the thoughts Danielle was projecting into his mind, and free himself from their hold on him.

"It is you who will pay, Eryndor. You will be judged by your peers and convicted. Then, and only then, will you be finally put to death for your atrocities," said Garrick authoritatively, as he towered over Eryndor and looked him the eyes. "We should have done this years ago, instead of banishing you."

"Good luck with that, Father," Eryndor sneered, his menacing face contorted with pure hatred.

"Adrian, open the portal," commanded William.

"Yes, William," said Adrian. He commanded a portal to open.

Assisted by the combined powers of Drakon, Zephyrion and Rhydian, Elara propelled Eryndor's body toward the open portal. She watched as Eryndor, the nine Lepidoptera Vampires, Adrian the Warlock, Garrick, and her four sons stepped through the portal, and then followed them through. Their mission to capture Eryndor was complete, and he would now face Norwegian justice once they arrived back at Olden.

* * *

A glazed-eyed, expressionless Hawk, who was crouched behind the bushes and had been watching the goings-on, frowned as he watched Eryndor and the others go into the portal.

Where are they taking him? Humph ... I wonder what Master will do to them once he is free?

He snickered and walked into the portal, not even considering if it would still be open when he arrived at the unknown end destination.

CHAPTER THIRTY-SIX

"Great work, everyone," said William, looking around the operations room of the Gramaze mansion, at each of their faces. "Today, we have not only helped save a community and country from destruction, but we have also gained the knowledge of how to fight mindless fuckers like Eryndor, with our strength in numbers from all types of Supes."

Everyone smiled and nodded in agreement.

"Tonight, we celebrate. There will be a special dinner in the large dining room for everyone to enjoy," William proclaimed, his gaze sweeping across the room filled with members of his formidable coven. A sense of relief washed over him as he realized that his coven had returned unscathed from their perilous mission. Gratitude swelled within him, knowing that there had been no casualties and that his coven remained safe and whole.

They all cheered loudly.

"Now, go and get cleaned up. I will see you all later tonight," said William. He watched them all leave the operations room, and the glass sliding doors close behind them.

William turned to Brock, who was working on the computer at the back of the room. "What have you found for me?"

"Not a lot, Sire. Hawk … he definitely came through the portal after you all did at Olden. But there is no sign of him after that. Do you think he is still under the mind-control of Eryndor?" said Brock.

"He could be, or … maybe he could be feeling ashamed of what he has done," said William.

"Hmm, maybe. I remember from previous missions, when I had been under mind-control, that even though I knew what I was doing was wrong, I still chose the wrong path. The type of leverage that keeps you under control is so strong, that you can't seem to break it," said Brock, his brow furrowed.

"Yes, I know that," said William. He walked toward the glass sliding doors. "Let me know if you find him, and what he has been up to, since he arrived back at Olden."

"Yes, Sire," said Brock, watching William, walk out of the operations room.

* * *

"Here you go, Xanthia. I thought you might like something to eat," said Lamiae, as she entered the bedroom carrying a tray.

Startled, Xanthia quickly sat up. With her heart racing, she pressed herself firmly against the headboard. She watched the tall brown-haired woman, who had her hair tied back in a bun, enter the room. With a mix of apprehension and vulnerability, Xanthia instinctively pulled her knees up to her chest. "No, thank you. I … I'm not hungry," Xanthia managed to utter, her voice quivering slightly. Her throat tightened as she struggled to find her composure, her eyes never leaving the woman as she cautiously approached, carrying a tray of food. A gulp escaped Xanthia's parched throat as she watched her gingerly place the tray on the bed.

"My name is Lamiae. I'm the household's cook," said Lamiae, her French accent apparent. She sat on the edge of the bed and looked at the concern on Xanthia's face. "Are you okay, my dear?"

"Yes."

"Is there anything in particular you like to eat? If you don't like what's on the tray, I can make you something else, if you like," said Lamiae.

"No … no, thank you," said Xanthia. Her eyes darted from Lamiae to the doorway, and then back again. Eventually, she placed her face down on her knees, closed her eyes, and started rocking herself back and forth.

Poor girl is scared out of her mind, thought Lamiae. She placed her hand on Xanthia's head and slowly stroked her strawberry-blonde hair.

Xanthia's body tensed, and an involuntary flinch escaped her as Lamiae's hand made contact.

"Don't worry, my dear. Everything will work itself out."

Her tearstained face looked up at Lamiae and she gulped hard. "How do you know that?"

"Well, I've lived here for many years, and I'm still alive. That's how." She smiled politely at Xanthia. "William and Renee have been really good to me since my family passed on, and if there is one thing that I know for sure, it's that I always feel safe here. The Gramaze coven might be different, my dear, but they've always treated me like family."

"Oh, right!" said Xanthia. She wiped the tears from her eyes and cheeks. "So, you don't have any living relatives, either?"

"No, my dear. They have all passed on."

"Just like me, then."

"Yes, but I have what I call my adopted family, here at the Gramaze coven. And like I said, they've been good to me," said Lamiae.

Xanthia relaxed a bit, and sat cross-legged in front of Lamiae. "What will they want me to do for them?"

Lamiae's brow furrowed. "You mean the Gramaze coven?"

"Yes." Xanthia searched Lamiae's blue eyes for an answer.

"Nothing! I would say that they want you to settle in here. They do care about you and your future, you know," said Lamiae.

Xanthia nodded, and tried to take in what Lamiae had said to her. The only other people that had ever cared about her and her future had been her parents, and now they were both dead.

"Would you like some of this food, my dear?" asked Lamiae. She pushed the tray closer to Xanthia.

Xanthia's nose took in the sweet aroma of the roast meat and vegetables, and she nodded in agreement. "Thank you, Lamiae."

"You are welcome, my dear." She picked the tray up and placed it directly in front of Xanthia.

Xanthia picked up the knife and fork, and cut into a roast potato. As the flavor hit her mouth, she said, "Mmm … tastes good." She had only just now realized how hungry she was.

"Well, I'll leave you to enjoy your food, my dear. If there is anything else you need, just dial two on that phone there." Lamiae pointed to the landline phone on the bedside table, next to Xanthia. "That is a direct line to my kitchen."

"Thank you … do you have to go?" asked Xanthia, looking into Lamiae caring eyes.

"I'm afraid so, my dear. We have a big dinner tonight in the large dining room. A bit of a celebration, I believe. So, I had better get cracking if I want to get on top of dinner," said Lamiae. She placed her hand on top of Xanthia's. "I will see you later, maybe, in the dining room?"

Xanthia's brow furrowed. "I don't know … I'm not sure." *Vampires … I don't want to sit in a room with a lot of Vampires that will probably want to drink from me.*

"Don't worry, my dear. You will be safe in the dining room. William and Renee will make sure of that," said Lamiae.

Xanthia nodded and said, "Thank you, Lamiae. You are so kind."

"Well, I had better go," said Lamiae, standing. "Enjoy your food."

"Thanks, Lamiae," said Xanthia. She watched Lamiae, walk toward the doorway, as she continued eating her lunch. Once Xanthia finished the meal, she decided to have a rest.

* * *

"Knock, knock," said Elsie, standing in Xanthia's doorway. "Can I come in?"

Xanthia smiled and said, "Yes, come in." She watched Elsie, walk into the room and sit on her bed.

"I wanted to come by and check on you. Are you going, okay?" asked Elsie.

"I think so. Well, I've stopped shaking, and I've eaten; that's a start," said Xanthia, noticing the tray of empty plates missing from the floor.

Humph, someone must have come and collected the tray while I slept. I didn't hear a thing, thought Xanthia.

Elsie smiled. "I'm glad. Would you like to go for a walk around the grounds outside?"

"Is that allowed?"

"Allowed … You are free to go anywhere on this property, I have been told," said Elsie, standing. "Come on."

Xanthia swung her legs over the side of the bed and stood tall. She placed her hand in Elsie's outstretched hand, and they walked to the doorway.

Xanthia's eyes darted everywhere as they descended the white marble staircase. *Wow, look at that glass chandelier hanging from the ceiling. It's beautiful.* As they walked toward the back of the house, Xanthia couldn't believe the lavish mansion and its surroundings that were set out before her. *This is something you only see in the magazines.*

"Hi, girls," said Danielle, as she walked toward them with Christian by her side.

"Hi, Danielle," said Elsie.

"What are you girls up to tonight?" asked Danielle.

"I was just showing Xanthia around the Gramaze house and grounds," stated Elsie. "I hope that's okay?"

"Of course, it is," said Danielle.

"You certainly have a lovely home here," said Xanthia.

"Yes, we think so," said Danielle, as she looked from Xanthia to Christian, and smiled. "I have lived here for over twenty years, and I never tire of this beautiful mansion, and the life I have."

"Me neither," said Christian. He smiled politely at Xanthia and Elsie. "We had better get moving, otherwise we won't make it to the dinner on time."

"Are you both attending the dinner tonight?" asked Danielle.

"I am," said Elsie. "It will be the first time I've had dinner at the Gramaze table. I'm looking forward to it."

"Umm … I don't know," said Xanthia, her brow furrowing.

"While you are staying here, you're welcome to eat dinner with us every night. You know that, right?" said Christian, who had been listening to Xanthia's thoughts.

"No, I didn't," said Xanthia.

"You are both welcome to come and sit with us at the table tonight," said Danielle.

"Oh, thank you. That is nice of you to ask," said Xanthia.

"Thanks. So, we'll see you later," said Elsie, as she looked from Danielle to Christian, and then Xanthia.

Xanthia smiled politely.

"Yep. Catch you later," said Christian, as he and Danielle walked on inside.

"They seem really nice," said Xanthia.

"They sure are. Come on, let's keep looking around," said Elsie, as she pulled Xanthia toward the back veranda area.

Xanthia's eyes lit up and her mouth dropped open when she saw the outdoor area set out in front of her. "Wow …

this is stunning." The home that she had been living in with her father was not anywhere near as lavish as this one. In fact, her home in the suburbs was really run-down.

"It sure is. Why don't we take a seat and enjoy the view?" suggested Elsie, indicating to the six-piece light gray lounge setting on the veranda, that had a low, dark-glass table in the middle.

Xanthia nodded and chose a seat that overlooked the whole backyard area. She had only ever seen this type of extravagant living on Netflix or in magazines. Set in the middle of a green manicured lawn was a rectangular swimming pool, its sparkling blue water highlighted by three lights positioned down the center of the pool, with water-spouts emerging out of them. "I feel privileged to be able to sit here."

"Yeah, I know what you mean," said Elsie, taking in her surroundings.

"Do you live here, too?" asked Xanthia.

"No. I live in the dorms next door. I attend the academy there."

"Oh, okay. So, what are you majoring in?" asked Xanthia.

"Umm … it's not that type of academy."

"Huh, what do you mean?"

"It's an academy for Legacies." Elsie took a deep breath. "It's for the children of supernatural creatures."

Xanthia gulped hard as realization hit her. "Oh, right. Does that mean you are one of them too?"

Elsie nodded and pursed her lips. "I'm a Griffin."

"What's a Griffin?" asked Xanthia. Her heart started to race.

"I can show you," said Elsie, as she stood up.

"Show me what?" queried Xanthia.

"This," said Elsie, as she spread her eagle wings, and her hands changed to talons.

Xanthia stood up quickly. *Oh, God, save me.*

"It's okay, Xanthia. I didn't mean to frighten you," said Elsie, as she quickly retracted her wings, and pulled her talons back into her hands. "Sit, please."

Xanthia did as she was asked, in fear of the repercussions. Pulling her knees up to her chest, she rocked back and forth, in anticipation of what might happen. "Please … I want to go back to my room."

"It's okay, Xanthia. I won't hurt you. Ever," said Elsie, as she sat on a single lounge chair across from Xanthia.

Xanthia continued to rock herself back and forth, and tried not to make eye contact with Elsie.

"I'm so sorry I frightened you," said Elsie, as she reached across and placed her hand on Xanthia's arm. "I didn't mean to. Please forgive me." She sat back in her chair and sighed.

Xanthia looked across at Elsie and noticed the hurt in her eyes. Placing her feet on the ground, she said, "It's probably me who should be saying sorry. It's just … well, you scared the hell out of me."

"Can we just forget this even happened? I feel bad enough already," said Elsie, looking into Xanthia's eyes.

"Sounds good to me." Xanthia smiled at Elsie. "Girl, your wings are huge. I thought … oh, don't worry about what I thought."

"I would never hurt you, Xanthia," said Elsie again.

With a furrowed brow, Xanthia had a flashback of when someone had flown her to the Gramaze mansion, and how their wings were just like Elsie's. "It was you."

"What was?" queried Elsie.

"You were the one who saved me and brought me here," said Xanthia.

"Well, sort of," said Elsie, remembering that night. "When you were found at Tassone Boardman's house, you were technically dead. A few of the Lepidopteras tried to revive you with their healing abilities, but they couldn't."

"Healing abilities! You mean the Vampires can heal people or …" she gulped hard, "Other creatures?" asked Xanthia.

"Yes. So anyway, we wrapped you in a sheet, and it was my job to bring you back here. But when I arrived at the Gramaze mansion with you, and handed you to Violette, you came back to life. The only thing I did is fly you back here."

"I remember …" said Xanthia, nodding. "I remember soaring through the air, and you holding me. I thought I'd gone to heaven. Thank you, Elsie."

"No need for thanks. I was happy to see you alive," said Elsie. As one of the noble Griffins, protection was ingrained in her very essence, an innate part of who she was. The well-being and safety of others, especially those she held dear, came as naturally to her as breathing. "Do you think you will stay with the Gramaze's?"

"Yes, that is a good question," said Renee, overhearing their conversation, as she stepped out onto the veranda.

Xanthia stood up quickly and took a deep breath.

"Sit down, child. There's no need to worry," said Renee, coming to stand beside her.

"Yes, Ma'am," said Xanthia, taking her seat again.

Renee sat across from Xanthia and Elsie, and calmly said, "I know it's a lot to take in … learning about supernatural creatures like us … but would you consider remaining with us?"

Xanthia swallowed hard.

"It will be okay, Xanthia. Just tell her how you feel," said Elsie.

"Umm … I would like to live here, but … I …" She looked down at her hands and fidgeted. "I'm worried that I would become someone's lunch," blurted Xanthia. She took a long breath to steady her nerves.

"I won't allow that to happen. Ever," said William, as he walked out onto the veranda. He had also been listening in to their conversation.

Xanthia jumped when she heard his deep voice.

"We want you to become part of our family, Xanthia. Believe me when I say Renee and I would love to have you come and live with us. We can provide for you and, care for you, and most of all, keep you safe," said William. "Please give it some thought before you answer."

"Yes, Sir," said Xanthia, as she looked at William and Renee, noticing the sincerity in their expressions.

"Well … I came out here to let you girls know that dinner is ready in the large dining room; that's if you want to join us," said Renee, standing.

"I would love to," said Elsie, standing. "Come on, Xanthia." She held her hand out for the young teenager to take.

Xanthia placed her hand in Elsie's. "Thank you. I would love to eat dinner with your family." Her scared eyes looked at William and Renee and then she smiled.

"If you decide to live with us, this will be your family, too," said William. "And family means everything to us."

"Oh, right," said Xanthia. *How nice!*

Elsie and Xanthia followed Renee and William inside to the large dining room, where everyone was already seated for dinner at a long wooden table.

Mmm … smells so good in here. Wonder what we're having for dinner, thought Xanthia, as she looked around at all the faces seated at the table.

Danielle stood up from the long table and said, "Come and sit with us, Xanthia and Elsie. We have saved two seats for you."

Xanthia and Elsie smiled, and walked over to Danielle, and took their seats.

William looked at Danielle and nodded his head. *Thank you!*

All good, Sire, mind-thought Danielle, as she nodded her head at William.

"Thank you," said Xanthia, looking at Danielle.

Danielle smiled at Xanthia. "You're welcome. There is a banquet of food over in the bains-marie for you to choose from. Just take what you want." Danielle looked from Xanthia to Elsie, and indicated to the sideboard over on the left-hand side of the room.

"Thank you," said Elsie. Standing, she walked over to the bains-marie.

"Thanks!" said Xanthia, standing. She followed Elsie over to the banquet of food that had been laid out to choose from.

Danielle nodded.

Hopefully she settles in here soon, Christian. Danielle placed her hand in Christian's.

Once Xanthia feels a bit more comfortable being around us all, I reckon she'll make some friends here. And maybe you could help with this, being that you know firsthand what it's like to feel this way; scared, that is, of the unknown, mind-thought Christian. He squeezed her hand and leant in to kiss the side of her head.

Yeah, I remember twenty years ago feeling the way she does. Not knowing who to trust, and feeling unsafe. It certainly feels like a lifetime ago, mind-thought Danielle.

Xanthia sat quietly and ate her food. Every now and then she looked down the long table and watched everyone. They looked like normal, everyday people, eating their meals and chatting. *Humph, normal!* Feeling a sense of relief and ease, Xanthia looked to where William and Renee were seated at the head of the table, and when they looked in her direction, she mouthed the words, "Yes. Thank you."

Reading her thoughts, William nodded once in her direction and smiled, knowing she had made a hard decision to trust supernatural creatures, and to even want to live with them.

You're welcome, he thought to himself.

Danielle, when she's ready, I want you to go with Xanthia and collect her clothes and belongings from her father's residence, mind-thought William, as he looked down the table in her direction.

Yes, Sire, mind-thought Danielle.

271

CHAPTER THIRTY-SEVEN

"He's been gone for two weeks. Where do you think Hawk may have run to, or be hiding?" asked Elara, as she looked out the large office window, and watched a sailboat moor offshore in Olden. Deep furrows of concern accentuated her forehead, revealing the weight she carried as she contemplated the whereabouts of her son.

"I wish I knew. But it's only a matter of time before he surfaces," said Garrick, as he came to stand next to Elara. "He won't last too much longer out there without help."

"That's what I'm afraid of, Garrick. He is, after all, only a boy still."

"There is nothing further we can do, Elara. Everyone has been informed to keep an eye out for Hawk, and if he doesn't want to be found, then …," said Garrick.

"Don't say it," interrupted Elara. "I don't even want to think about what may have happened to him. Do you think he's still in Olden?"

"Considering he's a great swimmer; highly unlikely. But if what Eryndor has told us is true, then we don't stand a chance of Hawk returning, ever," said Garrick. Deep down, Garrick clung to a glimmer of hope, refusing to fully surrender to the idea of Hawk's permanent absence, because he was still under the mind-control of Eryndor. However, the weight of Eryndor's revelations bore heavily upon him, casting doubt on the likelihood of ever seeing Hawk again.

"When is the council making their decision on Eryndor?" asked Elara.

"This afternoon, I assume. He has been found guilty, so now all the council have to do is make a decision on what his punishment will be."

"Hmm … considering Eryndor won't give up the location of the Twin Icefire Blades, we all know the council won't kill the little shit. Instead, they'll give him what punishment they see fit. In my eyes no punishment will be good enough for the atrocities and destruction he has caused in our villages. We are going to be cleaning up the mess he made for years."

"I agree," said Garrick.

"Have you heard anything from William Gramaze?" asked Elara.

"I spoke with him this morning, and still nothing. They have some sort of facial recognition program running in the background, hoping that they may find Hawk that way. William has even had Sully swim out into the ocean and telepathically call Hawk. That hasn't worked either," said Garrick.

"Knock, knock," said a guard, as he tapped on the wooden door to Garrick's office.

"Come," said Garrick, looking over at the doorway.

"Sir, the council have asked me to let you know they are reconvening, and require both of you to attend their chambers," said the guard, now standing before them.

"Tell them we'll be there in five minutes," said Garrick.

"Yes, Sir," said the guard. He turned and walked toward the doorway.

"Let's go, Elara," said Garrick, holding his hand out for her to take. He clicked his fingers to portal them to a little village in Norway, called Glittertind.

* * *

Garrick and Elara reached the cliff entrance, which was made of sandstone rock formations, and waited for the secret passage to the council chambers to open.

273

Place your hand on the rock. They heard a deep voice say.

Garrick and Elara both did as they were instructed, and watched a door-sized hole open inward.

Come ...

As Garrick and Elara stepped inside, the door closed behind them, sealing off the world outside. Daylight streamed in from an opening above, casting an ethereal glow over the chambers. The passageway walls, carved from sandstone and limestone, were solemnly adorned with the skulls of sacred Griffins who had passed before them, their presence a silent testament to centuries of legacy and honor.

Keep moving ...

"What is that?" asked Elara, as she listened to a few voices screaming for help.

Garrick shrugged his shoulders, as he looked around.

As Garrick and Elara turned the corner, their eyes widened in shock and disbelief at the scene that unfolded before them. In front of them was a corridor of lined limestone rock cells, stretching one after the other, with no windows and open bars, with prisoners locked inside. The oppressive atmosphere hung heavy in the air, accentuating the desolation within.

"I have always known what happens with Griffin who are convicted of crimes against our nation, but I didn't know that there was this many prisoners down here," said Elara, as she walked along, looking in each cell.

"Aww ... you have come to visit me," Eryndor sneered, his voice dripping with sarcasm, his gaze locked on his adopted mother and father. Behind the mystically forged metal bars, he stood tall, a figure shrouded in a tattered cloak that hung loosely over his body.

"Humph ..." said Elara, as they walked past his cell.

Keep moving ... thought the councillor.

When they reached the end of the passageway, there was a round, open room in front of them, where all the councillors were seated.

Sit ...

One of them indicated to a seat, which was on a limestone wall beside them.

Garrick and Elara did as they were instructed.

As these crimes were committed in your villages, Garrick and Elara, you have the right to be here and listen to what we have decided as punishment for Eryndor.

"We don't ask for any leniencies. In fact, Eryndor should pay for the crimes he has committed," said Garrick, matter-of-factly.

We have decided that Eryndor will not be put to death, even though he deserves to be for the atrocities and destruction he has caused. Instead, he has been given a life sentence. He will stay in the cell provided here, with no food or water, nor souls to feed on. What say you ...

The councillor's spectral maw did not move, but you could plainly hear one of them speak in a deep commanding voice to Garrick and Elara.

Garrick nodded in agreement.

"Why are you keeping Eryndor alive? The fucker needs to die," said Elara abruptly, as she stood up and questioned the councilors authority and decision. "He has already stated at the trials that he won't be giving us the location of the Twin Icefire Blades, and that would be the only reason to keep him alive. Again, I ask, why?"

That is for us to decide, NOT YOU, Elara Ironclaw. We are the law-makers here, and you will conform.

"But ..."

Elara mouth was sealed shut, so she couldn't talk.

Garrick's brown eyes opened wide, and his nostrils flared, when he realized that the councillors had sealed Elara's mouth. "There is no need for this," stated Garrick, as he stood up.

You will both leave, NOW.

The earth under them rumbled, and dust from the limestone formations rained down on them.

Garrick grabbed hold of Elara's hand, and they ran toward the entrance of the councillor's chamber.

As Elara looked behind her, she watched the eight councillor disappear, one by one.

When they reached the secret doorway, Garrick and Elara placed their hands on the wall, and the doorway opened for them to escape.

In the distance behind them, they heard Eryndor call out, "You won't stop me."

CHAPTER THIRTY-EIGHT

Hawk ...

Hawk's eyes opened wide, and his senses heightened when he heard the echoing voice of Eryndor. With a sudden surge of adrenaline, he swiftly stood tall, his body poised for action, ready to confront the anticipated presence of the Harbinger of Shadows. When he didn't see Eryndor, he breathed a sigh of relief and sat back down on the tranquil beach's soft sand beneath him, which lent a sense of grounding and familiarity, as the rhythmic sound of crashing waves filled the air, blending with the gentle sea breeze that brushed against his skin.

Hawk ...

Yes, thought a glazed-eyed Hawk.

I need you to go and collect the Twin Icefire Blades, mind-thought Eryndor.

Yes, Master, replied Hawk.

They are hidden at Garrick and Elara's home, mind-thought Eryndor, remembering where he placed them in the wall. *Where are you?*

Storvik, mind-thought Hawk.

Right! Let me know when you arrive home, and I'll give you the location of the Twin Icefire Blades, mind-thought Eryndor.

Yes, Master. Hawk walked toward the clear blue-green water, in a deep trance-like state, and dived into the shallow waves.

* * *

Sully sat on the cushioned window seat of Hawk's bedroom and rested her chin on her knees. As she watched the sun set behind the dark blue waters of Olden Fjord, and the pale orange sky started to fade, Sully wondered if she would ever see Hawk again. She had only returned to Olden in the hope that her presence may bring Hawk back home.

Where are you, Hawk? thought Sully, her brow furrowed.

Here!

Sully frowned when she thought that she'd heard Hawk's voice. Doubting herself, she sighed and shook her head.

Sully ... help me, thought Hawk.

Sully stood up quickly and looked all around the room. *Where are you?*

This time no one answered.

Hawk ... where are you? thought Sully. She knelt on the window seat and looked out over the bay.

Again, there was only silence.

Maybe I'm hearing things, thought Sully, shaking her head. But as she thought this, she spotted a bare-chested male running toward the castle. *Hawk?*

There was only silence.

Sully's heart pounded in her chest as she opened the window, and with her Lepidoptera Vampire speed and agility she jumped out of the window, landing on the grass below. *I have to know if it was Hawk or not.* As she turned around to scout out her surroundings, she spotted the bare-chested male again, running toward the side entrance of the castle. *Hawk!*

"STOP!" shouted Sully.

He stopped dead in his tracks and turned to look at her. "Hawk!"

An expressionless, glazed-eyed Hawk, looked straight through Sully, and didn't acknowledge her presence. Instead, he turned and again ran toward the castle.

"Hawk … STOP!" shouted Sully, as she ran at Vampire speed toward him.

Hawk's momentum halted abruptly as he locked eyes with Sully, who now stood defiantly in his path. The air crackled with tension as the intensity of their gazes met. Hawk's features contorted with bitterness and resentment, his eyes burning with a fiery disdain. "Get the fuck out of my way, Lepidoptera," Hawk spat, his words dripping with venom.

"Humph … who do you think you're talking to, fucker," said Sully, with her nostrils flared. She clenched her fists tight at the sight of his white glazed-over eyes.

Hawk didn't answer, instead he tried to sidestep around her, to enter the castle.

Sully pushed Hawk to the ground. "You will desist," she shouted.

Hawk looked up at Sully and said, "Unless you want to get hurt, Lepidoptera, you had better get out of my way." He jumped to his feet.

"Humph … I would like to see you try," said Sully. She gestured with her hand for him to have a go.

Hawk placed his hands over his ears and shook his head. "Sully, help me." His bourbon-colored eyes had returned.

"Hawk … Is that you?"

"Yes. Help me, please." He leaned into her for a hug. Hawk's demeanor bore the weight of both frustration and vulnerability as he spoke.

Sully leaned in to his embrace. "What can I do?"

"I can't control myself. I probably only have a few seconds before he takes over again," said Hawk. He stepped back and shook his head. "Get out of me, fucker."

"Who takes over?" asked Sully.

"Eryndor. He's in my head," said Hawk. He exuded a mix of weariness, resilience, and a determination to try and regain control of his own thoughts and mental space.

"Come on, let's get you inside, and see if your parents can help," said Sully, taking Hawk by the hand, pulling him toward the entrance.

But before Sully could even get him near the entrance, a glazed-eyed Hawk had returned, and swung a punch so fierce it knocked her to the ground and rendered her unconscious.

Your mission is the Twin Icefire Blades, Hawk. Nothing else, mind-thought Eryndor, who had been watching every interaction or thought that Hawk had, from his Glittertind cell.

Yes, Master, mind-thought Hawk, as he ran toward the side entrance.

Sully! screamed Hawk, from within.

* * *

"Sully ..." said Elara, who had happened upon her unconscious body lying on the grass.

"Huh!" Sully rubbed her head and sat up slowly.

"Dear child ... are you okay?" asked Elara, as she knelt next to her.

"I think so," said Sully. Her jade-green eyes opened wide when she remembered what had happened. "Hawk ..."

"We haven't seen him, dear," said Elara.

"He was here ... I spoke to him," said Sully.

"What? When?" questioned Elara. Her eyebrows furrowed slightly, signaling a desire for more information.

"Not sure how long ago. My head's a bit fuzzy," said Sully, rubbing the side of her head. "He asked me for help."

"Let's get you inside, and inform Garrick," said Elara. She helped Sully up off the grass, placed her arm around her back, and they walked toward the castle.

Garrick ... where are you? mind-thought Elara, as they walked into the large hall.

There was no answer.

Shit!

Elara turned to Sully and said, "Garrick isn't answering me. Are you okay to walk further without my help?"

"Yes," said Sully, who had healed herself with her Lepidoptera abilities.

"We will try his office, first," said Elara. She tried calling Garrick again, through mind-chatter, as they walked toward his office, but there was no answer.

Bursting through the office door, Elara found Garrick unconscious on the floor. Rushing over to him, she knelt beside his bloodied, motionless body and tried to rouse him. "Garrick …"

He didn't answer.

Sully knelt beside him and placed her healing hands over his unconscious body and his wounds.

Within seconds, Garrick woke.

"What happened here?" asked Elara, as she helped Garrick up off the floor.

"Hawk …" said Garrick, clutching his head, as he remembered their encounter. "He has turned *ond*." He looked at Elara with disappointment in his eyes. "And the strength he had." He shook his head. "I couldn't believe how fast Hawk's attack was, let alone how skilled he is."

"You do know that he is under Eryndor's control, don't you?" queried Sully. She watched Garrick, walk over to a couch near his office desk and sit down.

Garrick frowned. "No, I didn't know this. But that would make sense." He stood up quickly and walked over to the dark-gray-and-white-mottled wall behind his desk. Placing his hand on the wall, he felt for an opening. "Where is it?"

"What are you looking for, Garrick?" asked Elara, as she walked over to him.

"Before I passed out, I remember watching Hawk push open a secret compartment on this wall. But now, I can't seem to locate it," said Garrick, feeling the cold stone wall.

He turned to Elara. "The Twin Icefire Blades were inside the hidden compartment."

"Are you sure?" asked Elara, her brow furrowed.

"Yes, woman, I am sure." He raked a hand through his short hair and sighed. "I remember seeing the two wooden boxes, with their intricate patterns … fuck …" He shook his head when realization hit him. "If it's true that Hawk is under Eryndor's control, well that could only mean one thing … Hawk came to collect the Twin Icefire Blades for Eryndor. We need to warn the council."

Before another word was spoken, Garrick clicked his fingers to portal the three of them to Glittertind.

* * *

"Where are we?" asked Sully, as she stood next to the limestone rock formation cliffs and looked all around at the lush green surroundings.

"Glittertind," said Elara.

Garrick looked at Elara and said, "I think we're too late."

Elara spotted the open entrance and gulped, knowing the secret entrance to the council chambers was never left open.

As Sully followed Elara and Garrick along the passageway, she noticed that the walls were lined with skulls.

Shuddering at the eerie sight of them, she kept close to Elara and Garrick. *Why are these even here?*

"They are the skulls of all the sacred Griffin who have gone before us," said Elara, who had heard Sully's thoughts.

"Oh, right," said Sully, as she continued to follow them. "And these birds that are flying in and out of here; why are they dive-bombing us?" She ducked her head as the next one tried to peck at her scalp when it flew past.

"They're old souls, who are meant to guard the council chambers," said Elara.

"Oh, okay," said Sully, processing the information.

When they reached the end of the passageway, Garrick and Elara spotted the eight councillors, lying motionless, among the crumbled limestone formations of the boulders and rubble.

"Shit!" said Garrick, rushing over to pull the huge boulders off the councillors, and check if they were still alive.

Elara and Sully followed and helped to check each one.

Garrick ... said a faint voice.

Garrick pushed the rubble off the only councillor who was moving, and helped him sit up against the limestone wall. "Are you alright?" asked Garrick, kneeling in front of the councillor.

Yes, I'm fine! We all are; some of us have injuries that need to be taken care of by your healer. He indicated to Sully. *Eryndor has escaped. You need to stop him,* mind-thought the councillor, as he remembered how a powerful, almost-God-like Hawk, had broken into the cells and let everyone escape, including Eryndor, then caused an explosion, which brought down the entire inner circle of their chambers.

"I plan to. What happened here?" said Garrick.

It seems you have two sons that are now ond. *They're powerful together, and you will not only need to stop them, but you will also need to retrieve the Twin Icefire Blades they have stolen,* mind-thought the councilor.

"I will, my lord," said Garrick.

Remember our cultural history, Garrick, mind-said the councillor.

"What are you saying? I always remember ..."

The three spiritual objects, interrupted the councillor. His skeletal eyes bored into Garrick's skull, and placed some highlights of years ago into Garrick's mind, of when the three spiritual items were manufactured, and how they were forged with ashes from past Griffin.

"You mean the Twin Icefire Blades, the Golden Chalice and the Fae's Golden Ring?" asked Elara, as she knelt beside the councillor. She had been listening to the conversation, and knew her cultural history well.

Yes, and what I fear the most is, once they have the three spiritual objects, they will be able to bring back the dead. Our country won't survive, mind-said the councillor.

"What do you mean our country won't survive, my lord?" asked Elara, her brow furrowed with concern. "I thought that the council had all the power?"

He who controls the three spiritual objects, has control over the dead and will gain their powers. The havoc they can cause will make them unstoppable. I don't want to even contemplate what will happen if we can't stop them, mind-said the councillor.

"Shit, really! Do you know where the Golden Chalice and the Fae's Golden Ring are kept?" asked Elara, standing.

"Yes, I do," said Garrick, looking at Elara. He had been given the locations by the councillor. Turning to Sully he said, "Sully, can you stay here and help the councillors heal?"

"Yes, Sir. I am only too happy to help," said Sully, looking at Garrick. "Can you let William and Renee know where I am, and what I am doing?"

"No problem. And, thank you," said Garrick, standing. "We appreciate your willingness to help our councillors."

"You are most welcome," said Sully. She looked around at the ghostly figures of the eight councillors lying among the rubble, and gulped hard.

"Let's go, Elara," said Garrick. He grabbed her arm and clicked his fingers to portal them both back to Olden.

CHAPTER THIRTY-NINE

Hovering above the desolate expanse of the top deck of an abandoned oil rig platform, Eryndor's Harbinger of Shadows form floated in the air. His gaze swept across his devoted soldiers, their unwavering loyalty shining in their eyes. A sense of awe mingled with a surge of pride, as he observed the fervor and dedication that burned within them. Their willingness to lay down their lives for him stirred a complex mix of emotions within Eryndor.

Yet, amidst the overwhelming support he received from his soldiers, a shadow of longing clouded Eryndor's thoughts. He couldn't help but yearn for the same unwavering support and understanding from his family. The contrast between the devotion of his loyal soldiers and the absence of his adopted familial support gnawed at his heart.

You will pay dearly, Mother and Father, for what has transpired. Especially as I now have the Twin Icefire Blades, and your poster child, Hawk, thought Eryndor to himself.

"Tonight … we celebrate. Tomorrow … we divide and conquer," shouted Eryndor to his soldiers, who were standing on the deck below him.

The dedicated glazed-eyed human soldiers and glazed-eyed prisoners cheered loudly, and thrust their arms into the air, and continued to drink their alcoholic beverages in celebration of what they had achieved so far.

A mixture of frustration and despair washed over Hawk, as he stood next to Eryndor and listened to his detailed ambitions to conquer not just Norway, but lands far beyond. Looking over the sea of indifferent, glazed-eyed underling faces before him, Hawk let out a deep sigh, and reflected on the heavy burden he carried. He wondered if he would ever break free from the clutches of Eryndor's insidious mind-control, which dictated his every action and most of his thoughts.

After Eryndor concluded his speech and retreated to the lower decks, Hawk made his way to the edge of the top deck, finding solace as he leaned against the railing. From this vantage point, he gazed upon the vast expanse of the Norwegian Sea that stretched out before him, its waters embracing the shores of Norway. With a sense of longing in his heart, he observed the relentless dance of the turbulent waves, yearning to immerse himself in their embrace once more.

What is that? thought Hawk, when he noticed a barely visible shimmering wall, which was hovering close to the edge of the oil rig. He reached out to see what it did, and watched his hand disappear and then reappear, as he pulled it back toward himself. *Shit!*

"I have shields up around the whole oil rig," said Eryndor, as he watched Hawk pull his hand in and out of the shimmering wall. "We certainly don't want anyone knowing where we are, do we?"

Startled by his voice, Hawk said, "Right!" He turned to see Eryndor standing beside him, and then stood to attention.

"I see you are missing the ocean," said Eryndor, who had been listening to Hawk's thoughts.

"Yes, Master," said Hawk, nodding once, with his eyes averted away from Eryndor.

"Well, get used to it, brother. When I am finished with this world, there will be no more oceans, let alone supernatural creatures or humans," said Eryndor, sneering. He watched the look of astonishment on Hawk's face.

Over my dead body, Eryndor. Hawk's nostrils flared, but he didn't say a word, for fear of the repercussions.

"Cat got your tongue, brother," Eryndor taunted. "Oh, and just so you know, I can make sure your demise becomes a reality." He looked at Hawk with contempt.

Hawk shook his head and gulped hard. *I must try harder to block him from my thoughts.*

"Get yourself below decks and get some sleep. I want you bright-eyed and bushy-tailed tomorrow, Hawk," stated Eryndor.

"Yes, Master," said Hawk.

"Well, what are you waiting for?" stated Eryndor.

Eryndor watched as glazed-eyed Hawk nod once, and walked toward the open doorway on his right, which led down to the cabins below.

Hmm ... I wonder how you are still defiant toward me, Hawk. What power do you have, that I don't know about? I must keep my eyes wide open, thought Eryndor, scowling. He leaned against the railing of the platform and looked out to sea.

"My lord!" said a male's voice, from behind Eryndor.

"Yes!" said Eryndor, bluntly. He turned to see Albinus Giordano standing behind him.

"How can I assist you further?" asked Albinus. His white glazed-over eyes showed loyalty toward Eryndor.

"Climb to the peak of this platform structure and maintain a vigilant lookout. My desire is to avoid any unforeseen occurrences throughout the night," said Eryndor.

"Yes, my lord," said Albinus. He turned and walked toward the center of the deck.

* * *

With his hands resting behind his head, Hawk lay on the pillow, staring aimlessly at the flaking paint on the ceiling and remembered a time, not too long ago, when he and Sully had first met, and how they'd become friends, and then more when they were living in Marigot Bay together.

Sighing heavily, he thought, *Will I ever see you again, Sully?* He pictured her beautiful smiling face, and imagined looking into her jade-green eyes.

Fuck you, Eryndor. You always destroy everything.

His brow furrowed, when his thoughts were then turned to the day Eryndor appeared at the villa, and how he had kidnapped Sully, and ruined their chances of a better life. As his mind quietened, and he eventually fell asleep, Hawk dreamed of the days spent with Sully. Swimming in the villa pool, making dinners together, holding hands as they took long walks along the beach together, bathing together, and most of all, enjoying each other in Marigot Bay.

* * *

Sully sat with her legs stretched out on the window seat in Hawk's room at Olden, and looked out over the bay. A smile lit up her face as she remembered about their days of swimming together in the ocean at Saint Lucia, and all the wonderful moments they'd shared as a couple, before Eryndor entered their lives. She wondered if those days or nights would ever return. Sighing, she thought, *where are you, Hawk? Will I ever see you again?*

Elara stood in the doorway to Hawk's room and listened to Sully's thoughts.

She really cares for my boy. I, too, hope we get to see Hawk again one day.

Elara walked into the room and stood next to the window seat. "May I sit with you, dear?"

"Sure," said Sully. Looking up at Elara, she smiled and shifted over to make room.

Placing her arm around Sully's shoulders, Elara leaned in and said, "Hopefully Hawk will return to us soon."

"I hope you are right. I miss him so much," said Sully, leaning into Elara.

"I wanted to come and say thank you for helping the councillors today. I know you were a bit hesitant at first, but we do appreciate all the healing you did, and how you helped with the cleanup of their chambers. I'm sure you know from speaking with the councillors that they appreciated your every effort too."

"Both you and they are most welcome," said Sully, her voice tinged with weariness. She yawned as she leaned into Elara's body.

"Tired, my dear?" asked Elara, slowly pulling away from their connection.

Sully nodded yes.

"Let's get you settled into bed." Getting up, she walked over to Hawk's bed and pulled the covers back.

"Thank you, Elara." Sully yawned again and walked over to the bed. She was tired from all the healing she had performed today, and needed to rest her weary bones and mind. Lying down, she snuggled into the soft duvet and closed her eyes.

"Good night, dear girl," said Elara, as she tucked Sully in.

"Night!" said Sully. Within seconds she was asleep.

When Elara turned and walked toward the doorway, she noticed Garrick leaning against the door frame.

"How's she doing?" whispered Garrick.

Elara placed her index finger over her mouth. "Shh … she is worn out. She needs her rest."

Garrick nodded, and they both walked out of the bedroom, toward Garrick's office.

"What is happening tomorrow?" asked Elara.

"I have organized for the Gramaze Lepidopteras and a few of our experienced soldiers to go with me to retrieve the chalice tomorrow at first light," said Garrick, opening the door to his office.

"Good. The sooner we retrieve it, the better." said Elara.

"What do you mean, we?" asked Garrick. He sat in his office chair.

With her hand on her chest, Elara said, "You and I."

"I would prefer you stay in Olden. You'll be safer here. A few Gramaze family members are going to guard you," said Garrick, watching her reaction.

"Safer …" scoffed Elara, with her hands on her hips.

"Yes. I don't want anything happening to you, as well," said Garrick.

"How dare you decide for me what I will and won't be doing," said Elara, her brow furrowed.

"You know how vulnerable you are to Eryndor, Hawk, and the Twin Icefire Blades," stated Garrick, standing. "I won't allow it."

"Allow it! This is not your call, Garrick. I am coming with you all, and there is nothing more to discuss," stated Elara.

"Be reasonable, Elara. Not only will you be shielded here, but our people will rely on your guardianship. We must ensure the safety of our people and our kingdom, shielding them from Eryndor's minions, should they appear. You possess the strength and ability to accomplish this, and deep down, you know it to be true," said Garrick.

She looked at Garrick and sighed heavily. "Yes, yes, I know you are correct, Garrick. So, what are your plans to retrieve the chalice and the ring?"

"At this stage, I am only going to retrieve the chalice, which, according to the councillor's vision, is in Oman. I will worry about the ring later," said Garrick.

A silence settled over the room, heavy with unspoken understanding. Elara knew that once Garrick had set his mind to something, that there was no stopping him.

Garrick knew this task wouldn't be easy, but he was ready to face whatever lay ahead—for his kingdom, for his family. The weight of responsibility pressed against him, but he bore it without hesitation.

SNEAK PEEK AT BOOK TWO

Coming in 2025

Heritage Of Power

EMPIRE OF THE LEGACIES ACADEMY
BOOK TWO

CHAPTER ONE

As the sun began to filter through the mist-wreathed mountains, which reflected on the clear surface of the waters of Olden Fjord, a glimmer of the morning's first light sauntered through the window into Hawk's bedroom, and flitted across Sully's face. Feeling recharged from the best damn sleep she'd had in weeks, Sully opened her eyes, sat up, and fluffed her pillows. Leaning against the headboard, she looked out at the imposing yellow-and-orange skyline, and the calming ocean water of Olden, and wondered what the day would bring. Most mornings, her first thought was of Hawk.

Hawk ... I wonder where you are, and if you are okay? thought Sully. She breathed a heavy sigh.

Pulling the covers back, she stood tall and rolled her shoulders. *Mmm, that feels better.* Twisting this way and that, Sully stretched her arms toward the ceiling and walked over to the window seat. As she sat down, she noticed that there were a large number of Lepidopteras from her coven, which included her father, William, leader of the Gramaze Lepidopteras standing on the grass area below, along with Garrick, and some of his family and soldiers. All were dressed in battle gear. They were waiting near a blue-green shimmering portal, as Garrick addressed them.

Wonder what's going on there? thought Sully, with a furrowed brow. She listened in on the conversation below with her Lepidoptera hearing abilities.

* * *

"Right … gather around everyone, and listen up," said Garrick, authoritatively.

They all did as they were instructed by Garrick.

"Today, our mission is to retrieve a sacred golden chalice, which is an important historical artifact to our Griffin culture. It is currently situated in Wadi Tiwi in Oman," said Garrick, looking around at each of their faces. "When we arrive at Muscat via this portal," he pointed to the shimmering portal wall, "there will be a point of contact waiting for us, and they'll be able to transport us via road to Wadi Tiwi. From there we will need to find the golden chalice. I do have some intel on where the chalice is being held, but I am not sure if it is a hundred percent correct, because it has been many centuries since it was taken there, and no one has seen it for hundreds of years or more, that we know of."

"How far is it from Muscat to Wadi Tiwi?" asked William.

"It is about one-and-a-half hours' drive, and there will be some canyons to climb and water pools to navigate, before we arrive there. Now … as all of you know", he looked around at each of their faces, "Eryndor has escaped the councillors jail cells in Glittertind, and he has Hawk and others under mind control. If we come across them in Oman, our mission will be to bring Eryndor and the other prisoners back to Norway, so that they can be placed back in the Glittertind cells forever. If they don't come with us quietly, then they die. As for Hawk …" Garrick raked a hand through his short hair and sighed. "William and I will deal with Hawk. Am I making myself clear?"

They all shouted yes.

"Right … get your weapons ready, and let's go," instructed Garrick. He turned and walked toward the shimmering portal with his sword drawn.

Sully watched everyone follow Garrick and William into the portal, and the portal close.

* * *

Did you enjoy reading some of the first chapter of book two? Keep an eye out on my website **www.susanhoddy.com** for when book two of the Empire of the Legacies Academy series will be coming out in 2025

CATCH UP ON ALL THE LATEST NEWS AND UPDATES FROM SUSAN HODDY

Facebook: Susan Hoddy–Author
Instagram: susanhoddy
LinkedIn: Susan Hoddy
TikTok: Susan Houston 478
Threads   Susan Houston (Hoddy) (@susanhoddy)
Website: https://www.susanhoddy.com/

All readings, discussions, signings or appearances are done by appointment only.

If any libraries, schools, daycares, book stores or book clubs would like Susan to come along, and do a reading of some chapters and/or a discussion about her books to their group of passionate readers; you can contact Susan via her website and fill in the **Contact Us** form.

https://www.susanhoddy.com/contact/

For rights availability inquiries, including film and television options, please inquire directly with the author using the **Contact Us** form at her website.

https://www.susanhoddy.com/contact/

ACKNOWLEDGMENTS

This book would not be here, resting in your hands or on your e-reader, if it weren't for the following people. I owe all of them my deepest gratitude and love.

My book cover artist, Ammonia Book Covers, who worked tirelessly on the cover. Thank you, your cover is overwhelmingly beautiful, and I am so lucky to have found you.

My editing and formatting team at DP Plus—Debbie Phillips and Deb Klanfar—for providing me with invaluable critique and helpful instructions, and overall making my book better. Thank you so much.

My wonderful husband, Michael, for putting up with me, when all I spoke about for months was the characters, plot lines, and storyline of this book. Thank you for your patience and for everything you do for me.

My beautiful daughter, Samantha, who has always given me her advice, support and love. Thank you, Sam. I think one day you, too, might become a writer.

My many friends and associates, for all their support, feedback and suggestions. I appreciate each and every one of you. Many thanks to you all.

To my wonderful Mum, who passed away while I was writing the initial storyline of this book. Thank you for all the advice you have given me over the years, and the support you have shown me. I hope we get to meet again one day. I miss you every day. Love you, Mum.

ABOUT THE AUTHOR

Susan Hoddy is an award-winning author celebrated for her captivating blend of fantasy, romance, and young adult fiction. Best known for her Lepidoptera Vampire series, she brings a fresh and imaginative take on the vampire genre, weaving together supernatural intrigue, rich world-building, and compelling characters. She has also ventured into contemporary romance with her novel Security, showcasing her versatility as a storyteller.

Expanding her creative horizons, Susan recently embarked on a delightful new journey—writing and publishing a fully illustrated children's book series, The Adventures of Georgia and Cash, inspired by the joy of friendship and adventure.

Born in Perth, Western Australia, Susan has always been a dreamer at heart. She cherishes lively conversations with family and friends, spontaneous road trips with her husband, and quiet moments with a good cup of tea and a book.

After spending years working in various office roles, Susan decided in 2012 to follow her passion for storytelling. Earning a novel writing diploma from the Australian College of Journalism, she hasn't looked back since—continuing to craft enchanting tales where fantasy and romance collide.

AWARDS

In 2022 Susan won two book awards for *Attraction* and *Awakened* in The Lepidoptera Vampire Series.

***Attraction*, book one in the Lepidoptera Vampire series**, was chosen as the Silver Winner in the Fiction Romance category from MMH Press Book Awards.

***Awakened*, book two in the Lepidoptera Vampire series**, was chosen as the Bronze Winner in the Fiction Romance category from MMH Press Book Awards.

In 2019 Susan won two book awards for *Attraction* and *Awakened* in The Lepidoptera Vampire Series.

***Attraction*, book one in the Lepidoptera Vampire series**, was chosen as the Official Selection Winner in the Young Adult General Fiction category from New Apple Literary Fifth Annual Indie Book Awards.

***Awakened*, book two in the Lepidoptera Vampire series**, was chosen as the solo Medalist Winner in the Young Adult General Fiction category from New Apple Literary Fifth Annual Indie Book Awards.

OTHER SUPERNATURAL FANTASY BOOKS WRITTEN BY SUSAN HODDY

The Lepidoptera Vampire Series